Love
Letters
FROM A

F AT M AN

Love Letters

FROM A

NAOMI BENARON
winner of the G.S. Sharat Chandra
Prize for Short Fiction
selected by Stuart Dybek

BkMk Press
University of Missouri-Kansas City

Copyright © 2007 by Naomi Benaron
BkMk Press
University of Missouri-Kansas City
5101 Rockhill Road
Kansas City, Missouri 64110
(816) 235-2558 (voice)
(816) 235-2611 (fax)
www.umkc.edu/bkmk

Cover art: "Love Letters from a Fat Man" by Khadijah Queen
Cover and interior book design: Susan L. Schurman
Managing Editor: Ben Furnish
Author photo: Philip Raymond

BkMk Press wishes to thank Teresa Collins, Sandra Meyer, Chelsea Seguin, Emily Iorg.

The G.S. Sharat Chandra Prize for Short Fiction wishes to thank J. J. Cantrell, Leslie Koffler, Linda Rodriguez, Elizabeth Smith.

Previous winners of the G.S. Sharat Chandra Prize for Fiction: *A Bed of Nails* by Ron Tanner, selected by Janet Burroway; *I'll Never Leave You* by H. E. Francis, selected by Diane Glancy; *The Logic of a Rose* by Billy Lombardo, selected by Gladys Swan; *Necessary Lies* by Kerry Neville Bakken, selected by Hilary Masters.

Library of Congress Cataloging-in-Publication Data
Benaron, Naomi
    Love letters from a fat man / Naomi Benaron.
        p. cm.
    Summary: "A collection of short stories about family relationships and coming of age both in the United States and Rwanda during the 1990s Rwandan holocaust that offers a look at the wider subjects of race, religion, discrimination, and mental illness."—Provided by publisher.
        ISBN 978-1-886157-60-6 (pbk.: alk. paper)
        Notes: "Winner of the G. S. Sharat Chandra Prize for Short Fiction, selected by Stuart Dybek."
        PS3602.E6565 L68 2007
        813 / .6--dc22
                                                                 2007024370
This book is set in ITC Giovanni, Stencil & Caflisch Script Pro.

5   4   3   2   1

In memory of my parents,
Drs. Doris and Tully Benaron,
who taught me that justice
and love were worth fighting for,
and for Dan, who fights for me still.

ACKNOWLEDGMENTS

The stories in this collection were originally published as follows:
"The Chemical Nature of Things" —*Red Rock Review, CALYX*
"A Matched Pair" —*Green Mountains Review*
"Love Letters from a Fat Man" —*Tartts 2: Incisive Fiction from Emerging Writers*
"Lunch" — *Zinkzine*
"Indivisible" —*Sunspinner*
"The Vibrations of a Desert Rose" —*Big Tex[t]*
"God Spends the Day Everywhere" —*PRISM International Journal*
"Shedding Skin" —*New Millennium Writings*
"Directions"—*New Letters*

For the title story, I wish to acknowledge *Blue Angel: The Life of Marlene Dietrich* by Donald Spoto (New York: Doubleday, 1992) for historical information.

I would like to thank all my Antioch mentors—Brad Kessler, Frank Gaspar, Dana Johnson, and Susan Taylor Chehak. They have all helped me to spread my writer's wings, sometimes despite my vocal protestations. I extend my deepest gratitude to Stuart Dybek, who chose this manuscript as winner of the G. S. Sharat Chandra Prize. It is truly an honor. Gayle Brandeis has always been available to read my stories, offer encouragement, write letters, and share with me this wonderful passion called writing. Lorian Hemingway picked my story from a pile of manuscripts and stamped it with a bright red #1. My agents, Alana and Michael Lennie, have walked, run and swam with me during this long journey. Ben Furnish, managing editor at BkMk Press, has shared dog stories, provided a voice of calm in my storms, and, perhaps, has saved my life. Ah—but that is another tale. Susan Schurman and Sandra Meyer at BkMk Press have worked very hard to create a finished book from its raw materials. Khadijah, Queen of all things, created the cover and has been a true sister. For help with my Rwanda stories, I am particularly grateful to Pauline Mujawamarya, Roger Remera, Derick Burleson, Jean Nganji, and Rosamond Carr. Roz—you left us before I could present you with this book, but your spirit lives on through your children, your deeds, and my inadequate words. Meagan Knepp provided invaluable assistance with filmmaking details and helped me survive my first semester at Antioch. My sister, Susan Benaron, has read my work since we cuddled together in our parents' Big Bed, and has never complained. Meg Files, my dearest Pearl and first mentor, provided the inspiration for many of these stories. The book would not have been born without her. Barrie Ryan has been a spiritual guide, and it was her kick, planted firmly in my behind, that gave me the initial courage to proceed. This book would not exist without her. And to my husband, Daniel Coulter, I offer my deepest thanks for delicious cooking, faith, love, belief, support, and always a light in the dark days.

FOREWORD

Books of short stories—and, for that matter, of poems—can be divided between those that are organized around some unifying principle and those that are collections. The books that are unified are most commonly unified by place but they can be unified by reappearing characters, by overarching themes, by variations on a central image, etc. Each type of book, whether it be linked stories or a collection, has its particular beauties. The collection is by nature diverse and therefore unpredictable, full of surprises, or, at least, it can be providing, of course, that the writer's gifts are up to the task.

Those qualities of diversity, unpredictability, and surprise, and to that list add invention, abound in Naomi Benaron's collection, *Love Letters from a Fat Man.* Each individual story is graced by those same qualities, as well. As a collection, *Love Letters from a Fat Man* can seem romantic, tragic, comic, lyrical, whimsical, and moody by turns. The freshness of surprise comes from Naomi Benaron's powers of invention. I was especially impressed by how her stories are deeply imagined enough so that the invention always seems credible. Each voice rings intimate and true. Each new world created in the compressed length and time of the short-story form is vivid and real. This is a book that is rich in character, detail, and unified by a vibrant prose style and an empathy for its subjects. What's more, it is fun to read.

—Stuart Dybek
Final Judge
G.S. Sharat Chandra Prize for Short Fiction

Love Letters from a Fat Man

LOVE LETTERS FROM A FAT MAN

From: misslman51@aol.com
Date: Fri, 20 Feb 2004 04:20:51 EST
Subject: Greetings from Tucson, AZ
To: marleneinfo@marlenedietrich.com

My dear Marlene,

Forgive me for resurrecting you from your eternal rest, but I feel I must communicate my thoughts. As a sufferer of chronic and incurable insomnia I often ingest the fare of late-night movies. Tonight I watched a doubleheader of your films—*A Foreign Affair* and *Touch of Evil*—and was deeply moved, not so much by the films as by your beauty.

My name is Otto, coincidentally (or not) the third name of your father, Louis Erich Otto Dietrich. You must excuse my nosy nature; I have spent the past two hours discovering you on-line. To use a phrase that has found its way into the English language since your passing, I have "googled" you. It is amazing to me the series of parallels in our lives that draw us together.

I am a slim man and, I am told, handsome. My hair is blond, imperceptibly silvered, with the hint of a wave. Until my son died and my wife began to reclaim her affections morsel by morsel, I had the build of a barnyard rooster, all sinew and bone. However, I seem to have swallowed a whale. Otto Orca am I. The last time I tipped the cargo scale at my physician's office, I weighed in at 433 pounds, and blubber accrues at an alarming rate. I can no longer ambulate with ease, and caring for myself has become impossible. The simple task of tying my shoes requires the most undignified contortions.

Although *Touch of Evil* seemed quaint and moralistic, *A Foreign Affair* was of great interest to me. I was surprised by the empathy shown to the people of postwar Berlin. I watched enrapt, moments passing before the risk of losing consciousness compelled me to breathe. You will understand this when I tell you that my father was from Dresden. While he was occupied defending the *Vaterland*, his first wife looked up one night to see the sky become a storm of fire. I imagine her, transfixed by this terrible beauty, the air around her igniting as bombs screeched to earth, her arms around my two unknown half-brothers, all movement suddenly beyond the realm of possibility. Incineration would have been instantaneous, their ashes fusing with the rubble of the building—an eye for an eye.

I was a late edition, a second thought, born to the American nurse who cured my father of typhoid in a DP camp. My father became a good American citizen. Fascinated by the electrical nature of things, he earned a Ph.D. in electrical engineering. He decried the pursuit of war and worked for a well-known firm in the peaceful applications of his profession. He kept the insignias of the Reich hidden in a pouch of velvet. I found them after his death, tucked away in a dresser drawer. When I hold them in my hand, Marlene, they burn holes in my skin.

In contrast to my father, I have been at liberty to find employment in a military field. I am a physicist, studying the perfection of skin. Not the vulnerable covering of viscera and bones or the lunar whiteness that shimmers from the divine curvature of your legs. I study the skin of missiles. I strive for a combination of strength and slipperiness, if you will. A skin that will glide without friction, that hides from the searching eyes of radar and remains cool and intact despite unimaginable forces, to deliver its cargo to the upturned faces of mothers who watch with their young children tucked beneath their arms. An eye for an eye.

Due to my current condition, I have taken a leave of absence. The last time I attempted to drive my car, I did irreparable damage to vehicle and psyche. The space between stomach and steering wheel had become infinitesimal, leaving little room for the expansion of diaphragm that occurs with the intake of breath. Late for work and in a fury, I planted my feet and gave a violent backward thrust. I am a very strong man. My father, at age 75, was crowned the Strongest Man in the World, in the age category Seventy Plus. Fueled by adrenaline and a boiling anger at my recently departed wife, the poor seat was no match for my tantrum. I somersaulted backward, seat belt, chair and all, into the rear of my SUV. There I dangled, helpless and upside down, my sausage legs and arms waving: a monstrous insect from a late-night horror film. It is the strangest feeling, Marlene, to have tears streak up your forehead and soak your scalp.

I finally extricated myself, pushed the car back into the garage and closed the door, leaving the seat where it had landed—a twisted memorial to human rage. My breath came in violent shudders, and my heart had the sound and feel of a wrecking ball careening into my ribs. I trudged into the kitchen and turned the dead bolt. I made a vow: Here Otto shall remain, until they lift his lifeless form from the floor with their crane.

If anyone can understand this decision it is you, Ms. Dietrich. You who spent the last years of your life locked away in your Paris apartment, poisoned by the perceived ill will of humankind, drowning liver and kidneys in a gourmet alcoholic stew. Although I do indulge in a glass

or bottle or two of fine wine with my meals, this shall not
be my Weapon of Mass Destruction. I have embarked on
a journey to eat myself to death. No fan of cheeseburgers
and french fries, the sword I turn against myself is of well-
honed, quality steel. I shall annihilate myself one steak
Diane, one French-vanilla-ice-creamed-raspberry tart at a
time.

Yours in spirit and in flesh,
Otto

From: misslman51@aol.com
Date: Sat, 21 Feb 2004 08:27:37 EST
Subject: The Spirit of Opportunity
To: marleneinfo@marlenedietrich.com

Dear Marlene,
By now you are blinking in your newly awakened state
and wondering what has become of the world. Here on
earth, events catapult toward unimaginable conflagrations;
nothing new in that department. We continue to invent
excuses to destroy ourselves and improve the weapons with
which to accomplish this. Certainly I am as guilty as any,
earning my bread as I do from optimizing methods of destruction. But beyond the reaches of our floundering planet, the news is better.
On January 4, an adorable little rover named Spirit
landed in the crater Gusev on the surface of Mars. His
brother, Opportunity, landed in the vast plain of Meridi-
ani Planum on January 25. It is here that scientists believe
they have the best chance of discovering evidence of water
on Mars. After some initial problems, both vehicles are
prattling about, happily gathering samples and snapping
pictures.
I have read of your heroic performances at the front
lines during the closing year of WWII. The exploration of
new frontiers by our brave robots gives me the same tantalizing flicker of hope that the soldiers you entertained must
have felt. To a universe of death you brought light and life

and a pair of legs that were out of this world. In the midst of a drought of human kindness, two creatures of engineering genius ignite the hope of finding water on a desiccated and deserted planet.

Yours in anticipation,
Otto

From: misslman51@aol.com
Date: Mon, 23 Feb 2004 05:01:30 EST
Subject: Marta
To: marleneinfo@marlenedietrich.com

My dearest Marlene,
How are you? I am well, thank you, as well as can be expected. You are probably asking by now, how does such a fat man accomplish suicide by haute cuisine when surely he barely fits in his own kitchen? How does he chop vegetables for his sauté, pound veal for his Wiener schnitzel when his stomach protrudes like the prow of a ship before him? You are right to wonder, and please, have no fear of being frank. All that remains of my feelings is a hard-packed square of mud left to bake in the sun's heat. My wife, may she be eternally blessed, saw to that. And as we are on the subject, I have made a surprising discovery of my own! You, my goddess of smoldering perfection, suffered from bouts of chubbiness yourself. The temptations of all aspects of physical pleasure, it seems, hovered around you like a shadow. If I were inclined to reverse my own pitiful condition, I would do as you did and lie down on the floor for hours, turning the wheels of an invisible bicycle with my legs.

I digress. In answer to your question, a wonderful and shockingly beautiful young woman named Marta cares for me. From her name you would presume her to be of Spanish descent, but she is as pale as an Icelandic goddess. Her father, a lazy man, barely literate, filled out her birth certificate, and for expedience or from ignorance or exasperation, left out the *h*, and so it stands. Marta is tall, even when she slips off her platform heels and glides about the house in bare feet. She is thin; my eyes can trace the articulation of bones beneath the silvery shell of her skin. Her hair, like yours, is bronze.

Marta is between husbands, and so was glad for both diversion and employment. When she met me, her eyes widened as she calculated dollars in my bank accounts and days until my impending death. But we have come to an agreement on this account.

Marta, as she confessed in the lateness of an evening, her tongue slippery from several glasses of an excellent Medoc, finds her mates through the obituaries. She looks for older women whose final farewell is celebrated in the more fashionable funeral homes. She memorizes vital statistics, researches pertinent information on-line. (Marta has the MO of a brilliant scientist—she's a woman after my own heart.) Black-silked to the gills she approaches the grieving and vulnerable husbands.

"My mother went to school with your wife," she says. Or, "Your wife was my fourth-grade teacher. I remember..." And so on and so forth until she slides inside the poor sot's grief and asks if she can bring him a meal.

At this point, let me testify, it is all over. I have felt the tingle of her fruit sorbet against my teeth; the fiery caress of her chicken *alla diavola* has brought tears of desire to my eyes and an uncontrollable sweat to my brow. Were she to deny me, I would crawl across coals to lick a morsel of home-baked, buttered bread from her fingers.

I have taught Marta to play chess. She is a quick learner and has a fiercely competitive nature. As I march toward her king, her skin ignites, and her brows furrow in a delightfully seductive *v*. Lately I have been forced to bring out the timer, as without this distraction she would soon beat me. Last Wednesday she revealed a bold strategy, tricking me into thinking she would pursue a simple mate when in fact she sacrificed her queen and threatened me with disaster. Fortunately, somehow flustered by her success, she made a blunder on the next move and allowed me a merciful checkmate, rescuing a battered intellect from further blows. Marta forgave my conquest by presenting me with a bold Bolognese for dinner: buttons of porcini mushrooms crowning a mound of fresh linguine, Salade Niçoise and a loaf of bread shimmering with olive oil and roasted garlic on the side. For dessert she served cheesecake drizzled with intertwined ribbons of caramel and chocolate.

On Saturday I reserved the film *The Blue Angel* and a biography of the same name from the library. The Internet is a wonderful thing, Marlene! Truly one can live one's whole life with no more effort than the flick of the wrist, the click of a finger on a mouse. It is my prediction that future generations will develop the blinking watery slits of mole eyes, the pallor of salamanders wiggling about in caves. Marta picked up my treasures this morning and brought them. This afternoon I caught her sitting next to the window, bare feet pressed against the glass, skirt sliding up her sun-warmed thighs, reading the story of your life. She did nothing to reclaim her modesty when she saw me. She merely pursed her lips and wrinkled her nose.

"Did you know Marlene Dietrich was a lesbian?" she asked.

Her hand, supporting the open book (she had devoured nearly half!) rested in a fold of blue cotton pouched between her legs. I must admit to a flush that warmed my cheek, a drop or two of sweat that seeped into the furrows of my neck.

"I would appreciate your asking before you abscond with my books," I said, shuffling off toward the safety of my office.

"I was the one who got it," she called after me. I imagined her fingers casually brushing across the folds of her skirt as she readjusted her legs.

Tonight I will watch the most famous of your films, a bowl of buttered popcorn by my side. Hungarian paprika sprinkled on top provides a tantalizing addition, melting in red streaks that add a hint of sweetness and fire to the kernels.

But first I must ask you—is it true? I have heard of your affairs with men, but never a word of other diversions sampled. Of course I am open-minded, Marlene, but you must understand my history. My father was Aryan down to the mitochondria of his cells. Any tendency toward what he considered feminine weakness was answered with a belt. Sometimes, it seemed, he failed to remember who had lost the war. Well, enough. The stress of memory on my weakened heart causes uncomfortable palpitations; a gentle warning squeeze informs me it is time to cease. I shall bid you *gute nacht.*

Yours in admiration,
Otto

From: misslman51@aol.com
Date: Tues, 24 Feb 2004 06:00:16 EST
Subject: Cuckold Doodle-Doo
To: marleneinfo@marlenedietrich.com

My dear Marlene,
   How I weep! Were this letter pen and ink, blue rivers would flow from the page. I have watched *The Blue Angel* three times, and would have watched it a fourth had not my heart trembled with a weight of sorrow, threatening to burst from its "mortal coil." Your portrayal of Lola Lola, cabaret singer and femme fatale, has left me clawing for a breath of air.
   In the four o'clock stillness of my bedroom, my life takes on the shadowed cast of the Blue Angel's world. There is no sound beyond the groan of walls and floors struggling to bear my bulk.   No breath of child, no sigh of wife. To attempt sleep is useless; the ghost of Lola Lola's unlucky Professor Rath squats on my shoulder. Like this saddest of protagonists, I am a cuckold and a clown.
   I had a wife, Marlene. My wife was beautiful. She was taut: an ungrounded wire leaving a trail of sparks in her wake. She had a boy's haircut, bangs falling coquettishly over her eyes. She had the narrow hips of a young man

and tiny feet. Did she marry me for love or money or my Germanic beauty? Who knows. She was no cabaret singer, no Lola Lola perched on a stool. She was a teacher of high school mathematics, but like Lola Lola, she wove an inescapable web. I saw how men orbited around her, snared in her gravitational fields.

Was I like Professor Rath—a lonely, awkward man imposing his will on the world, peeking secretly into the sordid corners of life, undone by desire for a woman as indifferent to him as a mongoose to her prey? In the beginning, no. I was slender and tall, a crowing rooster, a leading man. But events beyond my control (perhaps) undid me, and I began to eat. In the end a fat man can be no more than a diversion, a freak amusement.

I had a wife, and she left me long before she left me. As punishment for my sins she began to deny me, one sweet taste at a time. I became a victim of starvation smothering in pâtés and mousse. I followed her from room to room, kissing her shadow. I cooked her elegant dinners and waited till eight, till nine, drinking wine at the table, playing Chopin, listening to the unanswered ring of her phone. I consumed her portions as well as mine and stewed in my own rage. I devoured desserts. Late at night, when she came home, I watched her from darkened doorways, a cigarette nearly burning her fingers while she read a book, traced the arc of a circle with her toes. I sniffed at the air for the hint of a man, the soured perfume of an embrace.

I had a wife, and could have killed her or, like Professor Rath, I could have died of grief. We make our choices; we lie in our beds. When Rath discovered his Lola Lola with another man he crowed like a rooster until crowing consumed him, transformed him into a beast of rage. He could have killed her then. The balance of plot could have tipped either way. Instead he willed himself to die alone in a darkened classroom, stretched across the desk from where he taught when his life was still his own.

Oh, where is Marta? I am in need of an omelet. With

fresh asparagus and a salty cheese—a feta or Gorgonzola
—to mask the taste of tears.

Yours in flesh and desire,
Otto

From: misslman51@aol.com
Date: Fri, 27 Feb 2004 03:58:46 EST
Subject: In Your Image
To: marleneinfo@marlenedietrich.com

My dearest Marlene,
    Felicitations. I am fairly well, thank you, although I
have noticed a new shortness of breath—a chortling that
accompanies the intake of oxygen—and my fingers have
grown puffy. Now that I am at peace with my decision, I
observe these changes with scientific curiosity, as detached
as a fly on the wall. Marta, who knows nothing of my plan,
has become alarmed and vowed to eliminate salt and red
meat from my diet.
    My rover friends, Opportunity and Spirit, have returned
pictures of a Martian sunset. From the surface of Mars the
sky appears indigo and is filled with dust. Soil samples collected from Opportunity have a much wider range of colors
than previously seen, but no evidence of water yet.
    You will be pleased to hear that Marta is quite enamored
of you. She has acquired a collection of movies and books
that are now strewn about the living room. She demanded
reimbursement, which I don't mind. This obsession of ours
injects purpose and direction into the stale atmosphere of
the house. Although the universe expands, my own world
becomes smaller daily.
    Marta has taken to plucking her eyebrows into a thin
arch that accentuates the almond shape of her eyes, and
this morning she appeared wearing a pantsuit, tie and fedora. She called me into the kitchen, and for a moment I
thought she had conjured up your physical being. I took
a step back, the floor reeling unsteadily beneath the two
boats of my bedroom slippers. There you stood, illumi-

nated by sunlight drifting through the drapes, your face a play of light and shadow as if a director's spotlight had been perfectly placed. You turned to face me and thankfully became Marta once more, a mirror in hand.

"It's perfect, don't you think?" she asked.

She did a slow spin. Pebbles of sunlight speckled face and suit. I remained speechless. She showed me the pictures of you parading around Hollywood in similar garb. How courageous you were to expose soul and spirit at a time when our sexual nature was kept in a well-locked closet. Hollywood was a far cry from the delicious decadence of prewar Berlin.

"I found these at the thrift store. Twenty-seven dollars." She twirled the fedora on her finger and replaced it at a provocative angle. "Two bucks for the hat. I thought you wouldn't mind."

Frankly, I was delighted and amused. My fingertips tingled, abuzz with desire to reach out and touch her skin.

After a breakfast of steel-cut oats with fresh strawberries and whipped cream (Marta is taking the issue of my health far too seriously!) the oddest thing happened. She cleared the dishes, brought an armful of books to the table and plopped them down. While flipping through pictures she suddenly stopped, her finger resting on a portrait of you with your daughter Maria. Confronted with the sultry gaze of your eyes, speech leaves me, and from the slackness of Marta's jaw I knew she was similarly affected. Your daughter stared out at us with a look of ill-controlled fury.

"She's jealous, that little one," I said.

Marta withdrew her finger as if burned. She looked at me, but said nothing. Stupidly, I continued.

"Jealous of the world for stealing her mother's love."

With those words, Marta slapped me. Her fedora flew from her head, and her pinned hair escaped to tumble over her shoulders.

"What do you know about it?" she said and walked out, leaving the fedora where it fell.

I sat for a moment, a beached whale, contemplating the act of hat retrieval. I picked up the book and went to my bedroom, my finger marking the page where an angry girl stared.

Beyond my bedroom window a family of Gambel's quail parades past, scratching seeds from the dust. In my imagination they are faithful to each other until death do them part. I have propped up the photograph of you and Maria on my desk beside a picture of my father, my mother and myself. The same pouting mouth and smoldering eyes stare back at me from my young visage. My father is straight-backed, as if preparing to salute the inspecting Führer. His arm is placed on my shoulder, but my body leans away.

Do not feel guilty for leaving the care and affection of your daughter to others, as you so often did. In the end, my Marlene, we are all abandoned.

And so, *auf Wiedersehen*, my dearest.

Yours, as always,
Otto

From: misslman51@aol.com
Date: Sun, 29 Feb 2004 23:06:27 EST
Subject: Duped?
To: marleneinfo@marlenedietrich.com

Dear Marlene,

As you can see, today is a rather special occurrence, the 29th day of February. The sky as well maneuvers into a portentous configuration. In three weeks' time, five planets will be in alignment. Mercury, Venus, Mars, Jupiter, and Saturn will thread themselves across the evening sky. The moon will hang from this string of jewels like a pendant.

Today was also an auspicious day in my own tiny universe. Today, in chess, Marta had me. She opened by setting up a risky queen's gambit. As usual I played the aggressor, pouncing on all pieces offered. But when we progressed to the endgame and she laid her finger lightly on the bishop, I saw with horror that mate in two moves was inevitable. She looked at me and smiled. She lifted her finger and responded with Kt X P check, a ridiculous move that allowed my knight to penetrate the territory of her king. I am troubled, Marlene. Deeply troubled. Had she not seared me with so pointed an expression, I could easily have dismissed her mistake as a lack of attention, an inability to follow through with an attack. But those eyes —your eyes—pinned me for the cuckold that I am.

How many men (and women) fell victim to your gaze? How many unwitting clowns, Marlene, crowing with a cry of presumed conquest, found themselves fluttering helplessly at your feet? It is always too late when we discover that freedom of movement is an illusion. We are maneuvered into alignment by a pair of irresistible eyes, a pair of legs with skin as luminescent as the moon.

Yours in deepest admiration,
Otto

From: misslman51@aol.com
Date: Thurs, 04 Mar 2004 05:05:12 EST
Subject: The Sins of the Father
To: marleneinfo@marlenedietrich.com

My Marlene,
I have been in bed for three days, too heavy to move. I swallow sorrow like bread. I expand beyond belief. Marta has finally rousted me, chasing me out with her dust cloths and vacuum cleaner. She claims my lair has become exquisitely foul, overrun by droppings of food that have turned into brightly colored colonies of fungus and mold. I attempted to communicate by laptop, an odd expression at best, for not even the most slender of Internet surfers places the computer there. But the word for me is particularly meaningless. Any semblance of a lap has been long buried by the geology of fat.

In the year 1944, you slept with American generals and sang to the soldiers of the *Vaterland*, concluding your broadcasts with a dedication to the Allied forces that you boasted were on the brink of destroying the Reich. Did my father, hunkered down on the front lines, hear your throaty German drinking songs and curse you? I would like to think so. In the year of my birth, 1951, you already had two grandchildren and appeared for what you were, a fading cabaret beauty, in *Rancho Notorious*, another in your string of failed Hollywood films.

In the year 1979, a year after your last film, *Just a Gigolo*, a child named Marta had a child of her own, a little girl. Had she kept her, she would have named her Amber. She told me this two days ago, perched on the edge of my bed, nibbling at a fingernail. When her father noticed the bulging belly behind her billowing shirts, he beat her until she prayed she would miscarry. She did not, but at her own request, she never saw her daughter. She wonders now about the color of her eyes, the cut of her hair, and perhaps, although she did not say, about the woman she has always known as her mother.

In 1992, the year of your death, I had a child: a son. Like his father he was a late edition, born to an aging father with a young woman as his prize. But unlike me, he was not an afterthought. His eyes were hazel and his hair was brown with an auburn hue. He walked at ten months and began to read before the age of four. Perhaps it was wrong, but we let him sleep nestled between us when he was terrified by nightmares.

I had a son, and when he was seven my wife left him in my care while she attended a conference. He had a delicate nature and was prone to exaggeration. A nick on a finger became a war wound. So you can understand why I assumed he had a touch of flu, an insignificant sniffle. My own father drove me from my bed when I shivered with fever; it was all I knew.

I had a son, and when he was seven he developed an infection, and the infection went to his heart, and beneath his pale and sweating skin his heart silently expanded until it no longer had the strength to pump life through his body. I had a son, and my wife left him in my care, and she barely had time to kiss him goodbye before he sighed and left us childless. When I held him in my arms, he was as weightless as a little bird.

On March 2, 2004, eleven years and ten months after your death, and one year, four months, three days and some odd hours after my wife, who never found it in her own diseased heart to forgive me, left me for more promising and fertile (and slimmer) ground, a little robot named Opportunity, equipped with all manner of scooping and digging tools, discovered strong evidence of flowing water on Mars. This conclusion was reached after analysis of rock samples showed the presence of sulfates and niches where crystals form, implying a wet environment.

The material seen inside these niches was shiny and bright. Here on earth, in Tucson, Arizona, in a desert in the midst of a drought, the forecast is for rain.

My Marlene, née Maria Magdalena Dietrich, pray for those of us who shuffle along on the skin of this planet you have left behind. I remain yours in affection and am attempting the faintest flicker of hope in a hopeless world, *meine Liebe.*

Otto

From: misslman51@aol.com
Date: Wed, 24 Mar 2004 08:00:01EST
Subject: Water on Mars!
To: marleneinfo@marlenedietrich.com

My poor Marlene,

In the end you could not sustain the illusion, nor could the illusion sustain you. You were nothing more than a play of light and shadow arranged beneath a spotlight. You amassed the weight of years as I amass the pounds of human suffering. You consumed Scotch at 10:00 in the morning. You stumbled and fell onstage, lacerating legs, fracturing femurs. In the end, the freedom that had sustained you imprisoned you. Terrified that a photographer would capture your traitor skin on film, you withdrew to your apartment and drank yourself to a lonely and furious death. Perhaps I am ready now to return you to your sleep.

Forgive my silence of twenty days, but here on the planet of Otto much has happened. World events continue to deteriorate, and the War Machine clamors for my services. My telephone rings off the hook.

Marta has discovered the Marlene Dietrich Collection at the Film Museum in Berlin, and she is determined to go. There are 15,000 photographs and more than 300,000 leaves of written documents on display, as well as countless personal effects including 50 handbags, 150 pairs of gloves, 400 hats, and 440 pairs of shoes. *Meine Liebe* Marlene, your closets must have shuddered under the weight of your vanity!

Since Marta is perpetually short on funds, she has decided that I will accompany her on her quest, and of course provide an all-expenses-paid vacation. She has calculated that I could be stuffed into an airplane seat if I lose 100 lbs. Amused at her request and ignorant of the capacity of her resolve, I acquiesced. She has rolled up her sleeves and gone to work. She threw out gallons of ice cream and absconded with wheels of fine French cheese. She divides steaks into infinitesimal portions, denies me butter on my baked potato, searches out the caches of Belgian chocolate hidden beneath my mattress, and hunts for evidence of illegal crumbs. I am forced to feed on troughs of salad with a tasty (although low-fat) vinaigrette. The final humiliation occurred when she brought the stationary bicycle of one of her departed husbands and set it up in the living room facing the television. I was terrified that I would upend the contraption or collapse the insufficient frame with my initial mount, but it has proven surprisingly well engineered. We have set up a stack of your movies, and I pedal and sweat as I watch you in your various incarnations of Marlene-hood slink across the stages of your life.

It is your last film, *Just a Gigolo*, that I return to most often. Surrounded by an entourage of handsome, cravat-adorned young men, you stare out with your black-lined and hooded, almond eyes and say, "Dancing, music, champagne: the best way to forget." In the darkness of a deserted café you stand next to a piano player whose silhouette fades into shadow. The ruinous brush strokes of well-lived years have been erased by the feathery touch of a black veil and the flickering shadows from a wide-brimmed hat placed at a provocative angle. With white-gloved hands clasped and a gold brooch fastened at your throat, you belt out your final song, the title song of the movie. From the deepest wells of human resolve you drink in the strength to sing as you have never sang before. *Life goes on without me*, you proclaim, the slightest quiver in your voice, and so it does, and so it shall when the terrible bulk of me goes up in flames to leave behind but a simple pile of ashes weighing nothing. I read in your biographies that tears flowed from all who watched the filming.

From the planet Mars, the news overwhelms me. My friend Opportunity appears to have landed on the shoreline of an ancient sea! The latest photographs of rock show bedding planes with ripples and discordant angles which, to the best of our knowledge, form only in the presence of flowing water. I have magnified the pictures, traced my finger along the delicate curves, and I concur. The possibilities for life, I learn, are found in the most surprising places.

I shall remain yours,

Otto

GOD SPENDS THE DAY EVERYWHERE

Ibye ejo bibara abejo
The things of tomorrow will be recounted by the people of tomorrow
—*Rwandan saying*

L ake Kivu, the ancients told, was formed on the hot,
dry plains of northwestern Rwanda when a selfish and
deceitful wife squatted down in her fields to relieve herself.
As punishment for her bad behavior, Imana made her waters flow until her fields were covered, and she drowned.
Her gourds and sleeping mat broke apart and became islands in the new, sweet lake. Fish leapt from the waves, and
the unforgiving land became soft and fertile.

Sister Joséphine recalls this legend when she walks
along the shores, picking her way across the slippery ledges
of rock, the scent of coffee blossoms a breath on her skin.
Sometimes, when it is early morning and only the fishermen and young children are awake, she takes off her shoes
and probes the sand with her toes. She picks up handfuls
and watches the sun glint from flecks of volcanic rock sift-
ing through her fingers.

Rwanda, she thinks then, is my home. She can't say the moment—or even the year—when this happened. When the spray and waves and sea-slicked cliffs that form the western coast of Brittany were tucked into a corner of her heart, and the warm current of Africa began to flow through her veins, became the pulse that rang in her ears from the time she awoke to the moment she lay down to sleep. Until last year, when the politics of hate opened a chasm in her calm and steady belief, Rwanda was the place where she could touch the face of God.

It is April now, the rainy season. This year Easter was early—it has come and gone. Sister Joséphine adorned the children in the orphanage with bright scarves and garlands of flowers. She decorated the church and the orphanage chapel with bouquets of lilies from her gardens. She prayed with her hands clasped tightly together and her eyes shut against the *abazimu* that wandered among the pews, restless and angry in death. With her face tilted toward the sky she waited for the slightest whisper of God's voice, but he was holding his breath.

The weather is as fickle as Sister Joséphine's faith. Some days rain bursts from the clouds in a fury, slashing paths through the terraced hillsides of Gisenyi, sending streams of red earth spilling into the lake. On these days the vegetables in her garden lift their leaves to the heavens, stretch roots into the softening soil. On these days Sister Joséphine once again feels the touch of God's finger on her forehead. But when the rains dry up and bean blossoms shudder and fall to the ground, Sister Joséphine has to dig in the dirt to find God; dig with her bare hands until they are scraped and bleeding.

The Banyarwanda have a saying: if you look into the eyes of a puppy before they are open, your child will be born blind. It was said that as a young girl, Enata's mother squatted in the sand on the shore of Lake Kivu to watch a bitch give birth beneath an overturned pirogue. Neither Enata nor her sister is blind, nor have they had an injury to the eye.

Every morning Enata watches Mount Nyiragongo from inside the orphanage gate, its teeth of fire and ash turning pale as the sun licks the lake, and light spreads across the waves in mercurial shivers. She sees the young boys run laughing into the water while their fathers wade out to the pirogues, empty water from the bilges with pails made of plastic bottles, unfasten the long poles that sway from the bows.

Every day Enata sees the soldiers stumble out from the barracks to begin their morning run, guns slung from shoulders, shaking sleep like a blanket from their bodies. The young Hutu boys, Clement among them, fall in singing behind the men, their feet sending up clouds of red dust. If she were to follow the procession she would come to a checkpoint, and the soldiers leaning against dusty jeeps would wave and call, perhaps raise their weapons into the air. If she were close enough she could smell the strong coffee on their breath, watch beads of sweat form a necklace around the throats of the Tutsi as they proffered their identity cards.

When Enata was ten, she saw the soldiers from the Rwandan Patriotic Front swoop into the town of Ruhengeri. She saw the Rwandan army fighting back, everyone running and shooting through the streets. She saw her father and mother pulled from a bus, dragged through the dirt. A gun butt to the head. The shudder of the machine gun against the soldier's body. The twist and fall of her father as he tried to protect his wife. Her brother—only four—wrenching free of her arms, running toward their parents, a cry flying from his throat, rising into the air as the bullets struck him. Her own voice fled forever into her fingertips. The Banyarwanda have no saying concerning the affliction of silence.

Sister Joséphine has finished her morning prayers. She steps onto the path and the breath of flowers greets her. Flowers she shipped from her convent in Brittany: lavender, alstroemeria, orchids, roses. Borders of thyme, basil, oregano, marjoram. She crushes leaves of lemon-scented geranium between two fingers, paints the scent across her cheek.

Along the lake shores and into the steep terraced hillsides, the gardens and coffee plantations of the *wazungu* are choked with nettles. Rocks jut from the soil. Feldspar teeth. Day by day the white families who have been her neighbors pack suitcases and flee. Banana trees wither. In the brittle chatter of leaves Sister Joséphine hears the bitterness of farewell: *murabeho*, they whisper: forever goodbye.

This morning a pale light washes the sky; there will be no rain. Red dust rises in the still air, and jeeps filled with soldiers idle in the narrow road. Something is wrong, Sister Joséphine thinks. There are no fishermen paddling out into the lake, no women washing clothes, no children bathing, filling plastic jugs and tubs with water.

From the orphanage she hears the children waking— rustling bedsheets, whispered supplications, shushed giggles. Enata stands alone by the gate, neck craned toward Lake Kivu, searching for Clement. Soon her sister Beata will open the door and run to her, and they will sign to each other in a language that—as far as Sister Joséphine knows—only God shares.

She wonders where the boys are: by this time they are usually strutting in the streets. Only last year they stopped by her gate every morning, flat bare feet shuffling, and she brought out baskets of sweet rolls steaming beneath a towel, passion fruit and slices of papaya quivering on a plate. Clement always waited until last, although his eyes never left the food. His hunger so natural that sight was sufficient to appease him. With a corner of the towel, Sister Joséphine hid the best roll for him.

Now the boys wear sneakers and Hutu Power T-shirts. One will have a radio, and the sound of Hutu Power from RTLM will tear through the morning stillness. Sweetened bread and a few slices of fruit no longer sustain their faith.

The cook screams in the kitchen. She runs out; soap bubbles stream from her arms. Sister! she calls. She is sobbing, and Sister Joséphine can barely pick the words from the slurry of speech. She takes the woman's hands in her own. Mukabera, she says. You must speak slowly.

President Habyarimana is dead, she says. Someone shot down his plane. The government's telling people to stay inside. They're setting up roadblocks all over the country and anyone caught on the streets could be shot. Mukabera stops, pulls in a mouthful of air. They're blaming the Tutsi. All Hutu, they say, should join the Interahamwe going house to house to kill them.

Sister Joséphine kneels in the dirt. God is deserting her, fleeing into the branches of acacia, spilling into the pebbles of light that fall between the branches.

Imana has abandoned us, Mukabera says, as if, along with her God, bright broken bits of Joséphine's thoughts escape from her body and clatter to the ground.

Enata turns from the gate and walks toward them. She holds her fingers to her mouth. Her dress ripples against her thin legs as she begins to run. Sister Joséphine sees in her eyes the dulled shock she remembers from three years ago when Enata and Beata first arrived: the unspeakable terror of witness. In an instant, the work of three years is undone—unraveling like a snagged loop of yarn from a sweater.

Come, she says. She rises, holds out her hand. She doesn't bother to brush the earth from her skirt. Enata takes one more step and stops.

Beata runs into the yard, as if signs from her sister's fingers had flown through the air, called her out. What's happened? she asks. What's wrong?

It's the end of the world, Mukabera wails. We're all going to die.

Sister Joséphine wants to slap her. She wants to beat her fists at the sky, throw rocks through the windows of the House of God.

Mukabera, we have to find courage within, she says. For the children's sake. They need to believe we can protect them.

Enata signs. If my sister can be with mama and papa, she will be happy, Beata says.

When Sister Joséphine was a child, she used to clamber to the edge of cliffs at sunset, open her arms wide and look out toward the sun as it careened into the sea beyond Pointe du Raz. Beads of spray clung to her skin. Wind lifted her hair, and anticipation thrummed inside her, a taut tendon. One day, she would think, the sun will catch fire in the sea. And I will be here to witness it. The thought made her giddy and light. Light enough to walk across the sea's surface and touch the skin of the sun.

Today the sun has caught fire and she has seen it. Whether God is with her or not no longer seems important. This thought terrifies her and calms her, both at once.

We'll eat breakfast, Mukabera, then we'll all go to the chapel. Imana hasn't deserted us. We need to keep that in our hearts.

Enata takes one hand, Beata the other. Two little birds, Sister Joséphine thinks, resting in my hands.

Sister Joséphine had been planting tomatoes when a fisherman knocked at the orphanage gate. Sister, I've brought you two little girls, he said. Enata and Beata trembled behind him, eyes half-closed. Their limbs and feet bled, open sores blooming. Mud crowned their heads, covered their ragged dresses. From the way the girls pressed against each other she understood them to be sisters.

What are your names? she asked. She kept her head down, hands at her sides. A posture she learned from her father, working with the new and frightened horses. What are your names? She offered a biscuit from her skirt pocket.

I found them crouched inside my pirogue, the fisherman said. They don't speak.

Enata took a step backwards, wobbled and fell. When Sister Joséphine lifted her, the child's head fell against the hollow of her shoulder. She remembered a young stork she found wounded by a rock, wing folded in against itself, a crumpled swirl of feathers on the path. She made a paste of fish and milk, smearing it on his beak until he learned to eat from her hand.

She fed the girls hot chocolate, gave them biscuits to dip in their cups. In the mornings they waited for her by the chapel door. Together they knelt and prayed.

Beata spoke within a week. When Sister Joséphine brought them books, she discovered they could read. In the classroom they sat in the front row. A fluid, whispered French rolled off Beata's tongue. Enata traced the words with her fingers. The pores of her fingers drank them in. It was a month before she smiled.

Sister Joséphine learned that they lived in Ruhengeri and their parents and aunt had been killed. They had come to Gisenyi to live with their grandmother. One morning, soon after they arrived, they awoke to find her dead. Killed, Beata said, by the grief in her heart.

Beata told her these things as if reciting verses from a book, but the story that surfaced in terrified glances, the startled flight from a loud noise—this remained as secret as Enata's signs. Sister Joséphine was patient. *Buhoro, buhoro,* the Banyarwanda said, *ni rwo urugendo*: little by little the bird builds its nest.

The first time Enata saw Clement he was fishing with his father. The children were walking with Sister Joséphine around the lake, and he stood in the bow of the pirogue, one hand on a long wooden pole, and waved. Enata did not wave back, but she remembered how he balanced on one foot like a crane and beat the surface of the lake with his pole.

Why does he do that? Enata signed to Beata. Why do the boys beat the water with sticks? Beata asked Sister Joséphine.

Sister Joséphine looked out across the lake. Enata wondered if it was France, and not Zaïre, that she saw in the distance. They're scaring the tilapia onto the hooks, Sister said.

The next day Clement came to the gate. He wore no shirt, and his ribs formed ridges between the valleys of skin. Enata was working with Beata and Sister Joséphine in the garden. Rose petals stuck to her feet: tiny pink toes. A basket of blossoms lay in the grass.

I want you to teach me to read, he said, holding a new schoolbook in his arms. Sister Joséphine wondered if it were stolen.

Enata, please open the gate, she said. She dropped a spent hydrangea stalk into the basket, smiling. Her hand brushed at a fly, leaving a streak of earth across her cheek like a second smile. Enata rose, walked to the gate with her head down.

The boy smelled sulfurous: a mixture of fish and rank lake mud. Scratches covered his legs. Sparkles of sand flew when he shook his head.

What's your name? he asked.

Enata turned her head toward the garden.

She doesn't speak, said Beata.

Why? She can't?

I don't know.

You can't?

He holds the book like you hold a child, Enata thought. She took the hydrangea from the basket and offered it to him. His fingers felt damp and soft, as if he had risen from the lake bottom. Words pushed against her fingers, but she didn't sign them. Instead she wrote her name in the dirt with her rose-speckled foot: *E-N-A-T-A*.

During the dry season, the skies of Rwanda sang—as clear and sharp as fine crystal struck with a spoon. The air thrummed with the scent of coffee blossoms, and Mount Nyiragongo breathed harmless puffs of steam. On such days Sister Joséphine returned from the market with bags of passion fruit, pineapples, mangoes, bunches of chubby, pink-finger bananas. On such days the sweetness of her life intoxicated her; she fell to her knees to thank God for sending her to do his work in this country.

In France her purpose had slipped through her fingers. It had been the nuns who cared for her when her mother became too weak and her father was forced to return to his fields. The scent of their lavender soap lingered in her hair after they brushed it. She inhaled the crisp smell of starch from the sleeves of their habits.

You must pray, they whispered, kneeling with her beside her mother's bed. The sprays of sunlight falling on their wimples in the darkened room seemed to her the proof of God's promise. A simple barter. She would become a nun. Her mother would get well.

She kept her bargain despite her mother's death. But working in the herb gardens at the convent, lost among the pungent tendrils of thyme, the hedges of rosemary with their fragrance of smoke, her prayers floated away. She called to God and heard only the breeze and rubbed-together leaves. Here in Rwanda the hillsides spoke to her. The syllables of her name rolled off the tongues of rocks, but it was her given name she heard: *Lé-on-tine.*

When Clement arrived with his books and asked her to teach him to read, she dared to imagine a sliver of God inside herself, as if she had the power to shape the wet clay of his limbs. She had seen him pause in the bow of the pirogue, leaning against his pole, watching the children walk by in their pressed shirts, school satchels bouncing on their backs. She gave him clothes from the boxes that came from France for the orphans. She cooked him omelets, shared her cakes and tea. She taught him numbers and sums. A hunger for food and for knowledge equally balanced in his soul.

Some months after Enata and Beata came, they sat at a table under a tree reading *Eloise in Paris.* Clement suddenly looked up and touched her eyelid, traced a line down to her chin. She didn't stop him.

You're so beautiful, he said. Too beautiful to be a nun.

Enata frowned and signed. Beata gave words to her shapes: My sister says there is no one more beautiful than a nun.

Enata was running back from her classes one morning when Sister Joséphine stopped her. She held out a package wrapped in brown paper.

Take it, Sister said.

Enata took it, felt the weight of it in her hands. It came from America. She sat in the dining hall with Beata, slid a knife beneath the tape. She put aside the row of bright stamps: strange flowers and birds. *Gorillas of the Lowlands and Mountains*, Beata read.

They flipped through the pages of photographs. Silverbacks with expressions of bored acceptance; their enormous sloped foreheads, their sad, wise eyes. Babies caught in a posture of chest-beating while mothers lounged on a carpet of nettles and vines. Black fur shone in filtered sunlight, fingers like leather gloves curled around handfuls of leaves.

Clement came out of the kitchen with his empty basin. Lake mud speckled his shorts, but his feet had been scrubbed clean. From the kitchen Enata heard Sister Joséphine packing tilapia in ice.

I want to be an animal doctor, he said. He touched a silverback's nose. Beata laughed.

Our father was a tracker, Enata signed. He went with the *wazungu* into the Virunga mountains. Once he took us. When the gorillas came close, you had to lie down on your stomach. My legs were on fire from stinging nettles.

Beata shook her head. No, she signed. I won't tell him.

Please. He always looks so sad. We should make him happy.

Enata remembered the tall, rubber boots, the blue jacket her father wore. A Yankees baseball cap that someone from New York had sent. The smell of damp leaves, the sweetness of wild celery on his fingers when he came home.

You can't be a doctor, Beata told Clement. Doctors are white.

Sister Joséphine says she'll help me. She says she'll give me money for school.

Rich *wazungu* pay for our school, signed Enata. I'm going to be a nurse.

Beata wrinkled her nose. You can't go to school stinking of fish, Clement, she said.

He picked up his basin. You don't understand that book, he said, sweeping it from the table. Stamps followed, fluttering to the floor.

Stupid girl: you don't speak English. He turned away.

Enata wanted to call him back. She wanted to tell him about the photographs the *wazungu* sent to her family. Her father hacking a path with his machete. Calling to the gorillas with a low, throaty cough, head bent forward, foot resting on a fallen tree trunk. A group of tourists kneeling, the trackers standing behind. Enata managed to save a photo, her favorite, tucked in her dress. She ran back for it after the soldiers came, after her Auntie came to take her and Beata away. They fled into the bush. When she looked back, the windows in her empty house looked like a gorilla's eyes: cavernous and sad. Bullet holes pocked the walls. Two days later, her Auntie stepped on a snake and died.

Kneeling beside her bed, Sister Joséphine recalls when President Habyarimana visited the orphanage. The children danced for him and presented him with a bouquet of flowers. Seated in a small and uncomfortable chair, he seemed to swallow up all the space around him, as if the boundaries of his body couldn't contain him. She was struck by his smile, the roiling, liquid laugh that welled from his belly. He walked down the rows of children and shook their hands. He gave them candy. His soldiers milled about among the gardens, guns swinging sleepily.

Now he has been blown out of the sky. Sister Joséphine imagines his spirit rising with the smoke of his burning plane. She closes her eyes and prays for his soul. She prays for the soul of the country.

In the kitchen the radio screeches. Lists are read of people to kill. Addresses are given. Sister Joséphine recognizes the name of a pediatrician she met at a conference in Kigali.

The name of a professor who has been speaking out against Hutu Power.

The children are waiting in the chapel. What can she tell them? Last night she sat in her cell and read St. Paul's letter to the Corinthian Church. *The weakness of God is stronger than man's strength.* She nodded her head, drew comfort and order from the words. Last night she would have said to the children: Have faith. God's love will protect you. But between night and morning, this country she has wrapped about her like a cloak of holiness has been picked up, shaken, and flung against the rocks. She hears a faint tap on the windowsill and looks up to see a bird hunting for bugs. His head bobs from the puff of bright feathers as he drums against the concrete. The sound of his beak, she thinks, is not unlike the sound the rain made on the roof of her childhood home.

Sister Joséphine tries to recall a message from St. Paul. She tears apart the softness of vowels, hunts inside the hidden corners of consonants. She can't discern the strength of man or God. She finds only a swamp of weakness. The smoke of burning houses is all that reaches heaven now.

One Sunday, after church, Clement asked Enata if she could come to his house for a meal. When he came to get her, he wore a clean, pressed shirt and a pair of shorts that was too big. Lining up in front of their doorway, his family looked scrubbed and shining.

They sat at a long, wobbly table, coarsely shaped. Clement's mother poured water from a steaming kettle over their hands. A little girl in a pleated dress held a basin. They ate spicy grilled tilapia with their fingers. Platters mounded with fried plantains and crispy potatoes shining with oil were passed around. The eyes of nine brothers and sisters watched Enata as she ate, followed the movement of her hand to her mouth. Bottles of Fanta wept onto the plastic tablecloth.

Why doesn't she talk? a brother asked.

She doesn't want to, Clement replied.

Why do you live in the orphanage? Are your parents dead?

A nod.

Did the Tutsi cockroaches kill them?

Enata thought of her Tutsi grandmother. The smoke from her pipe and the words of her stories curling into the air in late afternoon. The sweetened tea and Belgian biscuits, a thin coating of chocolate melting on the tongue. When you are eight, you have not yet cut these scars across your heart: *Hutu, Tutsi.* When you are eight and your parents are pulled from a bus by men with guns it does not matter who they are. She wiped her noisy fingers on her skirt, silenced them in her lap. The youngest brother, kneeling in the chair next to hers, touched her arm and looked at her plate. She smiled. With his tiny hands he removed the last flakes of fish from the bones, put them, one by one, in his mouth.

After lunch they walked down to the lake. Bubbles rose from a hot spring, steam swirling into the papyrus. Nearly naked boys bathed with filthy bars of soap. A film of soap, oil and sunlight shimmered on the surface; a dead fish floated. Squatting in the mud, a boy dunked a potato speared with a stick. Enata laughed without sound.

Put your toe in the water, Clement said.

She plunged her big toe into the pool, withdrew it quickly, hopped on one foot. It felt as hot as the water she poured from the kettle for Sister's tea.

They waded out onto a rotting dock. The timbers creaked and swayed beneath them as if they were on a ship. Pirogues rocked in the shallows. A man hoisted a net, paddled out into the lake. A group of little girls waved, the bright rags of their dresses lifting above their knees.

I want to learn your language. Will you teach me?

Enata nodded. A hammerkopf lifted off from a branch of eucalyptus and glided across the lake. His flat brown head bobbed toward the waves.

Umukobwa, she signed and pointed to herself. Girl. *Umuhungu.* Boy. Clement tried the shapes with his fingers. *Yégo,* Enata signed. Yes.

That's what we make the canoes from. He pointed to a stand of silver-trunked trees on the hillside. We call them *imiseke.*

Her fingers made the sign for *igiti, tree. Tree,* Clement signed. She pointed at the lake. *Amazi,* she signed, water. She embraced the sky, the lake, the hills with her arms. She held her hands together in prayer. *Imana,* she signed. God.

A convoy of soldiers crawled up the road, leaning out from open-backed jeeps and trucks. Clement leapt up laughing, made a machine gun out of air. He mowed down papyrus, banana trees, oil palms, the boy cooking the potato, the ragged giggling girls.

What's the sign for gun?

Enata squinted. With her half-closed eyes she sent him far away and made him very small. She had no sign for gun. Instead she made the sign for *uburozi,* poison. *Urupfu,* death.

They found the puppy tied to the orphanage gate a week before Christmas. His body was a cage of bones, his shoulder blades tiny wings. He shook and cried. After they washed and dried him, they brushed his fur with a brush made from coconut fiber until he shone like charcoal. He ate fistfuls of *ubugari* dipped in soup, a sweet potato and a piece of fish. His belly expanded until they thought he would roll down the hill.

They stood on the porch. A steady rain fell. The sound on the corrugated roof was like Enata's mother singing when Enata was small. Her grandmother used to sit on a chair in front of the door with her pipe, telling the stories of the lion-woman, Nyavirezi, and her children: Nyavirungu, daughter of volcanoes, and Ryangombe, the powerful king. Her brother cooed in his sling. Her father squatted with his knife and a piece of wood. The shapes appeared slowly, and Enata and Beata guessed what they would be. A truck. A boat. A mountain gorilla with her baby. Sometimes he spoke of the *mzungu* lady, Dian Fossey, who lived with the gorillas and made them famous. He had been her tracker until she was murdered.

Enata signed and pointed to her fingers. At first Beata stared, silent and frowning. Enata signed again, loped out into the rain and beat her hands against her chest. Beata laughed and clapped her hands together.

Digit, she said. We'll call the puppy Digit.

On the window ledge above her bed, the small wooden gorilla that her father carved had squatted, protecting Enata while she slept. This is Digit, her father had said. He was Mademoiselle Fossey's favorite: her child.

Digit was missing for days before Enata found him lying in the flower garden. When he tried to come to her he stumbled and fell. She carried him to Sister Joséphine and they made him a bed. They took him to the infirmary. Sister Joséphine boiled fish and mixed it with sweet condensed milk. For a week he lay on his blankets. Enata slept in a cot beside him. She dipped her fingers in the sweetened fish. Digit licked them with his soft, hot tongue.

On the day Digit died, Clement came to see her. He had joined Hutu Power, and he wore sunglasses, American jeans, a T-shirt that said *Hard Rock Cafe*. On his feet, a new pair of boots.

He rarely came to read books anymore, and when Sister Joséphine questioned him he replied that big things were going to happen in the country. Secret, powerful things. Only stupid people read books, he said. Soon we won't need them any more.

But he dug a grave for Digit, laid him gently inside. He made a cross from *imiseke* wood with *Digit* painted in blue letters. Two weeks later he came with a dog carved in ironwood. Enata recognized the high, pointed ears, the tail curled into a question mark.

Mukabera is cooking a pot of sorghum porridge. It is thin and has a sharp, sour smell: it is turning into sorghum beer. Sister Joséphine opens a cupboard, takes out a tin with a few packets of sugar inside. She has abandoned her black skirt, put on a pair of men's trousers. Spirals of tea-colored hair escape from her scarf.

In the past three days families have been arriving at the orphanage for protection. Children sleep four and five to a bed. People squat in hallways, lie down on the floors. The news from the countryside is bad.

Today it is raining: black squalls burst from bloated clouds. Water splashes into the pans and basins placed beneath the roof for collection. Water tears at the soil of the garden—now nearly picked clean—disgorges mouthfuls of mud. Sodden ghosts wander among the bean stalks. There is no power, no phone. Piles of garbage tilt behind the buildings.

Sister Joséphine pulls on her raincoat. Today the soldiers are allowing people to go to the market. They're nearly out of food. Mukabera gives the pot of porridge to Enata to bring into the dining hall. She rolls an extra fold into her *pagne* to protect her clothes from the mud.

No, Enata signs. I want to go with them.

Sister knows without waiting for Beata what she has said. Enata, you can't come. You're needed here.

A light shines in Enata's face. Sister recognizes the burning wick of God. The wick that sputters in her own chest.

Before the war began, the shores of Lake Kivu glistened—bejeweled. Gardeners worked in the gardens of the coffee farmers, the executives from Primus Beer. Belgian women sat beneath umbrellas sipping tea and iced juice. Sister Joséphine would wave, call them by name. Tourists at the Palm Beach Hotel lounged in beach chairs, ate passion fruit and pineapple from delicate china. Euphorbia and eucalyptus screened them from the sun.

Today, two more houses have burned. Blackened timbers lean against each other. There is no glass left in the windows; they gape like the empty sockets of a skull. Unhinged shutters slap.

The rain falls harder. It slams into the streets, stains Sister Joséphine's sneakers red with mud. When she descended the hill from the orphanage and saw the men with machetes and guns, she sent Mukabera back. The road was thick with them; they loomed beneath the trees, lined the paths and drank their beer. I don't think your identity card will protect you now, she said.

She knocks on the doors of shuttered shops, walks on when no one answers. Down a small dirt path where huts squat beneath pale-leaved acacia there is a little shop where Sister Joséphine goes to buy the crumbly cookies from Kenya that the children love. She knocks, and a woman lets her in.

Good morning, Sister, the woman says. She is tall and thin, her face sculpted from ironwood with a delicate blade: the features that inspired the Belgians to designate the Tutsi as the chosen tribe.

Good morning, Pauline, Sister Joséphine replies. *Amakuru*? How are you?

Ni meza, I'm fine.

As if they stand in the sunshine and the world still makes sense.

Do you have any bread? Some powdered milk?

The woman disappears into her house. Sister Joséphine hears a radio: a song praising Hutu Power.

Here, Sister, take this.

In a sack, two loaves of bread, a folded piece of newspaper from which flakes of powdered milk spill. A packet of Kenyan biscuits. Some sugar. Sister Joséphine reaches into her bag for her coins. The woman stops her.

Pas d'importance, Soeur, it doesn't matter. In a few days' time I will be dead.

Enata stands at the locked gate. A red swollen sun rolls on the eastern horizon. She climbs over the bars and runs down the hill behind the orphanage. She hopes Beata will not wake and find her missing.

The *ta-ta-ta* of gunfire rattles the ground. *Abazimu* rise like mist from the lake. Their abandoned bodies roll on the waves. The ghosts are singing: their voices chatter from the treetops. They brush against her skin. They catch in branches, snarled nettles, palm fronds. Enata gathers the large heart-shaped *umuravumba* leaves in her scarf.

Last night the killing began. People calling out, banging on the gate, pleading for shelter. Gangs going house to house with spears, machetes, nail-studded clubs they named *nta m pongano y'umwanzi*, no mercy for the enemy. The living crawled out from the piles of dead. Smoke filled the night sky. With the water she has saved in her basin, she will boil the *umuravumba* leaves and make a tea to treat the wounds.

The Banyarwanda say about God: *Imana yirwa ahandi igataha i Rwanda*, God spends the day everywhere but comes home to sleep in Rwanda. Sister Joséphine steps across the bodies in the road. Eyes and mouths open, they offer up their innocence to her. Body of Christ, blood of Christ. Flies lift in a cloud.

Soldiers and militia toss bodies into piles. They sing as they heave—a rhythmic chanting. Identity cards and bright scraps of clothing swirl in the dirt. She shouldn't have come out, but there's no more water. There are so many wounded lying in the halls. They have no more cloth to make bandages, no way to clean the gashes.

Standing at the edge of the road Sister Joséphine recognizes two doctors from Médecins Sans Frontières. They lean out from a ridge overlooking the lake. She calls to them, takes a few tentative steps onto the bloodied sand. They don't hear her—they're counting bodies in the water. With them is a journalist, counting in English. His voice has a flat, singsong quality, as if he's reciting a children's verse. She thinks of the orphans playing a game they learned from an American tourist.

Eighty-three, eighty-four
shut the door
Eighty-five, eighty-six
pick-up-sticks.

Sister Joséphine awakes to the sound of singing. A crazed, wild song. Notes torn from the throat of a lion. She pulls on pants and a shirt, runs outside. A mass of men and boys pushes against the gate. Women dance. The night sky sizzles with torchlight, and machetes leave incandescent, circling trails.

She can name most of them. She held them in her arms when they were small and sick and their mothers brought them, trembling with fever, to her door. They left milk, fish, fruit as payment. They sang to her in greeting as they worked their fields.

What do you want from us? she asks.

We hear you're hiding Tutsi. We've come to fumigate, one says. There is laughter, an incomprehensible torrent of shouts. A beer bottle sails over the wall and shatters beside her feet.

The air staggers with *urwagwa* fumes, the strong banana beer. The men sway and lean into each other, eyes glittering. She can count their missing teeth.

Sister Joséphine hears a door open. She turns to see Enata walk toward her, hands held out, palms up like a painting of Jesus, the burst of gold around his head, the shining stigmata. The men push against the gate.

It's the stupid one, a woman calls. The mute. Hey, stupid—are you a Tutsi cow? Can you speak to save yourself?

We are all God's children, Sister Joséphine says. If you want to kill someone, kill me.

Enata comes to the gate. Her eyes glow in the light of the torches. Her body trembles with light.

For a moment the crowd pauses. Sister Joséphine detects a slight backward shifting of bodies. She dares to pray they will be spared.

We don't want to hurt you, Sister. We only want the *inyenzi*. We're taking them to a safe place. If you bring out the Tutsi cockroaches, the rest of you can live.

A shrill cackling erupts. Then a surge, a freak wave. The gate tears from its hinges; the sea pours in, unstoppable. From the dormitories Sister Joséphine hears the screams of children, the keening of the women. She pulls Enata inside the circle of her arms.

Stop, she shouts. Stop where you are. Miraculously, they do. She smells the hot stale sweat, the sour beer, a metallic synapse of excitement. I ask you in the name of God to leave, she says.

The dark curve of the sea parts, reveals a luminescent vein of earth. Clement emerges, steps across this path. He appears to Sister Joséphine to be floating toward her.

Enata pulls free. She stands in front of him, arms outstretched. Her nightdress quivers in the breeze. The ends of her headscarf quiver against her shoulder.

Tell them you are Hutu, Clement signs. His fingers are wood; they can't get around the shapes of the words. He doesn't know the sign for *mbabarira*, forgive me.

There are no Hutu, no Tutsi in God's eyes, Enata signs. The words glow in her fingertips: her hands are flames. Torchlight ricochets from walls, palm trees, the bruised ghosts of Sister Joséphine's flowers.

Behind him the crowd shifts, presses forward. Torchlight glints from the nails in their clubs. They begin to chant. Clement senses that in a minute they will break into a run.

She's Hutu! he shouts. If he moves toward her, they will kill him too.

Tell them, he signs again.

Enata kneels, palms together, bows her head. Her lips move without sound. Sister Joséphine kneels beside her. She prays that in the few moments she has managed to bargain from God, the children have run into the hills. She prays that he will find a way to keep them safe in his hands. She prays that Enata will feel no pain.

If you can kill us while we pray then God help you, she says. There's nothing more I can do.

Sister, he says. You could save so many.

No, Clement. It's not for me to judge who can live and who must die.

Clement lowers himself onto his knees. At least the gift of dignity is his to give. A gun glints from the waistband of his trousers.

Sister Joséphine, will you pray for me?

Yes, Clement, I will.

They pray, then Clement rises. He puts the gun to her head. Sister Joséphine was twelve when her mother died. She walked with her father to the cliffs. The wind pulled at her, and she tilted toward the edge of the precipice. The upwelling spray cooled her cheeks. Papa, she's not really dead, she remembers saying. I can feel her in the water and the wind. She's turned into the breath of God.

From a nearby tree Sister Joséphine hears the sound of a bird. She can see him from the corner of her eye. A small green bird perched on a yellow trumpet flower. She sees that Enata watches him too. How odd, she thinks. He must mistake the light of torches for the rising sun.

Indivisible

There are five fingers on Dee's left hand. Five fingers on the right. Her nails are clean, and the chewed tips are imperceptible without close scrutiny. Good. She kicks her feet free from the sheets and raises them in a V. Five toes on each foot. Nine toenails perfect and shining, one a barnacle-scarred scallop shell, the victim of a recent marathon.

She analyzes her hands and feet in the wash of Houston lights that filters through the hotel curtains. An anemic yellow light. The light from the clock radio is nausea-green. Prime numbers. Primary colors. Primal scream.

Dee stretches her arm toward the light switch but pauses mid-air. In the darkness she feels the ridge of fresh scar between armpit and left breast. Nothing new. No new growths multiplying in the terrible darkness between midnight and 5:20 A.M. No new clusters of uncontrollable cells expanding by powers of two. She feels one more time, sweeping her fingers in tiny circles across her flesh. Inert. Her cells, her breasts, her life. She turns on the lamp.

The numbers on the digital clock radio read 5:20. Twenty divided by five is four. Two hands plus two feet.

The number five seems suddenly and terrifyingly signifi-
cant, as if the universe itself expanded and contracted in
beats of five: *in two three four five, out two three four five.*

In her house in Dallas it is also 5:20. How many miles
from Houston to Dallas? She guesses around 200. The
flight takes approximately fifty-five minutes. An estimate,
but still: *you see?*

Five is also a Fibonacci number, the series of sums of
the previous two. One, zero plus one, one plus one, one
plus two, two plus three. Dee breathes in this truth: the
natural world spirals in an endless Fibonacci sequence. The
numbers of leaves, petals on flowers, the secret inward curl
of the nautilus shell. The number of pairs of rabbits multiplying, multiplying.

When Dee left her house, Clay sat at the kitchen table,
pulling thick skeins of hair into Rasta braids. Sheet music
lay scattered on the floor. She had to step over it, wobbling
on her thin-spiked heels, to kiss him good-bye. She wonders
if he is home sleeping now or out prowling for the nearest
available female, sampling the just desserts of a jazz musician's gig. Musicians. They will promise up and down their
sad, sweet riffs, but they will never change.

She does not have to leave the hotel until eight. Her
presentation is at nine. They are sending the manager of
Research and Development to pick her up in his fancy gas-
eating car. Special Dee, whippet-thin, with her oil company
job, her fancy Ph.D., her melon-gold curls and sexy black-
stockinged-high-heeled legs. They will never guess that her
breasts are inert and a melon-ball shaped lump has been
scooped from her hungry flesh.

What to do, what to do with this stretch of time.
Reading is impossible; her mind flips and spins on the
sentences, spirals off on its own untraceable journey. Her
lecture is packed in neat memorized boxes of words. She
knows it down to the smiles and pauses that will make her
audience laugh.

There is a pool in the bowels of the hotel. It opens at
6:00, but today she can't swim. Seven days out of the pool

following a biopsy, said the doctor. It has only been four. Looks good, said the doctor, ninety-five percent sure, but she knows better, knows how men and statistics lie.

Why did mammogram lead to ultrasound lead to needle lead to knife? Why did descriptions zigzag from "diffuse" to "suspicious" to "inconclusive?" Dee imagines evil-looking cells in trench coats making shady deals.

The pool is twenty-five yards long, three lanes wide. Dee swims here whenever she is sent to lecture in Houston, wowing the fat red-faced Oil Men who float in the Jacuzzi stew with her swim-team perfect butterfly. Back and forth Dee flies, her body undulating with her powerful dolphin kick. *Streamline off the wall, kick two three four five.*

They will never guess that she is forty-seven with a child of her own at Harvard, intent on his own fancy Ph.D. They will never imagine the nights, husband Missing In Action, when she stood in the darkness by the child's bed, breathing in the sweet hay smell of his dreams, trembling at the café-latte perfection of skin—the harmonic mixing of Clay's dark wood tones, her Irish-linen-whites—in paralyzed awe of his very creation from two simple cells.

Lester. Young Lester, Clay had joked. Dee allowed him this name, this tribute to the great jazz legend. Clay held the accidental gift of their union in his arms, dreaming, she knew, of those tiny fingers sliding up and down the scales of a saxophone. Never, she vowed. *Never, Never, Never.*

Dee swings her feet onto the carpet. She rises, stretches, takes a few deep breaths. She walks toward the bathroom but stops abruptly two steps, maybe three, short of the bathroom door. She realizes two things: first that she has counted her steps, and second that sometime between the hours of midnight and 5:20 A.M. she has come to believe that her life must proceed in countable units divisible by five. She has taken eleven steps. Had she understood her predicament sooner, she could have traversed the distance in ten bold paces.

What shall she do? If she takes a step backward, does she subtract or add? Is a march in place zero or one? Despite

the urgent press of her bladder she sits naked on the floor
and begins to cry. No, she says, swallowing sniffles. Not
now. Rules—she must establish the rules. A step backwards
is subtracted. The smallest stomp of her toes is added. This
last thing she concedes unwillingly. It seems like cheating
but is necessary, she knows, to conceal behavior that may
be construed as bizarre.

She pushes herself up, takes a small step backwards and
bounds onto the bathroom tile. She feels a warm trickle
against her inner thigh. On the cold white seat she allows
herself to weep in terrified, uncontrolled gulps.

Dee is no stranger to counting. Swimming since the
age of five, she counted strokes, laps, seconds shed from
her times. She and her sister Rachael counting cars from
the window of the station wagon on the way to practice. In
school she built worlds from the unfaltering predictability
of math.

During the times when her father was drinking, tearing
through her evenings with his furious binges, she began
to count steps, dogs in front yards, cracks in the sidewalk.
How many stepped on 'til you break your father's back?

When the punishments started, her body folded in a
stiff V across a stool, she catalogued the blows from his
belt that seared her bared buttocks like a brand. At night,
huddled in bed with Rachael, Dee would guide her sister's
fingers across the fresh wounds.

Dee wipes her cheek with the back of her hand. She
turns up the shower until it nearly blisters. She scrubs her
thighs until they are lobster red, lathers face and neck with
five swift strokes, steps out and surrounds herself with the
elegant white towel. She takes up her brush. How many
strokes to ensure healthy hair? Was it fifty? Per side? Her
hair is beginning to thin; it comes out in thick, snarled
clumps at certain times of the month. She fears that fifty
per side will leave her bald.

The hotel gym opens at 6:00. There are rows of gleaming
handled treadmills and exercise bikes with enormous front

wheels. Dee hates the sweaty closeness of gyms, prefers to set out by herself along the black gumbo trails around the lakes.

She remembers when Lester was three or four her sister came to visit. Rachael sat at the breakfast table with a newspaper and a cup of tea, her milk-skinned daughter bouncing on her thigh. Young Lester sat spread-legged on the floor crashing trucks together, his woolly curls a-tangle. "They found a body at the lake, Dee. A body. Right where you were running." Rachael looked up with rabbit-scared eyes.

"Death is death," Dee shrugged. "When it comes it comes." It was the first time she had said it aloud, the first time she realized it was true.

She didn't tell Rachael that it was only the current of Lester's heart that pulled her along, kept her afloat through evenings of guessing the hour when Clay would come home. The current of Lester's heart and the wonder she saw in his eyes at the very existence of the world.

The years, Dee realizes, have made her cautious. She dresses, puts on her shoes and heads for the hotel gym. She has no desire to end her life on a filthy Houston street. Cancer, at least, has a tragic dignity about it. *Does* it? She reconsiders. *Seems fifty-fifty to me.*

There are four people in the gym. Two older men walk on treadmills, last night's beer bouncing in bellies that hang over the elastic of their shorts. A woman with headphones and a praying-mantis waist lifts weights; a man with a ragged Exxon T-shirt and bulging calves rides a bike.

Dee hoists herself onto a treadmill. For sixty minutes she counts her steps at 7:50-minute miles or calculates the Fibonacci sums as high as she can manage in her head. The rhythmic sums comfort her. Their smart, crisp edges push away cancer and march over visions of Clay's earth-dark arms entwined with the limbs of coeds. She can't fill in the tones of the students' skin—it doesn't matter. The point is that their skin is smooth and shivery as satin beneath Clay's hands—both qualities that hers has lost. From the headphones notes of the *Brandenburgische Konzerte* drift into her blood and calm her nervous heart. No jazz for Dee today.

The telephone confronts Dee when she unlocks her door. It seems larger than the television, larger than the comfortable armchair, as large as the room itself. Look at me, it says. I am your connection, your mainline to the world, your bearer of news. Seize me in your fingers if you dare.

She sits on the bed and pulls the cell phone from her purse. Ridiculous, she knows. There were no messages at midnight. Clay is sleeping or fucking, and her surgeon to the rich and famous won't be in his office before nine holes of golf. She turns on the phone and checks.

Sleeping or fucking, the hotel phone whispers. Do you have the guts to know? Can you run this little experiment to its conclusion?

Dee lifts the receiver, puts it down, lifts again but keeps her finger on the button. *In two three four five, out two three four five*, she breathes.

Before the pea-size lump presented itself to the underside of Dee's third finger, she was ready to leave. Enough is enough, she said, for the three hundredth or three thousandth time. To hell with this love thing that slides its fingers inside my ribs every time I turn my back. Enough is enough is enough. She made a list of things to take, things to do, words to say.

She can't remember the last time they made love. Sex, yes. But sweat-drenched teeth-grinding screaming-out love? A faraway dream.

The blame is partly hers, she knows. She can drink all the soymilk she wants, stuff her squirrel cheeks with boiled salted soybeans till the cows come home, but her hormones are jumping ship. Tiny estrogen molecules scurry like rats from the flushed, open pores of her skin. And Clay follows their trails to the tree-shaded houses and apartments near the campus of Southern Methodist University. There the wild but well-bred girls of Texas study music and other arts from a locally famous professor: a kohl-eyed saxophone player with hair that sprouts like kudzu vines from his head and delicate fingers that dance up and down atonal scales of air.

Dee lifts her finger from the button and calls. Five rings. I'll give him five rings, no more. On the fourth ring she hears the phone picked up, dropped, picked up again. "Clay," she says. It's all she can manage.

"Mellow-Dee, what's up?" He hasn't called her that in years. She hears puzzle or worry in the sleep-thick whisper. She never calls home.

"Clay," she says again like some stupid schoolgirl. She listens for the telltale rustle of a sheet, a dream-muffled female sigh. "I'm scared." She puts her fist in her mouth. She hadn't meant to tell the truth.

"What is it, Baby?" She hears him sit up. She thinks of his warm skin and wants to cry.

"Clay, would you notice if suddenly I had no breasts?"

She has not told him about the lump. Rita, her computer tech, drove her to surgery. A foot thing, she said. I'll be sort of groggy tonight. On the way home she wrapped her foot in gauze. She wore a T-shirt to bed, turned breast and tear-salted cheeks away.

Dee hears Clay's belly laugh and starts to giggle herself. She clutches her stomach and squeezes her thighs together to keep from losing control.

"Dee, what are you talking about? For a genius, you are making no sense a-tall."

Dee wipes away a tear, then two. "I just miss you, that's all. I wonder sometimes if you miss me, too." She hears shuffling, but she thinks it's him.

"I'll see you tonight, Baby. Only nine hours away."

She looks at her watch. "Ten. With luggage and traffic, ten."

"I love you, Dee." She hears him yawn, imagines his long body stretching.

"I love you, too," she says and pushes the button down.

Well? inquires the phone. Was he alone?

Inconclusive, she answers. Ninety-five percent sure.

The hotel breakfast presents Dee with a new set of challenges. She wants cereal, but does she have to count the flakes? Chex are easily counted, but she hates them. She prefers granola but could not manage the sums. Her hand wavers above the row of cheery boxes, reaches for Blueberry Lo-fat Granola. Count, her brain commands. She chooses Chex. At the table she pulls an eight-ounce carton of soymilk from her purse.

Her feet in their sensible shoes are hidden by a long skirt with spiraling Indian patterns. Her high heels and short dress are packed in her bag. How could she five-step in her shiny black spikes?

Chex are larger than she remembers. She picks up a teaspoon, puts it down, asks the waitress for a soup spoon.

"I'm starving," she explains, at the woman's slight smirk.

The Chex float away like rafts on a sea of milk. In desperation, she scoops an uncounted mound into her mouth. She nearly chokes, spits the half-chewed pulp into her napkin.

For the first time tiny fingers of fear tickle Dee's ribs. They poke at the lobes of her lungs. How long will this go on? Will she have to count drops of chemo as they drip into a line in her chest? Will she have to wonder *sleeping* or *fucking*, as she heaves up her breakfast, pulls out handfuls of hair at the bathroom sink? She picks up a newspaper and pretends to read.

The date on the paper is May 17. Tomorrow, she realizes, is the twenty-second anniversary of the night she met Clay. It is also the twenty-second anniversary of the eruption of Mt. St. Helens, and the night she knows with absolute certainty that Lester began his life from the encounter of two erupted cells.

I knew him, Dee kept whispering into her margaritas. She had been saying it, thinking it since morning, when she heard about the mountain and the dead geologist, incinerated in a sulfurous blaze of pyroclastic ash. She was four years into a graduate degree and three hours into a good honest drunk. She began to fall in love with the saxophone player when he played his Charlie Parker riffs, the notes blowing and cascading in a fiery explosion of their own.

"Buy the sax player a drink," she told the waitress, gulping the last of hers. "Tell him it's from me, a volcanically eruptive fan."

"Thank you," he said when he sat at her table. "To whom do I owe this honor and privilege?" Dee felt the warmth of his body seep into her own, smelled his sweet hot sweat.

"Dee," she said and tipped him a toast.

The sax player tipped back his head, laughed with his wide mouth. "Dee. Dee. Are you mellow, Dee? Are you mellow-yellow-Dee?"

At her apartment Dee showed him pictures she took of volcanoes in Indonesia, the aftermath of earthquakes in the Philippines.

"The Ring of Fire," she said and showed him the map on her wall, pointing out the red circles and triangles that represented the earthquakes and eruptions lining the Pacific Rim.

She showed him pages of her thesis with their scrolls of equations. She told him how the symbols soothed her, transforming the violent chaos of the earth into elegant order. Clay traced the symbols with his finger and smiled. He began to hum.

"It's like music, Mellow-Dee. Some crazy atonal composition." He blew his saxophone of air into the fiery night. "You know, we're inevitably united because math and music are two halves of the same beautiful whole."

Dee began to cry. Margarita-sweet tears dripped onto Clay's arm. She told him about the dead geologist, how he worked in the lab across from hers at school, how she had gone to his presentations, talked to him about the magic of magma bubbling down a slope. She told him how his eyes burned when he spoke of the privilege of witnessing such primal power released.

Clay held her and rocked. He kissed her hair. "Blaze-of-glory, Mellow-Dee—what better way to go?" He sat her up, traced a grand explosion with his hands.

At that moment Dee understood two things: first, that Clay was absolutely right, that she herself would be happy to pass from this world in a similar manner, and second that she must be bound forever to this crazy music-making man whose wild gestures she would never be able to quantify.

Dee's cereal has become a soggy mess. It is impossible to scoop her sums of five without pushing them onto the spoon with her fingers. There are also fractions of Chex to deal with, which demand new rules. Toast would have been the optimal choice, but people in the hotel business seem to think that whole grains are a foreign plot. She feels certain that the insipid white substance that passes for bread would turn to paste by the third chew. She has lost her appetite at any rate. She pushes away her bowl and signals for more coffee. She tries to drip countable drops of cream, gives up, pours for five seconds. Look at the bright side, she thinks. A fascinating experiment concerning the physics of food. She pulls a folder of overheads from her briefcase, organizes them for the twentieth time.

At twelve minutes to eight Dee sees the R&D manager in his dark blue suit and bright red tie. A rebellious lock of gray hair swoops across his forehead. He enters the restaurant with long, fluid strides. No quantified steps for him.

She stands and waves for him to join her. It's a lady's prerogative to stay rooted by her chair. She scoops up her slides, returns them to her briefcase, pulls out a one-page summary of her talk. She notices a slight tremor in her finger, stuffs the latest urge to cry inside her chest. When did shining confident Dee, rising female star in the male Kingdom of Oil, become a sniveling mess?

"Hello, Dee, good to see you again," the manager says and smiles. He takes her outstretched hand.

Shake two three four five. "I've been looking forward to it," she lies. She drinks a third cup of coffee. Her nerve endings jangle with raw electric current. She never has more than two.

At the revolving lobby door Dee sees it is raining: a misty rain that washes sky, trees, road with gray. She unfolds her raincoat, slips hands inside their proper holes. The manager pulls an umbrella from his briefcase, snaps it open above Dee's head. Dee jumps at the noise. She ducks inside the SUV through the opened door, smells air freshener and a hint of smoke.

"Sorry, wife's car. Mine's in the shop." With a wave of his hand the manager dismisses smoke, Glade, backseats sticky with candy and soda.

We cannot help our lives, she wants to say. I believe this: our fate chooses us. We do not choose our fate. Instead she nods her head and smiles.

The manager pulls away from the hotel, fights traffic onto the freeway. Dee counts trees, their rain-heavy Fibonacci-leaved branches bowing toward her. A solitary bird lifts off from its perch, flaps shining bituminous wings. Crow or raven, Dee wonders. She can never keep them straight.

The car accelerates to pass. For the briefest flash of time Dee wills their vehicle into oncoming traffic. Blaze of glory, Clay. Good-bye. But life pulls her stubbornly back. Our fate chooses us; we do not choose our fate. Incineration by volcanic eruption, the scattering of her parts by fiery explosion of SUV, these are not her endings to claim. She plods through one day after another one step or five steps at a time. Although her story was written when a snow-capped mountain blew its top.

"*Boy*," Dee's father said at her wedding. He jerked his thumb toward Clay's parents, who had gotten up to dance, and then tossed back another bourbon. "You say they're both doctors?"

"Yes, sir." Clay slipped his shoe inside Dee's satin dress, explored her calf with his foot. She wondered if dark skin flushed.

Her father threw an arm around Clay's shoulder. A pugilistic fist dangled from the sleeve of his tuxedo. Clay's foot was yanked like a lever, gave a kick Dee knew he didn't mean.

"So what does that make you—*the black sheep* of the family?" He chortled.

Dee's mother patted and soothed, slid the glass beyond his reach. Rachael chewed her fingers and wheezed into her champagne. Clay's shoe reclaimed its territory, prowled upward toward Dee's thigh. He smiled, drummed his fingers in an Elvin Jones rhythm on the tablecloth.

"You can move the Man from Mississippi, but I'll be damned if you can remove Mississippi from the Man," he chanted in his velvet voice. Inside the calderas of his eyes, bright magma smoldered.

I disown you, Dee vowed, watching her father's face turn from red to purple. I disown your fists, your belt, the weakness of your life. She counted cups, spoons, best friends. She counted the empty glasses by her father's plate. She counted the kicks of tiny feet inside the round, white bulge of her belly. A breaststroker, she thought. I know a perfect frog kick when I feel it.

"I think I'll work for an oil company," she said into the candlelight of the fancy hotel room, the last thing that would ever be paid for by her father. Clay worked at the floral-patterned buttons at the back of her dress.

"Oh, my Mellow-Dee, what's happened to those brave dreams of research on the Ring of Fire? What about those beaming young students waiting to hang on your every word of wisdom?" The dress slithered down her body, fell in a heap at her feet. It made a sound like the rustling of leaves in the wind.

"You teach, I'll get rich," she said. She placed a hand on her belly and counted big fat dollars rolling into a bank account, making piles of money for a college education.

Clay worked her backward toward the bed. He opened her with his hand.

"You can take the girl away from the money-man, but man-oh-man just try and take the money away from the girl."

He sang to the rhythm of his movements. Dee felt tiny frog feet kicking in sync.

"Here we are," says the manager and opens Dee's door. The smoked-glass windows of the corporate office wink. The entire structure tilts toward her in the mist. She dangles a foot, tries to make herself move. *In two three four five, out two three four five.* It's a swim meet, she tells herself. Like diving off the blocks. She juts both feet forward and jumps. Her shoes make a tiny splash on the wet pavement.

Dee dismisses herself by the manager's door and heads for the bathroom. Safely inside the stall she practices deep breathing and hugs her chest. Her fingertips search the ridge of her left breast one more time. Four more hours and I can call.

In the meeting room people wait with pens and paper, mugs of undrinkable coffee. Dee counts four women—one more than the last time she was here. Four plus one makes five. There are six rows of chairs, four rows deep. There are four empty seats. She misses her tiny dress and smoky stockings. She feels like a grandmother in this skirt.

"Good morning," she says. She walks to the desk at the front of the room, toe-stomps and sits on top, feet dangling. She shuffles through her overheads and slides.

The manager introduces her and offers her coffee. She shakes her head and pushes herself off the desk, sending her organized and sorted presentation tumbling to the floor. Slides and papers scatter. Crouching on her haunches, head bent forward, she counts them as she puts them back.

"Can we dim the lights?" she asks. Her voice squeaks: a ridiculous falsetto.

In the darkened room, with her equations shining on the overhead, her muscles finally relax. She speaks of Laplace transforms and Fourier domains. With her mathematical magic she changes the music of sound sources towed by ships into pictures of oil-filled domes many layers beneath the surface of the sea. She shares her integrals and differentials but keeps her Fibonacci secrets to herself.

"That was fascinating," says the woman Dee hasn't seen before as she collects her papers after the talk. The woman is wearing a bright orange skirt and a red silk top. *Doesn't go with her hair,* thinks Dee. *But I'll bet her breasts are whole.*

"Thank you." Dee slips her folder into her briefcase, glances at her watch. *I can check my messages now,* she thinks.

"I don't know if you remember me. I was a first-year grad student when you were finishing up. I went to your thesis defense." She pauses, smiles. "You were an inspiration."

Another cop-out, Dee wants to say. *I will tell you this: you should never lie to your dreams.*

Her fingers are out of control. They are dancing, making their way toward scooped-out breast to check for the fiftieth time. She presses them into her armpits instead. She thanks the woman again and backs toward the door. *Am I in negative territory here? Shall I count in sums of minus five?*

By the time she gets to the airport in Houston she has checked her messages three times and called her surgeon once. He is out to lunch with his important friends. *Did she detect a note of sympathy in the nurse's voice? Is the woman already counting the number of months until Dee croaks?* She starts to call Clay, turns off the phone, fights back her hundredth tear. *What on earth has become of me,* she sobs. *Strong Dee, swim team captain Dee is drowning in a vat of brine.*

The plane takes fifty-eight minutes to get to Dallas. Dee retrieves her bag and reaches for her phone. *I will call when I get to my car,* she says. *If the number of steps is divisible by five, it will be a good sign.* After one thousand eight hundred and ten she still seems continents away. *To hell with it. Like it or not, I am giving up.* She begins a high-step jog, bag bouncing behind her on its wheels. She breathes freedom into her lungs.

When she is safely in her car, she turns on the phone and calls. She would need a high-speed sensor to count the beats of her runaway heart.

"Just a minute, I'll put you through." Does Dee hear doom buzzing through the line? Did she blow her one chance at salvation when she ceased to count her steps? She sticks a finger in her mouth and samples a corner of her nail.

"Good news, Dee. It's benign."

Dee lets out her breath in a rush. "Are you absolutely sure?"

The doctor laughs. "One hundred percent."

Dee thanks him twice and disconnects. She rests her head on the steering wheel and allows herself to cry. She believes they are tears of joy. Her mascara leaves gummy rivulets on her cheeks.

The windows in Clay's study are open despite the rain that has followed Dee home. She can hear the throaty tones of Billie Holiday and Clay's sweet alto sax. Dee leans against the car door, listens and watches. The rain feels cool and fresh. The light is on, and she can see the forest of Rasta braids bending into the magic of notes.

I would miss him, she realizes. An immense loneliness, impossible to calculate. She walks to the door on shaky legs. She ascends uncounted steps.

"Hey, Baby, welcome back. What's happening?" He stands and bows, motions her into the room.

"I'm home." *Well obviously, you fool*, she thinks. She sets her bags down, steps toward him.

Clay puts his sax in its stand, embraces her. He takes her hand and leads her toward the bedroom. "Yes, if you're still wondering; I really did miss you."

Dee slips off her shoes, yields to his pull.

"Sorry about that phone call. I was feeling a bit strange." She sits on the edge of the bed. Clay coaxes her backwards. Sinking or swimming, she wonders.

"I almost left you," Dee whispers into the dark curl of his ear. "I think if you hadn't been home this morning I could have done it."

"I know it, Baby," Clay sighs. "I could feel it in your skin." He slips off skirt and pantyhose in one smooth movement. "That, and I found your list on How to Leave Your Man."

The buttons of her blouse are opened one by one. She wriggles free, unhooks her bra and tosses it onto a chair. Clay brushes the inside of her thighs with his lips, tickles her stomach with his fuzzy plaits of hair.

This admission is his gift to me, she thinks, his offering. She allows herself to sink into the snowy whiteness of sheets.

His fingertips inch over the curved cage of her ribs. Lover man, oh where can you be, asks Billie from the other room. He's here, replies Dee, ninety-five percent sure.

Clay continues his upward scales until he finds her breasts. He sits up suddenly when the fingers of his right hand meet the unmistakable ridge of scar.

"Benign," she says. Six letters. The product of the two Fibonacci numbers that precede five, but not the sum. Benign is indivisible by five.

THE CHEMICAL NATURE OF THINGS

I t's not bad here, really, but when I told my friend from chemistry class where I work, she made monkey faces.

"*One Flew Over the Cuckoo's Nest*! Hey, Nurse Rat-Shit!" she roared. "Where's Chief Broom?"

Like I've never heard that before. I took out my car keys and jangled them in her face. "Remember—it comes down to this," I said, "the separation between us and them."

I work nights, so I have to mop the floor after dinner, and it's my job to count the sharps. That's the hardest part because there are thirty-nine patients on the floor, and lately my mind slips and slithers down its own path, which has little to do with knives or forks. Sometimes I have to start over three or four times to make it come out right.

Let me clarify this: sharps is not an accurate term here. I eat dinner on the hall, and I can tell you that it takes ten minutes to slice off a chunk of overcooked beef, three healthy stabs to spear a boiled-to-death potato with a fork.

"Are you sure, Lillian?" Nancy the psych nurse asks. "You counted right?"

"Nancy, I have a college degree," I say for the millionth time. "I can count to thirty-nine."

I know what she's thinking. I know what all my friends think. But this job's just a little setback. A glitch in the not-so-well-oiled machinery of my life. I have higher ambitions for my nametag than *Certified Nursing Assistant.* At this point I invariably get the story about the girl who stole a fork and went to the bathroom. She peeled layers of skin like an onion from her wrist until the pearl blue of vein pulsed in her fingers, then she peeled some more. By the time they found her, head slumped over the blood-slippery toilet, she had lost nearly a quarter of her blood.

I tell Nancy that was before my time, and there's no way she can blame me. I tell her when a person puts her mind to something, it doesn't matter how many times you count the sharps or check the toothpaste tubes for drugs. *Her will be done.* I never tell her that these truths have carved caves in my heart through which wind passes like a sigh.

This job is good for me, because I'm back at school now, and most nights I have plenty of time to study. I'm going to be a doctor, I say. Nancy smiles. S*tupid little CNA,* her white teeth whisper. But I mean it. I will.

I sit on the hard chair in the back of the nursing station under a neon light that pops and sizzles. I can feel the chemical thrum of light vibrating through my teeth. Neon, noble gas, tenth element in the periodic table, atomic weight of 20.179. It has a closed inert shell of electrons and is stable. I think of a nautilus shell, folded in on itself, shining in shallow tides.

Lithium is an alkali metal and extremely reactive. It is mined from lepidolite, a pink-to-lilac rock with a pearly luster. Third in the periodic table, atomic weight of 6.941. Such a tiny thing! It could have saved my mother's life.

Every door has a window. When I make rounds I have to shine my flashlight into the dreams of each patient. These dreams fly down the beam of light; they rattle against my skull. When I catch open eyes, I know that thoughts have swallowed sleep whole. I can see them: the hungry ghosts of guilt shuffling across the bed.

Sometimes I feel these ghosts brush against my skin, and I have to stick my hand in my pocket to touch the keys. The brass is cool against my fingers. I take out the ring and jingle them like magic coins.

Everyone must be in his own bed. No one can be in someone else's bed. There will be no eating no crying no reading. There are pills to make you sleep to make you behave to make you smile to make you eat or keep you from eating.

There is a pill to make the ingestion of alcohol a violently intolerable and potentially fatal mistake. *The longer a patient remains on therapy, the more exquisitely sensitive he becomes to alcohol.* Now that I have discovered the *Physicians' Desk Reference*, the key that unlocks the language of drugs, I read these words over and over. But how can I stick my fingers through the weave of time and unravel one particular knot of my life? Not even the medicine of words can heal the past.

If you violate the rules, we will give you a pill. Perhaps it will be the right pill, perhaps the wrong pill. It doesn't really matter.

Nancy dispenses the pills in little plastic cups. She lines the cups in neat rows on a tray. Seven rows of five and a row of four. If you need to be here, you need to be on meds.

The pills glisten. They are as cheerful as smiles. Nancy writes the name of each patient on the appropriate cup. They are arranged in alphabetical order. They are checked and crosschecked to avoid mistakes.

"Come and get 'em," I call as the patients line up in the hall. "Candy for sale." Nancy hates this. She says the treatment of the mentally ill is serious business and should not be made light of. I say we are all stewing in our own soup and we have to grab at any rotten morsel of happiness that floats by.

Nancy watches the patients swallow their pills. Certain patients must open their mouths and lift their tongues. If you are suicidal, you will horde your pills in a sock in your drawer. Perhaps one night you will swallow fistfuls, or perhaps you will only count them before you go to bed. Either way. You have an exit strategy, a key to the lock, and this allows you to sleep at night.

If you are bipolar or God speaks through the fillings of your teeth, you will spit your pills into the soil of plastic plants that spread branches into the corners of the rooms. You will want to feel the sharp edges of your illness vibrate against your ribs. You will want to feel your universe slice your chest. These pills, you say, blur the lines of sleeping and waking until I walk in a fog. I take these damn pills, you say, and I can't *feel* myself *think.*

My mother drank because the earth could not hold her. She climbed stars like a ladder, and the sun exploded in whorls of light inside her head. My mother bought jewels and furs that my father returned. She blazed through nights, cigarette embers a trail behind her, burn marks on fingers, two frightened children watching from closets and stairwells. She called dead German relatives and presidents of European countries on the phone.

My mother floated up attic steps to her studio and threw pots with feral shapes. She made magical glazes with an alchemist's flair. The finished pieces froze skin to clay, seared blisters on fingertips. She sold them for enough to keep her sensitive skin swathed in silks and cashmeres. She set sheets and curtains on fire. She was terrified of showers and gas.

My mother drank because she refused to believe that a soft metal with a purplish tint, a lonely electron spinning in its outer shell and an atomic weight of 6.941, could save her. If she could choose again, would she swallow pink pill or gray and yellow capsule from her plastic cup? No, she whispers when I search for her among the sighing stars. I would spit them into potted plants or nurses' faces.

Would I stop her? Would I check beneath her tongue? I want to say yes. I want to believe that salvation or redemption, at least, was possible. But who was I to decide that when she stepped from an attic window she could not fly?

The orderlies from *admit* bring the girl at 3:00 A.M. I am reading about valence electrons, the twirling planets that orbit an element's outer shell. The nucleus of an element is surrounded by shells of electrons like layers of an onion: a certain number to each layer. A valence of plus one means a sole electron circles a completed shell. A valence of minus one misses one electron to complete the outer shell and become stable and inert: a noble gas. It is these valence electrons, I learn, that determine the chemical nature of things. It is these electrons that determine the future when two elements collide.

The girl is wrapped in a blanket. When we approach her, she wriggles free and tosses blanket from body as if shedding skin. She is naked, and her own skin is as translucent as the plucked wing of a bird. I trace her sharp bones with my eyes. Her hair is matted into oily ropes that form a Tesla coil in the space around her skull. I hear the arc of current between hair and head. *This girl's electrons are spinning out of control*, I think. *A nuclear explosion is imminent.*

"Get her to *iso*," Nancy commands. The girl kicks and flails as the orderlies grab her. She is drowning in her own soup. Her arms are sketched with jagged lines: white adhesive strips cover red skin. They are superficial cuts, but bleeders. She tears at patches with her teeth, flings drops of blood onto orderlies, blanket and floor: paint on a canvas. Her face blooms with crimson branches. She has scratched down to muscle and bone.

I know you, I think, my breath stolen by the vision of this girl. I remember myself as a young girl with a razor blade held between two fingers, my mother's death bleeding from me in bright red drops. I sliced a portrait of my family—a heart and three X's—into my skin. A wounded heart was all that remained of my mother. A father and two daughters had been X'd out. My face festered, but you had to look closely. I knew to hide scratches under feathers of hair. *Dirty girl selfish girl: too stupid to save a mother.*

Nancy has been expecting her. There is a vial of Ativan on the tray, a glinting syringe. "Lillian," Nancy calls.

"Richard." Richard is the other CNA. His body is a banyan tree; his trunk-like arms and legs root him to this world. In one swift movement, Richard scoops girl blanket blood into his arms. One good squeeze and her bones will snap like twigs.

He carries her to isolation, tosses her onto the bed. A dim lightbulb in a cage hangs from the ceiling, and the walls are padded. There are padded leather straps on the rails of the bed.

Richard elbows me, whispers into my ear. "A sandwich or three short of a picnic basket, this one."

I shake my head. *Just one electron short of a full shell,* I think.

"Four-point restraint," says Nancy. "Lillian, get her arms."

She tries to scratch me. I feel the dry parchment of her skin against my gloves. The three of us tie her hands and feet to the bed, but it's me she accuses when Nancy slips sleep into her vein. She raises her head, looks at me, spits in my face.

"Stupid fucking bitch," she screams. She begins to laugh and I laugh too and soon we are both laughing so hard I'm afraid Richard will tie me in a knot and throw me into the bed next to this girl.

My mother drank because she had a direct line to every socket in the house. Alternating current, not blood, flowed in her veins. My father finally called the hospital when she fell down two flights of stairs. When the ambulance doors closed, I felt a door slam shut in the house of my heart.

They dried her out and sent her home, shining and new. She had a mouthful of good intentions and pockets full of Antabuse and Lithium.

Lithium does not flush well. I saw bright pink dots twirling in her toilet. My father, a physician who lacked the potions to heal her, forced Antabuse down her throat. *The longer a patient remains on therapy, the more exquisitely sensitive she becomes to alcohol.*

How long had she been drinking when we found the carpet of her studio covered with vomited blood? Who knows. The window was open because my mother needed more air more space than this filthy world could provide. The rag of her shed body slept in the bushes below.

Every door has a window. *Iso* is no exception. There is no need for my flashlight here because the light must be kept on. At first I think the girl is sleeping, then an eyebrow raises, a lid blinks open. She beckons with her head, the only moveable part of her restrained body. I am not supposed to do this, but my key is already in the lock. I slip inside.

She is wearing pink pajamas now. She looks like a wild-haired doll, her furious artwork hidden by fluffy sleeves. The pajamas must have come from the blue backpack tucked in the corner next to Nancy's desk. I imagine this girl's parents, sleepless now, pacing the halls of a house that is no longer safe. Grief and guilt stalk them, thieves in the shadows.

The girl swims to the surface through seas of Ativan sleep. "Pssst," she says. I step closer. "Fuck you," she says. "Bull Fuck You Shit."

She looks at me head on. Her eyes glint like minerals I have seen that form in the molten mantel of the earth. I plunge in and find no bottom: only layer after layer of beautiful green.

I think of a gift my mother brought me when she returned from a trip to India. It was a round box carved from a shell. Inside the shell was an elephant, also carved from a shell. The elephant opened to reveal a smaller elephant and so on until there were six shimmering elephants of descending size in my palm. It did not seem a fair trade for a month of abandonment.

"But look, look" my mother whispered. She crouched beside me, wiping tears of outrage from my face. Flames of her thick red hair burned my cheek. "You can see the moon and stars of India shining in their skin."

I hold my keys to the girl's face and jangle them. A coil of my own red hair, AWOL from the requisite braid, touches the sheet by her shoulder.

"Look," I tell her, "you can see the moon and stars of India shining in the brass."

She laughs. "Bull Fuck You Shit."

"I'm with you," I say. "Bull Fuck Me Shit." I want to believe that this girl, with her out-of-control electrons and a valence of minus one, will be okay.

Vibrations of a Desert Rose

I

Beethoven was a Jew," my mother said. She was still well then. Her face glowed with life, and the thick crown of braids she always wore gave her the look of European royalty. She sat in her wing chair, dark blue with gold jags that reminded me of lightning on a summer's night. She wore a calf-length dress made of some shimmering fabric. Folds of flowers draped across the legs of the chair. Her feet were up on the ottoman, moving to the music.

We were listening to the *Missa Solemnis* on one of those Indian summer days. "Sanctus," her favorite movement, played. Soprano and tenor voices swooped through the blue-tinged dust, swam through rays of afternoon sun. The buzz of music and heat made my skin vibrate.

"Ma, he was a Catholic. This is a fucking Mass."

"Aach! *Klug vi der velt.* You're as smart as the world. Listen!" With an imaginary baton she conducted an avalanche of strings. The notes filled her with a holiness I knew I would never reach. "Only a Jew could suffer like that." She looked at me, held a hand to her heart and smiled. "And soar above it."

Beyond the window the backyard slid toward the line of spruce that hid our property from the street. I could still make out the outline of the garden my dad and I planted all the years of my childhood. The rectangle of grass was greener there: a denser, more vibrant hue.

Today a gray slush turns from rain to snow and back again, bends the branches of chestnut and copper beech. Dead leaves cover desiccated grass. I remember my mother in October and bawl like the orphan I am. The *Missa Solemnis* is cranked so loud the speakers burst with sorrow. *Sanctus Dominus Deus Sabaoth!* Floors and furniture tremble, but still my mother's sanctity eludes me. *Hosanna in excelsis.* I can see her in the empty wing chair, two wings of misbehaved red hair flaring out from her braids. She has the same smile she kept through six months of chemo and two months of dying like she knows something secret and sacred, and she is not going to tell. Not ever. All I want is to touch her, just touch her, one more time.

Soon my successful sister will descend from the skies and glide through the oak pocket doors of the living room. I know I should get off my ass and meet her at the airport, but I can't. My mother's death weighs me down like wet earth, filling up the space inside my skin.

"Take a cab, Lisa," I say. You who were too important to help my mother die, I think.

My sister is not too important to see how the money gets divided. She gets a bank account for herself and college funds for her two children. I get to live in the house, I get the car I used to transport her to doctors and poisoning appointments and I get a trust fund that my sister oversees. I, who can be entrusted with my mother's life and long journey into death, cannot be trusted with money. I have not yet earned my Ph.D.

I am brilliant—more so than my sister—but I have these *episodes*. The equations I try to solve don't make sense anymore, and I can't sit still because I keep tripping over all the space-junk in my head. I promised my mother I would take my meds, and I keep my promise day by day. Still, the ultimate purpose of theoretical mathematics eludes me. I am hanging on to my Harvard education by the curly hook of an integral sign.

II

I'm sitting in a bar in Kermit, Texas, with a guy named Peaches whose feet stink so bad that when he took off his boots in the truck today I thought something had curled up and died in there and I said so. "I Musta Died and Gone To Texas" wails from a jukebox resurrected from *The Twilight Zone.* A few tottering guys in cowboy hats sing along.

It's been four weeks since the Challenger exploded, dusting the earth with the ashes of spacecraft and astronauts. That's it, I said. Life is too short to sit and think about Riemann Surfaces and String Theory. I called my sister, promised her I'd come to Dallas, threw a knapsack into my inherited Volvo, locked my mother's ghost up for the winter and headed south. I met Peaches in a bar in Savannah, and when he asked did I want to work on a seismic crew in Texas I said what the hell, hopped in his truck and signed on.

Peaches keeps trying to kiss me. I keep swatting at him, and if I take one more scooch toward the edge of my barstool I'll fall flat on my ass on the barroom floor and disappear beneath sand, cigarette butts, and peanut shells.

He wants to scare me. He fishes his slingshot from his back pocket, cocks it and lets fly. Stale barroom air whooshes by my cheek. He's ordered two servings of Rocky Mountain Oysters—full dinners, not the appetizers. I look around for a sympathetic female eye, but as far as I can tell I am one of three women who is not here in a professional capacity of one form or another. One is playing pool. She's as thin as a fence post and waves of her black hair keep caressing the table. There's a stack of quarters on the rail and I wish I understood the physics of her fingers because no matter how her balls leap and spin, they drop into impossible pockets. The other woman rides the horse of our line foreman's knee. Her cowboy hat perches crookedly on a loose interpretation of red hair, and her complexion has a slightly greenish hue. I think she's more in need of Dramamine than emotional exchanges.

When the oysters come they're no different than any of the other anonymous chicken fried things appearing on every plate with every meal. I look Peaches right in the eye, pick up a quarter-size medallion of bull's balls with my fingers and pop it into my mouth. I expect gristly resistance, but my teeth sink in with a sigh. The taste is almost delicate. A subtle, nutty flavor, my palate says, but my brain keeps repeating *testicle*, and my stomach is in revolt. I have to make an exit before I heave onto the cowboy-booted toes of Peaches' odoriferous feet.

I decide the time is right to make contact with Lisa, who must be wondering where I am. I give Peaches a peck, testosterone-filled mouth and all, and mumble about the place where women go to readjust their powder.

I feel like I'm stepping into a bad Western. The sky sizzles with stars, and sand dunes undulate on either side of a highway stretched from one vast emptiness to another. Tumbleweeds drive down the wrong side of the road. A living, crawling collection of them sticks in a barbed wire fence where it waits to swallow dogs, cowboys, pickup trucks, the Eastern Seaboard.

I call collect and my sister accepts the charges. We've been through this before.

"Hi, Lisa. I guess you wonder why I'm not in Dallas."

A sigh. "Well, the thought did occur to me, Syl. Where are you? We've been worried."

I spit remnants of masticated testicle on the ground. "I made it to Texas. I got a job; I'm okay." I decide not to tell her I'm a juggie, stomping geophones into the ground with a crew of escaped and not-yet-convicted criminals.

"Syl, I don't like the way this is sounding. I wish you'd get in your car and come to Dallas. We have a job for you here. A real job that uses your talents." I hear the wail of a little girl, a muffled conversation and a kiss. "Adrianna says to tell you hello."

I hear a shouted "did not" in the background. Those kids hate me. "Tell her hi too." Here's the part she won't like. "Lisa, I don't have the car anymore. I traded it for a sailboat." There's a minute of silence before she answers. She's thinking about the silver Volvo, how well it would have fit in her garage.

"Okay," she says. I hear her take calming breaths. "Did you say a sailboat?"

Maybe my diction is off from the remains of mountain oysters. I tell her I was freezing so I took the southern route but by Savannah I was sick of driving and this guy I picked up hitchhiking was sick of sailing so we traded. I thought sailing would be easy. My undergrad degree is in physics. A force vector here, a little mass-times-acceleration there and boom! Off you go.

"Sylvia, you didn't sail to Kermit." Brilliant, that woman. No wonder she's amassing fortunes in the petroleum industry. "Where's the boat now?"

"I sank it." I hear a stifled gasp.

"Did you say you sank it? Are you all right?"

I am writing equations in my head, thinking of solutions free from police or doctors or Lisa jumping into her BMW with leather seats and driving to Kermit at 30 miles per hour over the speed limit.

"Lisa, it turns out Chaos Theory is crucial to sailing. It's difficult to predict where in relation to the wind a boat will end up, given the turbulence that occurs along the lee side of the sail. Especially with respect to rocks, which are not always visible from the sea surface." *Quod Erat Demonstrandum.* I don't mention the variables of rotten wood and missing caulking. A long pause follows in which I feel the words form in her brain and I mouth them with her as they come through the receiver.

"Sylvia, are you taking your meds?"

"Of course I am." I don't mention I have switched pink pills for the resinous buds of cannabis harvested from between the corn stalks in Peaches' daddy's farm. It works quite well at keeping the electric buzz to a tolerable leakage of current between the ears.

"Okay, Sylvia. I want you to promise me you'll keep taking them. I know you promised Mom." The dirty bitch. How dare she. "And I want you to think about coming up here. No. Just come. I'll drive down and get you if you want; really I will."

Poor Lisa. I am forever drilling potholes into the smooth highway of her life. I wonder if she's tracing the call. I blow a kiss at the receiver and hang up.

Peaches sways through the door with Renegade the chain-man. Renegade works for the surveyor, determining the points on a seismic line with a measuring tape called a chain. Renegade has chains tattooed across his biceps and around his neck, and mats of dirty blond curls that look more like a rug than human hair. "I'm full as a tick," he says, patting his paunch.

"Hey, Silver," calls Peaches. I told him that was my name. He ensnares me with one hand and pulls his stash out with the other.

A neon Lone Star Beer sign washes his cheeks with blues, reds and yellows. Sparks of light synapse from the fuzz on his cheeks, refract from the glassy blue of his narrowed eyes.

"I was gonna put Silver on the Vibroseis crew," he says, giving my shoulder a squeeze. "She tells me she has a lot of experience with a vibrator."

The Vibroseis, I have learned, is a truck the size of a small ocean liner. It has enormous wheels and a steel plate that sends vibrational signals into the earth where they reflect from subsurface structures like layers of a cake. It's picked up by instruments called geophones, or jugs, as well as by teeth, bones, viscera, and extraterrestrials. Renegade roars and pokes his tree trunk of an elbow into me. The vibrator is an endless source of amusement when there's a woman on the crew.

We climb in Peaches' truck and drive toward the motel. "Roll me one, sugar," he says and hands me his stash. I feel the chill of Renegade's gaze slide over breasts, thighs, the place between my legs where Peaches' hand is going.

Renegade is not pleased when we let him out at the Motel 6 and do not follow. Peaches tosses him a baggy to appease him and off we go. His hand hits the jackpot and I feel a white-hot zing arc into my belly so hard I have to bite my lip to keep from groaning.

"Get a couple a Lone Stars outta the cooler," he says, not moving his hand.

The moon is high by the time we park by the side of the road in Monahans. It's about three days past full, a Texas-sized football kicked into the curved surface of stars unfurling above the dunes. Peaches holds up the barbed wire with his boot and I know where this is going and I slither into the land of no return, cold sand scraping my belly. There's a hint of sage in the breeze, the sharpness of tannin from the scrub oaks that push up stubbornly from the desert floor.

Sand dunes shimmer in every direction and I crane my neck, listening for the ocean's roar. I could be on Cape Cod, where I spent my childhood summers. I could be careening down mountains of sand, my mother at the top of the dunes in a yellow dress, her crown of braids hidden by a wide-brimmed hat. I start to shiver and can't stop.

Peaches has a blanket, and we climb to the top of a dune. The sand here is gypsum; it's white as bones. He takes a toke from a joint, breathes it into my mouth. I inhale him from his hair, gold and fine as corn silk across my face, down to the tight wires of hips and crotch and thighs that rest between my legs. We take off our clothes and I must be upwind of his feet because he looks and smells as sweet as the fruit of his namesake. I still shiver despite the heat of his body that spreads like a grass fire up my spine.

"Baby, you tear me up," he says. We lie on the blanket staring at the sky. A cellophane wrapper skitters across the sand, catches in a clump of grass. Trucks roar past on the road and I pretend it's waves and suddenly I'm suffocating under the weight of space and moon and stars. I sit up to catch my breath and my hand hits something hard and sharp. I dig it out from the sand and hold it up in the moonlight.

It's some kind of mineral. Light glints from a series of pale pink planes that curve outward from a central core, back into themselves and each other. It looks like a flower made from a Mobius strip, endlessly folded so I can't tell where one dimension ends and another begins. I think of gravitational fields radiating from the surface of a black hole, sheets of force peeling off into seas of black space. I pull back my hand before this thing burns holes through me. Peaches laughs and picks it up.

"Spooks got you? It's just a desert rose." He grabs it, scrapes it across my cheek. With his slingshot he fires it into the distance. I hear a ping against the trunk of an oak and then the hardness is gone from his face and he kisses me, cups my chin in his hand.

"You are one pretty gal," he says.

"You mean that?"

"Silver, I am serious as a heart attack." He climbs back on. I feel the hot pulse of him as he slides inside, and I wrap my legs around him because I am terrified that without this anchor of flesh and bones I will slip between grains of sand into a universe devoid of everything except empty West Texas sky and wind.

It's 5:00 A.M. and Peaches is in the parking lot honking the horn and the guy from the front desk is standing in the doorway yelling about my open door. What the hell do I think this is, he says, some place of prostitution and all I can think of looking at his turban as I pass my brush through snarls of red hair is that goddamned desert rose and layers of the universe peeling off like paint from the walls in this hellhole where sleep is impossible because the wind rattles against the windowpanes and the perpetual motion machine of road vibrates my brain awake every time I close my eyes. "There's *no air* in here," I tell him. "How can I sleep with a closed door when something keeps stealing *the air*?" I look the guy right in his third eye and he braces his back against the doorway.

"Don't you understand," I ask, "that elementary particles are like musical notes vibrating along taut strings of space? And humans are the vibrational nodes in this Grand Unifying Theory. As such we need *air*."

Well that does it because he is backing away now and I tell him yes please I would very much like that free cup of coffee. Peaches keeps honking and Renegade tosses his coffee at the stairs. I wonder why they don't throw us out on our asses until I remember that the oil bubble has burst, and a sticky black pall of unemployment has settled on the Permian Basin. If we are the only game in town they will let us play.

"Well lookkit Jew," says Renegade when I open the truck door. He flicks his tongue across his lips.

"What?" I wonder which part of my body whispers *Jewish*. I slide in. The smoke, marijuana and tobacco, is as thick as a New England fog bank. I haven't tightened the lid on my cup, and hot coffee sloshes onto my jeans.

"Well-look-at-you," he says, curling his mouth around each word. He is sitting too close. He smells musty, like well-composted leaves or an old fur coat.

Peaches smiles at me. "Hey, Silver," he says, drawing words and smoke into his lungs. He hands me the joint, which is a good thing because my tongue tastes of metal and the faulty soldering job of my cerebral wiring is starting to come undone. He turns to Renegade, and that hardness is back, turning blue eyes into slits of ice. "Watch it," he whispers.

Renegade flicks a speck of ash from his Harley Davidson jacket. "The hell I will."

It's time for me to check out, so I snuggle up to Stevie Ray Vaughan on the tape player. He slides guitar notes in and out of my body like he owns me. "It's floodin' down in Texas," Stevie moans, and I half wish it would. Renegade pokes me.

"Stevie's a good ol' boy." He pins me with his reptilian gaze. "Even if he sings like a Nee-gro." He pokes me again as he says the word and then waits, unblinking. I don't have the guts to take him up on his offer and call him what he is, so I wiggle in my seat like a worm. "Fuckin' Yankee," he says anyway.

I peer through the darkness at the detritus of the oil bust.   Behind chain-link fences, spotlights illuminate junked cranes, derricks, drills. They lurch out of the desert like strange trees. Cannibalized trucks sink into sand, tumbleweeds collecting against deflated wheels.

When we stop next to the recording truck, Renegade pushes past me. The survey truck is there, engine idling, and he jumps in. In the luminous glow of the cab I see him jerk his head in my direction. He rolls down his window and spits, and I hear laughter.

Carl, the recording-truck engineer, opens the doghouse door. Lights blink from a bank of instruments. The line foreman comes out, coffee in hand, and offers a cup to Peaches. I lean against the truck and watch them talk, shifting their weight from one foot to the other. Breath and steam mingle in desert air so sharp it slices through lungs like a straight razor. I blow on my fingers, shove my hands in my pockets. I'd like to open the hood and curl up beside the engine. I remember my parents sipping coffee beside the fireplace, sharing the Sunday *New York Times*, and a sudden urgency of missing them explodes inside my chest.

"Get your ass in gear," says Peaches. "Let's load up the jugs."

He slams down the tailgate, and we heave up heavy coils of recording cable, hasps of geophones and wires. It's a good thing there was a Viking somewhere in my ancestral woodpile. I grew until my eyes were level with my father's hairline, then I grew some more. I have his college-boxing-champion muscles, my mother's fire-red hair. Years ago I discovered I can talk dirty, put in a brutal day's work, toss down drugs and liquor with the best of them. Peaches will never imagine the towering brick house, bookshelves lined with indecipherable texts, two girls trailing in the shadows of professor parents with chairs to their names.

The horizon is tinged with pink fuzz when Peaches and I get to the first station, marked by a red plastic flag. The emptiness of the place is a breath expanding and contracting against my skin. Bunch grass shivers, and sand swirls in tiny tornados around a few skinny trees. In the distance, pump-jack arms seesaw, a lone windmill turns. I kick at a rock and wonder how cattle survive.

Peaches hoists the recording cable and begins to lay out the line. I put on work gloves, grab the hasp of geophones and struggle with the tangle of wire. He puts down the coil and comes to help me, leaning his body into me. Electric heat sears my skin.

"Here, sugar, you still ain't got it right. Like this," he says, guiding my hands. "Make sure the jugs go in straight or you'll bend the pegs."

The peg is what couples the geophone to the motion of the earth. Bend it and the signal changes from smooth sinusoid to a messy series of spikes and jags. Peaches dangles the geophone, peg down, places a foot squarely over the top and stomps. The peg sinks into the sand. He bends down and clips the takeout into the recording cable. He walks with me, laying cable, to the next wooden stake. He nudges me. "You try."

I mimic his movements, but someone snuck in a layer of caliche and the peg crumples.

"Ah, shit," he says. He digs a shallow hole with the heel of his boot, stomps in jug and wounded peg, covers it up. "Have to do." I clip in the takeout. He slips me a canteen of water and a package of donuts and hoists the cable onto his shoulder. "Be careful," he calls, not looking back.

By the time I find Peaches parked beneath a cottonwood with a Dr. Pepper, I have settled into my stomping rhythm. It coincides with the beat of "I'm Cryin'," which has stuck in my head since Peaches turned off the tape player and silenced Stevie Ray. He pats the ground and takes two sandwiches from the cooler.

"C'mon, babe. Sit a spell."

We eat ham and cheese, drink Dr. Pepper and take a few tokes from a joint. Sheep-backed clouds drift across the sky, and my thoughts bounce off them like signals careening off layers of rock. I think of that desert rose again, its perfect symmetry, unseen dimensions unfurling from its core. My eye just catches something moving behind a far clump of bushes. It's a coyote or a fox, a pup. It plays with its prey, leaping into the air and pouncing. It takes my breath. It's all I can do to tap Peaches on the shoulder and whisper.

"Look," I say, and before I know it Peaches is up with his well-armed slingshot in his hand, and he takes aim. "Coyote scum," he says and shoots. The puppy teeters and falls. I look at him, at the twitching body. My mouth is open but for a moment no sound comes, just a gasping, retching knot of air. Then it bursts out of me and that creature's soul jumps into my body and I scream and scream until Peaches knocks me to the ground and presses his hand over my mouth.

"Fucking bastard," I yell into his palm. "Fucking bastard." His free hand is on my belt buckle and he is panting hard and then his finger is inside and I am as limp as the coyote as his mouth replaces the hand against my lips and my jeans are down around my boot tops. Still I can't take my eyes off the coyote and I pretend it's sleeping in the sun as the two of us come and tears pour down my cheeks into the thirsty ground.

He pulls out, gets up and wipes his hands. "You tear me up, Silver," he says, tossing two hasps of geophones onto the ground by my feet.

I point to the body. "You can't just leave it there."

He cocks his head, looks at me like I'm insane. He bends down, uncoils a few feet from a new spool of recording cable and screws the cable heads together.

"Watch me," he says and walks away, streaming cable behind him.

I wish I had a shovel, but I don't. I walk over to the coyote and touch him. He looks like a sleeping puppy, front paws curled together. Sunlight illuminates tiny wisps of hair inside his ears. His fur is the color of sand swirled with gray, as if he had been created from the desert landscape and would sink into it again. There is a caved-in place above his eye and a trickle of black blood congeals around the nose. "I'm sorry," I say. I drag him behind the bushes. He's not stiff, but the warmth is gone.

I pick up the hasps of geophones, clip one to my belt, grasp the other in my gloved hand. The coyote tears a black hole into my universe. He prances along the Schwarzchild Radius that marks the edge of a black hole's gravitational pull. Light pours from his eyes in the pattern of a rose. The pattern lodges like a burr under my skin while I stomp jugs into the center of the earth. Stomp and clip to the pattern of a rose.

The sun is a fevered red by the time I spot the truck in the distance. Clouds of dust blur its edges. The engine's gunned and the wheels bounce off the ground. Peaches takes aim and doesn't veer until he power-slides, spitting me with dust and rocks. There is a half-crazed whoop from inside the cab. The truck bursts with juggies. They pour from the windows and overflow the bed of the truck.

"Hop in, sugar," he says. I muscle in and someone hands me a joint. I don't need it because the fumes are enough, but I take it. I look at Peaches' hands on the wheel and all I can see is his fingers closed around the slingshot, the black hole of the coyote's eye.

On the third toke it hits me. It's the pattern thing. We're laying out cable wrong; that's what my brain has been trying to say all afternoon. The geophones are like elementary particles vibrating on a string. We collect data in a line, everything vibrating along two dimensions. But if we lay cable like a rose, we unfold a multitude of dimensions. This could be a breakthrough. Not only for geophysics but the detection of particles in other dimensions. It could eliminate the need for particle accelerators, bring together the divergent fields of experimental and theoretical physics, win a Nobel Prize.

I want to tell Peaches what I've discovered, but the image of his back receding into the desert, the uncoiling snake of wire, is enough to shut me up. When we get to the recording truck, I'll tell Carl. He's an engineer. He'll understand. I think of a promotion. I think of more money than my sister will ever make. I imagine tearing up the papers for the trust fund and leaving them in a pile at her feet.

The doghouse door is open and Carl is marking a strip of seismic record with a pen. Peaches has us roll down the windows long before we get there, and he parks downwind. All that is left of the sun is a fuzzy brushstroke splashed across the horizon's edge. My hands tremble, but I don't know if it's from the inside out or the outside in.

We unload. Peaches and two other guys stand by the doghouse door and talk. I want to push past them but I stand with my back pressed against the warm hood until they shake hands and walk toward the truck.

"Be right back," I say. I knock on the door and Carl invites me in and looks me over. I feel as if my clothes are wearing thin from the constant traffic of eyes that travels up and down my body. "How them boys treatin' you?"

"Fine," I say and I tell him about my theory, careful to stick to seismic lines and keep the far-reaching consequences to myself. He puts down his pen, takes off his glasses, licks his lips and swallows.

"Miss Silver, I believe we are way ahead of you. We've been shooting 3-D seismic for years." He stands up, walks toward me until I have to lean backward to preserve a corner of air. "Tell you what. Why don't you quit worrying your pretty head about what kind of job we are doing *up here*." He says this as if *up here* is rarified, something pure I could never attain. "How's about you stomp jugs and leave the *thinkin'* to us."

He sniffs at my face and the collar of my jacket. "And I advise you to save your extracurricular activities for your extracurricular time." He mimics the motion of toking on a joint before pushing past me and leaning out the door. "Peaches," he calls, "I need to talk to you. You can wait in the truck," he says to me, slipping his gaze between my legs.

At dinner Peaches is silent. We are eating cheeseburgers at a table with the other crews and Peaches tosses back shots between Lone Stars and a knot in his jaw keeps working long after he finishes chewing. Renegade cracks jokes and Peaches laughs with his mouth but not his eyes and he swipes at a stain of ketchup that makes him look like he is coughing blood. There's a sandstorm outside and the wind slams fistfuls of the stuff against the windows, blows trash inside every time the door opens. I asked for my burger medium-rare but it's still struggling to its feet inside the bun so I drown the poor thing in beer before it sizzles to death in the acids of my stomach.

Renegade throws his arm around my shoulder. I look at Peaches and Renegade looks at him, too. Peaches takes a bite of burger and fixes us with those eyes that sighted down the skull of a puppy. He chews slowly, swallows, puts his Lone Star to his lips. I try to duck from Renegade's grip but he squeezes hard. I open my mouth to bite but he's onto me. He squeezes my jaws closed.

"Well I'll swan," he says. "Ain't you a wild thing." He lets me go.

I get out of the truck at the motel and I want to leave but my body won't let me. I stand by the door of the cab and Peaches comes over and kisses me hard. He puts a hand on my ass and pulls me into him, grinds until desire reaches critical mass inside me, sucking in bones, breath and night air.

"It's been swell, Silver." He starts to walk away, stops, turns toward me. "You tear me up." And he is gone, taking the stairs two at a time.

This is going to be a long night but I have a lot to do. I wish I could open the window in my room. I wish I could find a classical music station; I need some Beethoven to calm my nerves. Or jazz or blues or anything that's not country or screeching evangelists. I find a pen in the drawer but no paper. I pull out the Bible and start writing equations in the margins. I start simple: Maxwell's equations. And presto—God gave us light. I move on to the Uncertainty Principle. And God saw that even he could not simultaneously predict the position and momentum of a photon. I'm a bit rusty, but soon I'm tossing geophones along Reimann surfaces, and by the time I realize someone's pounding on my door I have turned the word of God into a space-time continuum.

I expect Peaches or maybe the night manager but Renegade pushes in. He sways, nearly falls, and I believe if I light a match he'll detonate. He grabs me, throws me down on the bed.

"Get the fuck out," I say. I look around for something to throw.

"Well lookkit Jew. Miss prissy." He starts for his zipper.

I scramble up but he slams me back. He's on top of me before I can move. He pins my wrists with one hand and shoves the other one into my crotch so hard I fly backward, hit my head against the headboard. He tears at my jeans and I can't breathe and my whole body buzzes. He leans toward my face like he is going to kiss me. I arch my neck, bring my head forward as hard as I can. I feel something give in the bridge of his nose. He lets my arms go and I think he'll give up but he punches me hard. Once between the eyes and once in the jaw. A field of stars explodes in my brain.

"Fucking cunt," he says and rips the fly of my jeans open. Blood from his nose drips onto my exposed belly.

"My father is the president of this company," I say. "I'll have you in jail so fast your head'll spin." He stops and looks at me. His reptile body doesn't believe me, wants to keep going, but his simian brain tries to process the information. He presses me into the bed.

"So you're the one," he says. I don't know what he's talking about but I nod. "You told Carl about the pot and had him fired."

"Yup," I manage, as if this conversation made sense. "He said he quit but I figured he was bullshitting." He presses again but zips, gets up. "Fucking cunt whore bitch," he says and is gone.

I'm shaking so hard I drop everything I pick up but it doesn't take long to pack. I put the Bible in my knapsack and reach for my wallet so I can leave some money for the bill. No point in showing the night manager my festive face. My back pocket's empty, and I remember Peaches with his hand on my ass. I wonder if I'm going to cry.

I have to keep wiping blood from my nose and the vision in my left eye is blurred and my mouth won't close right. I pick up the phone and call Lisa. She answers on the fourth ring even though it's 1:00 A.M.

It takes me a minute before I can speak, but Lisa waits. She knows who it is.

"Well, it looks like this job isn't going to work out, Lisa." There's no wondering about it any more. Tears stream from my eyes: the closed one and the open one.

"What's the matter, Syl? You sound awful."

"Abscessed tooth. It's killing me."

"Stay where you are, honey," she says. "We'll come and get you. Please. Don't move."

"That's okay," I tell her. "I'll take a cab." I hang up, leave the key in the door and pull it shut. The wind has gone to sleep, leaving a film of sand on asphalt, bushes, parked pickups and "Don't Mess With Texas" bumper stickers. I'm on the road in fifteen minutes, and my thumb is out.

III

A trucker gives me a ride to I-20 and I barely have my backwards-walking-rhythm going when a van speeds past. It swerves into the breakdown lane and backs up. I wonder if I should duck into the bushes but suddenly there's a female face at every window. The women yell and beckon. I start to run but my face hurts too much so I slow to a jog. I see New Mexico plates and the side door slides open and a chorus of voices calls "Get in, girl," so I do.

It's like forest inside the van. The girls are all wearing shirts that say Lady Pumas and there are gym bags and basketballs and basketball shoes taking up every inch of floor space. There's not one of them who could sit up straight without a head injury. Driving the van is a red-faced man, a brick wall with sculpted pillars for arms and legs. He peers at me over the top of his glasses.

"Hi," he says. "Set to go?"

I squeeze into a seat that is already being shared by two women and a fuzzy teddy bear. The overhead light goes on as they roar back onto the highway and they are all staring at me. I wipe blood from my face and the woman next to me hands me a Kleenex. Her skin is the color of the milk chocolate my mother used to get from Switzerland. Two long pigtails trace shadows across her cheeks in the blinking beam of light.

"Child, what happened to you?" she asks and the women shout back "She walked into a door," and they start laughing and pretty soon I'm laughing too.

"We're going to Fort Worth," she says. "A basketball conference at TCU."

"Yeah, we're gonna kick some ass and eat us some beef," someone shouts from the front seat.

The Kleenex woman reaches behind her and drags out a cooler. "Soda?"

I reach for a Dr. Pepper, change my mind and grab a Coke. She points to herself. "Lakesha," she says, "Lah-Key-Sha," as if I come from another planet and may not understand. "Yvonne," she says, pointing to the woman next to her who is big enough to take up the entire seat by herself and has a grin as wide and friendly as the state of Texas. Lakesha holds up the teddy bear. "Teddy," she says.

"Sylvia. Pleased to meet you. I'm going to Fort Worth too." I sip soda through my misshapen mouth, trying not to drool.

"We're the Lady Pumas," Lakesha says, in case I missed their shirts. "From Las Cruces. New Mexico State University." She points to the driver. "And that's our fearless leader, Coach Duncan."

Coach Duncan waves. I see his glasses reflected in the rearview mirror. "Don't forget chauffeur par excellence," he calls out, wiggling the steering wheel.

The rest of the Lady Pumas introduce themselves and go back to talking and eating, now that the oddity of me has worn off. Lakesha offers me a sandwich. The smell of meat makes me queasy, and I decline. I settle back against the seat. "Change that damned radio station," she yells in response to some country singer's wail. The stations swirl and spin through the night, and for the briefest moment I swear I hear the notes of Beethoven like a slight shiver across my tympanic membrane. I inhale the stale heated air of the van and pretty soon I am drifting in and out of sleep, comforted by the steady buzz of conversation. The *Missa Solemnis* floats into my dreams like an old friend. *Agnus Dei, qui tollis peccata mundi, miserere nobis. Dona nobis pacem.* Grant us peace.

When I wake up we are pulling off the highway, heading for the friendly lights of a rest stop. My face throbs in time to the bass of some rock 'n' roll song and my left eye won't open. I'm sure it's glowing purple in the dark. I touch my upper lip with my tongue and feel crusted blood. Lady Pumas are coming to life, stretching long limbs across seats, elbowing each other in the ribs. A Coke appears under my nose and I shake my head, afraid of how much it will hurt if I open my mouth to speak. The van doors slide open, and Pumas explode through them before Coach Duncan has come to a stop.

"Hey! Wait 'til after the conference to break your damn legs," he yells.

"We're just trying to beat you to the ladies room, Coach," a blond woman with an enormous 'fro calls over her shoulder.

I slide out behind Lakesha. She reaches over me to slam the door shut. "Damn, girlfriend, you're tall enough to join the team." She lifts my chin toward the fluorescent light. "You look like shit. How do you feel?"

"Like shit." But I don't, really. It hurts less than I thought to talk, and despite my facial trauma my body thrums with some incandescent light of its own. Lakesha slips a Kleenex from the sleeve of her sweatshirt, spits on it and begins to wipe the blood. The tender gesture catches me off guard, and I am suddenly a little girl again, with muddy tear stains on my cheek. I remember my outraged screams as the spit-moistened tissue in my mother's fingers bore down on me.

"Do you have a place to stay?" Lakesha asks when we climb back into the van. "You can crash with us if you want; we don't bite, not even Coach Duncan." She catches a loose strand of hair and tucks it back into her pigtail. Her freshly-scrubbed face shines as if it had been brushed with honey. There is a calmness in her half-closed eyes that I can almost touch, and her gaze unmasks me until I have no choice but to tell the truth.

"I don't have any money."

Lakesha laughs. "That's all right. Neither do we."

The doors slam shut and we're off again, speeding toward Forth Worth. I'll spend the night with the Pumas, maybe hang out a few days and watch the games if they invite me. Then I guess since I'm so close I should head to Dallas and stay with Lisa for a while. She's probably pacing by the phone and wondering if she should call the cops. Or maybe she just hopped right back into bed and doesn't give a damn. Maybe I should head to Savannah instead and try to reclaim my Volvo.

I'd like to go to sleep, but the whoosh of cars passing in the opposite direction is resonating with the frequency of my brain, and I feel like an undamped harmonic oscillator. I think about Lisa in her immaculate house with her faithful husband and two beautiful bright children. *Men ken keyn mentshn nit derkenen, biz men zitst nit mit im oyf eyn fur,* my mother used to tell me. To know a man well, you must ride in the same wagon with him. I wonder what it would be like to come home from work every day, gather a family for dinner, waltz through bedrooms tucking little girls in and telling bedtime stories, retiring to read beneath a fluffy goose-down comforter. I've never been on the grown-up end of that. I wonder what it would be like to live a life not spent skittering on the edge of someone else's universe.

The radio hums softly in the background now, and I let my head fall onto Lakesha's shoulder, pretending to sleep. Hurtling through the black hole of highway space I imagine myself as a stretched string, vibrating between two fixed ends. I think about vibrational nodes, those places along the surface of a standing wave where motion ceases, and I realize that the safety of Lakesha's shoulder is such a place. This is what we are all searching for, I want to tell the Lady Pumas, the truth of it filling me like the hint of flowers I breathe from the hollow in Lakesha's neck: the still pools where holiness whispers, as ephemeral as the vibrations of a desert rose.

A Thousand Dances

For Remera, because he rose from the lake and he lived.

Imana yirwa ahandi igataha i Rwanda.
God spends the day everywhere but comes home to sleep in Rwanda.
—*Rwandan Saying*

I t is raining here. Lightning explodes from black clouds. Thunder shakes the rocks. "I came to bear witness," Ingabire says. She walks shivering through a river of mud, her body a skin of flames. She calls for her mother, her father, her sisters. She knows they were together in a place not far from here. She knows she has walked until there was no feeling left in her legs and her heart turned to ice.

Ingabire steps over rocks, trips over bodies. Some are moving, some are not. Mount Nyiragongo rises from the muddy landscape like a jagged tooth, breathing fire and smoke. Blue plastic tents flap in the wind. People, wandering in and out of the mouths of tents, stare at her with eyes like wounds. She is lost, surrounded by the mouths and eyes of wounds.

A man watches from the entrance of a tent. She thinks it is her father, steps toward him and sees it is not him. His eyes blink in a face of mahogany bark. Perhaps he is an *umuzimu* walking among the living. Perhaps she is an *umuzimu* walking among the dead. He approaches. She smells smoke and wet leaves.

"Come with me," he says.

"I'm looking for my sister. She came back to watch me dance. Now she's not safe."

The man touches her arm, beckons her to follow. "None of us are safe now," he says. Ingabire walks behind him with her bare feet like two boats of mud.

"You're full of fever," he says.

"I've burned up," she replies. "There's nothing left of me but flames."

The man takes her to a tent with a red cross on the side. Ingabire thinks it is a church. She wonders if she is home in Butare.

"*Allô, docteur,*" he calls.

The man who comes out of the tent is young and wears a white coat. He's not a priest. She thinks he's a soldier. She tears free and tries to run. Her muscles flow away from her like water, and she lies in the mud between the feet of the two men. She is too tired to ever move again. She feels their hands under her back and her legs and the cool of their fingers on the flames of her skin and she is lifted into the air and the rain. She is brought inside the tent and put on a blanket and she closes her eyes against a world that will never be still again.

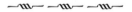

Ingabire has lived and danced in Paris. She has danced in Brussels, London, and Rome. Shivering with fear in the musty spaces of backstage, her sister Violette would gently coax her until she was ready to tie her *inzogera n'ikinyuguri* around her ankles and wrap her *umukenyero* around her waist. Gently she would tap her feet until the tinny sound of the bells took her home, and she could take Violette's hand and burst through the curtains into the blaze of lights where together they danced, feet lifting from the floors of banquet halls and concert stages. Even on the cleanest floors she was aware of a faint chalk-grain feel, the feel of the rust-tinted clay of Rwanda that finally succeeded in pulling her home.

THE DANCE OF UMULIRO, FIRE

Ingabire dreams she is dancing. She dances the *Umushayayo*, the slow swirling dance of her country. She wears the traditional *umukenyero*, the red cloth wrapped tightly against her body. White fringes flare, keeping their own rhythm to the movement of her legs. On her ankles the *inzogera n'ikinyuguri* sing the rhythm of her feet. A white ribbon tumbles across a bare shoulder.

Her arms wave like papyrus in a breeze. Her feet float in a haze of dust. She circles, head thrown back, fingertips extended, and the glass-blue sky swirls. The sun gasps with heat. Ingabire dances for her life.

In a stand of reeds along the shore Ingabire sees her family. Mother. Father. Violette. Devota. Flames of sun lick the waves. But where is Gasore? He's so young: not yet five months. He should be bundled in a sling against Devota's breast. Ingabire sees his body twirl and spin on the lake. He is a pirogue, a dugout canoe gliding on the surface. He is floating for his life. Ingabire tries to breathe, but her lungs fill with blood. She breathes in the blood of her country. Her country bleeds for its life.

—m— —m— —m—

"Are you Ingabire Colette?" the man in the dirty white coat asks. He wears a stethoscope around his neck. He holds the metal against her chest and asks her to breathe. Fear rattles in her throat. He puts his hand out to touch her, and she screams.

"*N'ayez pas peur. Je suis médecin.* I'm a doctor; you're safe now."

Above her, blue plastic sags: a ragged flap of sky. Rain beats against the tent. Water weeps from the roof onto her skin. The doctor's words fall like water into her ears. She tries to sit, but a roaring fills her head. Lake Kivu shouts a sea of curses that bang against her skull.

"Mama? Papa?"

"You came alone. You told the old man who brought you here you crossed Lake Kivu in a pirogue. He said he didn't know you, but he knew who you were."

Ingabire shivers. She is as hot as the sun, as cold as a river of ice.

"Take this," the doctor says. He lifts her head, puts a pill in her mouth. "You're burning up with malaria. You need IV treatment, but we don't have it. We don't have anything." He puts a bottle of water to her lips. *Amazi.* The pill is a bitter stone that sticks in her throat.

"I'm so thirsty," she says. "I could swallow all the rain from the sky."

THE DANCE OF UKUGURUKA, FLIGHT

Ingabire arches her back, turns her arms into wings. A fish eagle wheels above the lake. The sun shining on the rust-colored wings gives it the appearance of bleeding, shedding its life into the waters. Black wingtips arc toward the heavens to form a silent prayer. *Mana mfashe*, God help me. The bird's white head gleams. Flee, he cries, there is nothing left but bones.

Ingabire executes a series of jetés and pirouettes in the shadow of the eagle. The bones of her feet are hollow: the bones of a bird. Faster and faster she leaps. Volcanic rocks scoop the skin from her feet until the shores are red with her blood. She follows the rocks out into the water, out toward the far shore where the country of Zaïre rises. Zaïre is a green jewel in the distance. Zaïre is a gaping mouth waiting to swallow her. *Urupfu rurarya ntiruhaga.* Death eats and is never full.

"Mama," she calls. "Papa." She hears only the silence of stones. She slips; her feet kick and jerk as if she were dancing on logs. She looks down to see arms and legs entwined like gnarled roots beneath her feet. Lake Kivu is choked with bodies, and Ingabire dances to Zaïre on this bloated sea.

—₥— —₥— —₥—

The first time Ingabire remembers dancing, she was floating in the warm lake of her mother. She felt the drumbeat of her mother's heart, and of their own accord her tiny feet began to move, tapping the rhythm of life with her toes. Ingabire heard the chop of her mother's hoe, the drone of cattle, and the slippery notes of her sister Devota's dreams. In the evening, the voice of her father rippled through her skin; on Sundays the hymns from the ochre-walled church on the Avenue de la Cathédrale flowed through her veins. Sounds mixed and swirled in the waters that surrounded her, and Ingabire danced and floated, reached her fingers toward the world.

When Ingabire was born, she came out feet first, her toes moving and stretching in the cool air of dawn.

"A bad omen," her aunt whispered. She made the sign of the cross.

"A special child," her mother replied. "She is blessed with a sacred gift, so I will call her Ingabire, the blessed one."

Ingabire's mother bundled her in blue and gold cloth. Ingabire cried and kicked. Her mother kissed her and held her to her breast. There she heard the familiar sound of her mother's heart and was comforted. She felt cold air and warm skin, smelled the tang of sweat, the sweetness of milk. Her toes curled and uncurled as she drank.

Above the house the sun bloomed, bursting through the towering plume of clouds and the taut pink skin of sky. Ingabire felt its pull. The leaves of the jacaranda stretched across the roof. The scent of blossoms sang in her nose. Ingabire stretched her feet toward the ground.

It was two weeks before Easter when Ingabire was born. By Christmas she could walk by herself to her father's outstretched arms.

"Come, little daughter. Run to me," her father called.

Ingabire's sapling body waved; she stretched the branches of her legs: first one then the other. Her new muscles felt half fluid, half solid. This was a feeling she never lost.

The thunderous heartbeat of rain on the roof filled the house. The thrum of rain propelled her forward, pulled her on a current of music and love until she collapsed inside her father's arms. Devota and Violette, running beside her, clapped their hands.

"You see," her mother said. "I was right. God has a purpose in blessing us with this child."

Ingabire nestled against her father's chest. Her body swayed with the rhythm of his breath and the song of the rain. Her feet moved with the pulse of her country. Rivers of rain fell on the earth. Red clay ran down the hillsides and filled the rivers and streams.

—〰— —〰— —〰—

"I can never forget watching you dance," the doctor says. "It was in Kigali, the night President Habyarimana was there."

Ingabire looks at her feet. Blood and mud have formed a crust. Part of a toe is missing. She tries to move her toes, but they are stone: they don't belong to her.

"Habyarimana turned into flames," she says. "His plane exploded in the sky."

The doctor offers her water, and she drinks.

Ingabire's body floats on the narrow cot. She's a pirogue spinning through the lake. Violette is a cloud rising from the soft curve of wood that is her body. She sings and casts a net into the waters. The net gleams with fish.

"Why did you come back, Violette?" she calls. "There's nothing here but death."

"Was your sister with you?" the doctor asks. "Your mother and father?"

Ingabire does not want questions. She wants to hear the notes of prayers rising from the church, the explosion of drumbeats from Devota's drum rising through the soles

of her feet into her flying legs her spinning body her arms
that could reach out and hold between them the rage of the
world.

She touches the doctor's sleeve. "Doctor."

He kneels in the rippled edges of her fever. "What is
it?"

"I want to tell you," Ingabrie says. She begins her story.
the words float in the damp air.

— ⁓— — ⁓— — ⁓—

"We were hiding in the forest when the soldiers caught
us. With their brown skin, their shirts with the green-
brown pattern of leaves, they seemed to rise form the earth.
Uri umuhutu cyangwa umututsi? they shouted. We held each
other tight; we shivered and said nothing. Devota and Gasore, Violette, myself. Are you Hutu or Tutsi? they shouted
again. We curled our Tutsi fingers into tight fists. Gasore
would not stop crying. His fear shook the treetops."

— ⁓— — ⁓— — ⁓—

Ingabire turned her world into dances. She turned earth
and plants into arabesques, terraced hills and banana groves
into leaps and pirouettes. She stood in Violette's shadow as
her sister practiced ballet, and the shadow moved her legs,
her arms. Ingabire stretched and grew. Inside her veins the
blood of her country mixed and swirled. She had the broad
face and almond eyes of her Hutu mother, the long delicate
body of her Tutsi father.

"Mama, am I Hutu or Tutsi?" she would ask, tugging
on the folds of her mother's *pagne*. "What difference does it
make?" her mother said. "We're all Rwandan."

But when they went to see her aunt in Gisenyi, Auntie
spat in the dirt. "You'll see," she whispered when Ingabire's mother couldn't hear. "The Tutsi can't purge the regal
blood from their hearts. They'll try to rule us again."

"No, Auntie. My father's a teacher. He studies trees.
He's not a king."

Ingabire twirled. She intertwined her fingers above her head to shape a crown. Faster and faster, until she spun away the storms from Auntie's eye.

In the early morning Ingabire walked with Devota and Violette by the shores of Lake Kivu. They stopped by the gardens of the beautiful houses where the *wazungu* lived and called out to the gardeners and maids.

"Who lives here? Where do they come from? What do they do? Our auntie works for Mme. LaForce. Madame's husband is the most important man in the place that makes the beer. "

Mme. LaForce's house was at the southern edge of town. Sometimes, as a special treat, Auntie would take Ingabire and her sisters to work with her. In front of the house stretched a thick lawn. Ingabire wiggled her toes in the grass and laughed at the tiny fingers tickling her feet. One day she and Violette made up a dance to the gardens. They turned their arms into branches, their fingers into flowers. They dipped and swayed and slid their feet through the grass. Devota clapped her hands and sang. When they stopped they heard applause.

"Beautiful! Magnifique!" Mme. LaForce shouted. She sat in a wicker chair sipping iced juice by the garden's edge. A shadow from her hat danced across her cheek. "Jacqueline, you must bring the girls to perform at my parties."

"Certainement, Madam," said Auntie. A spark of sun flew from her gold tooth.

Violette showed off her arabesque, her graceful ballon. Three days later they came in their *imikenyero* to dance for the Belgians and their American visitors. Devota brought her drum and two ironwood sticks.

"I want to go to France," whispered Violette as they held hands and watched the guests applaud. The women wore tiny shoes that lifted their heels and made them walk on their toes. The men wore jackets and ties. Sweat shone on their foreheads, and they patted them with white clothes that poked like little hats from their jacket pockets.

"What are you talking about? Rwanda is your home."

"Rwanda is nothing," Violette replied. She bent forward in a bow, sweeping away her country with her arms. "You can't be a real ballerina here. You have to go to Paris." Ingabire curtsied. She covered her feet with her skirt and tried three small steps in imaginary *mzungu* shoes.

On the way home Ingabire heard the waves slither out toward the center of the lake. Eucalyptus leaves chattered, shedding rivulets of moonlight onto the sand. Coffee berries shone on the hillside, like glistening drops of blood. Their scent brushed her skin. Frogs sang from the shadows.

"Violette, you can't leave. Tell me you were joking. Don't make me scared."

Violette turned and stamped her feet. "I'm going to be famous. I'll marry a rich *mzungu* and have a huge house and silk dresses and I'll dance up and down the stairs."

Devota laughed and beat her drum. "*Mzungu* Violette," she sang. "Fancy white girl, what will you do with the color of your skin? Where are all the black girls in your fancy French ballet?"

"*Je suis* Fancy White Girl," Violette called back and pushed against Devota's arms.

"No, I am Fancy White Girl," said Ingabire, and she did her high-heel walk with her *umukenyero* hiked up to her knees.

The water exploded as a fish eagle plunged into the waves, a flash of silver gleaming from its claws when it rose again into the night. Someday an airplane will take my sister away from me, thought Ingabire as she watched the white head of the eagle turn to a point and disappear. After tonight I will lose her, little bit by little bit.

—⁓— —⁓— —⁓—

"You're one of the lucky ones," the doctor says. Ingabire shakes her head. Pain flashes behind her eyes. She sees the soldier, feels the gun pressed to her temple. She touches her fingers to the scabbed wound.

"Forgive me. I only meant because you have a cot."

The tent overflows with people. Between the cots people lie on rocks that shred their skin. Their moans are the only song left of her country.

"Zaïre?" she asks.

"Yes. You're in a refugee camp near the border." The doctor sighs. "You need blood. We have no blood. We don't even have clean water to wash your wounds."

"Violette flew to France in an airplane. She has a French husband and children the color of sand."

The doctor has bent to examine her foot. Her words fly up through the tent and catch in the clouds that hang above this place like so many dirty rags.

"My sisters have become birds, but I am a cockroach crawling on the jungle floor. *Inyenzi.* I have no wings to fly away."

The doctor wipes her forehead. Ingabire breathes in the coolness of his fingers and speaks.

"We are Hutu, I said to the soldier who had spoken, standing in front of my sisters with my mother's Hutu face. If you are Hutu, why are you crawling around in the jungle like cockroaches? He put his gun to my forehead. The others laughed. Where are your identity cards? he said. We've lost them, I said. There were so many roadblocks. We were trying to save time and got lost.

"The soldier hooked a finger beneath my chin, lifted my face to his. He traced the outline of my nose. Your hand, he shouted. I held my fists against my belly. Show me your hands. Another soldier seized my fist, uncurled my fingers. The others crowded in behind me. I heard a thud, like a woman pounding washing against a rock. Devota screamed, but Gasore screamed no more. The soldier bent my fingers back until I was dizzy with pain. Hutu nose, inyenzi fingers. He pressed the gun between my eyes.

Let's see what you're made of inside. He shoved me down into the vines and stinging nettles. He was so heavy on me I thought I would drown. I prayed for it. Next to my face an orchid witnessed my shame with its creamy monkey face and unblinking purple eye, its indifferent stare, as the soldier pushed himself between my legs and tore me in two."

—ᵚᵚ— —ᵚᵚ— —ᵚᵚ—

Ingabire held tightly to her blowing skirt. The sounds of planes, trucks, busses and people tumbled together in the morning air. She pressed against Violette, breathing in the unfamiliar smell of her European clothes. The stiff fabric of the blouse scratched her skin.

Devota, Mama, and Papa loaded bags onto a cart. Cousins, aunts, and uncles formed a procession behind them, the children turning their feet black with the dirt of Kigali streets. Violette took Ingabire's face in her hands.

"Don't cry, petite. Next year we'll dance together in Paris."

"Violette, I don't want to dance in Paris. My feet wouldn't know what to do. I have to dance in Rwanda. "

Violette's finger followed the salty path from eye to chin. "*Petite folle*, you can't turn your back on a gift. If Mme. LaForce wants to sponsor you, you have to take it."

She bent down, pressed her cheek against the corner of Ingabire's lips. Her skirt made a strange shushing sound, and her body moved in the way of the *wazungu* women at Mme. LaForce's parties, with her back straight, her imprisoned legs folding into a V.

"It's getting so dangerous here," she said. She gestured at the soldiers. "We should all leave before the country explodes."

A plane revved its engines, swallowing Violette's words with its high-pitched wail.

A soldier stopped them at the gate. "Identity cards," he said. A machine gun hung from his shoulder. He placed a hand on Violette's arm, and Ingabire saw fire in her father's eye.

"See what you'll be missing, Violette?" He handed his card to the soldier. Her mother took her card from her bag. Ingabire saw the warning brush of fingers against her father's hand.

The soldier took the cards. He read them and handed them back. Her father's card fluttered to the ground by the soldier's boot. Her father stood a moment before bending to retrieve it, eyes a slash on the soldier's face. Ingabire let out her imprisoned breath.

"You're the lucky one, *ma fille*," he said as they headed toward the concourse. "We've become a nation of slaves. The only thing disappearing faster than the forests is our freedom."

Ingabire heard her cousins fumbling in bags and clothing for their cards. Fear and rage turned into a dance inside her. Her feet tapped a pattern half flight, half fury.

"*Imana ikurinde*," Ingabire said as she stood on the dazzle of concrete beside the plane, shouting her words into the storm of engine noise. Her arms were vines about her sister's neck.

"I'll be safe. You're the one who needs God's protection. Promise me you'll come as soon as you finish school."

"Yes, I promise. I'll come to study, but I'll never stay."

Violette ducked her head through the loop of Ingabire's arms. "Dance for me every day, and I'll dance for you. It'll be like dancing together."

"I'm dancing for you already, Violette, but it's a dance of sighs."

Violette pressed her lips to Ingabire's ear. "I'm so afraid for all of us," she said.

Violette stepped onto the metal stairway. She held her arms out to her family, waved, then turned away. Her new shoes made bright hammer sounds as she leapt from step to step. Ingabire heard their distinct staccato for a few seconds before the tap-tap mixed into the general percussion of farewells: Devota's fingertips on the skin of her drum. *Murabeho, murabeho,* goodbye.

Ingabire felt Violette's tears on her neck. She drew her finger through them and brought it to her tongue. The taste of salt remained long after the door to the plane clanked shut.

"Papa, is it true the *Mwami* had a thousand cattle?" Ingabire asked as they passed the sign for the Royal Palace in Nyanza.

Her father laughed. There were eight of them pressed together in her cousin's car. The windows were open, and the breeze swirled around them. Devota dangled her scarf from her fingers to twirl in the wind. A luminous scarf of dust rose from the road.

"*Oui, ma fille. Mille vaches pour les mille collines de Rwanda.*"

Ingabire watched the blur of terraced hillsides, the stone teeth rising from the earth. Women climbed the steep paths to fields of legumes, maize, and sweet potato, descended with heavy sacks balanced on their heads. Men shouldered bunches of bananas. A procession of people lined the roadside pushing and pulling produce and five-gallon containers, carrying machetes and hoes.

We are a nation of constant motion, thought Ingabire. This motion is the blood moving through my veins. It feeds my muscles, propels my arms and legs to dance. What would I dance in Paris? Square buildings rising into colorless sky? Earth bound beneath a prison of concrete?

"Mama, Papa, I'm going to make a thousand dances for my country. And I'll dance one dance from the top of every hill."

The car slowed, stopped, crept forward again. They joined the tail of a long beast of cars wheezing exhaust and panting in the shimmer of road. Ingabire pushed across her cousins to lean out the window. At the head of the beast was a checkpoint manned by soldiers. Beside the soldiers a family leaned against a wooden cart filled with vegetables and held their hands in the air, their identity cards offered up.

"A nation of slaves," her father said again.

"Etienne, leave it be," her mother whispered and patted his hand.

Ingabire saw a pulse of anger beat against her father's throat. By this time Violette was flying across the broad elephant-ear shape of the continent of Africa. She could rip her identity card into a thousand pieces and fling them from the window of the plane. A thousand glittering flecks of ice laughing and dancing across the sky.

THE DANCE OF AMAGUFA, BONES

Ingabire is dancing the 999th dance of her country. Her feet stomp; clouds of dust rise. Her black skirt flares; the sleeves of her black blouse quiver in the oily, tumultuous air. A red sash winds about her waist.

Devota plays her drum with drumsticks made of human bones. The skin of the drum is a human face, and the voice of the drum is the voice of Rwanda. It shakes the trees, stirs the hot liquid earth inside the mountain called Nyiragongo.

Lightning arcs between sky and ground, splits the swollen clouds. Flames of water strike the earth. Little Gasore, clinging to Devota's breast, cries tears of blood.

Ingabire raises her hands above her head, presses her palms together, arms forming the shape of a mouth. The shadow of the dance slips inside her. It grows and swells until there is no room left for anything except this dance. The dance surges through her arms and legs. She leaps and spins and reaches her arms to the drowned sky.

As Ingabire dances, the earth grows dark with blood. The cries of her people rise through the soles of her feet and she slashes the air with the blade of her fury. Ingabire dances a thousand stories with her body. A thousand stories for the uncounted people mixing their bones with the bones of the hills, their blood with the blood of the hills. The rivers bleed. The lakes boil. Bloated bodies tumble toward the sea. Ingabire dances until she is empty, until there is nothing left but bones and sky. She collapses in a clattering heap of bones. She looks for Mama and Mapa. She searches for her sisters. There is no one here but the *abazimu* with their breath of ice, their fingers of smoke, watching from the forest's edge.

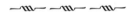

"I've brought you some food," the doctor says, holding a bowl of porridge. A film of oil floats on the surface. It has a sour, fermented smell. Ingabire turns her head away.

"Your fever's down. You should try to eat."

"Only death eats now," Ingabire says. She has drowned. Her body lies heavy and swollen at the bottom of the lake. Sardines with stinging mouths feed on her eyes.

"At least a sip of water. For me if not for yourself. Please, take your pill."

Ingabire cannot move. How can she command her body into motion when it is only bones and mud? The doctor's fingers are at her wrist, searching for life. The *abazimu* crowd around her cot, shouting to be heard.

"I can never forget watching you dance," the doctor says. "I couldn't bear for Rwanda to lose your gift."

There is warmth at her wrist, a flicker of a beat. Ingabire curls her fingers until they touch the doctor's hand. "Death is very hungry," she says.

The doctor folds her hand into his. She feels a tug, a gentle current buoying her up from the mud. She lifts her head, swallows water and pill, a spoonful of porridge. "Doctor," she says. "Death has eaten my name." The doctor puts down the bowl.

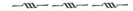

"In the forest I became a crab crawling between giant lobelia, through ferns, a tangle of liana and stinging nettles. I moved because I had to move, because my hollow legs had a will of their own because I could not look back because death nipped at me like a dog because I heard Violette and Devota pleading, Go, go. You must keep going. You must not stop. I went forward because if I looked back I would have shattered into a thousand pieces of shell and bone scattered in the leaves of liana, bearing witness to nothing."

—〰— —〰— —〰—

It was the bracelets that Ingabire saw first: seven malachite bracelets on the outstretched arm.

"Violette!" she cried and broke into a run, pushing through the sea of people at the gate. "I can't believe you've come," she said as she felt the flush of her sister's cheek against her own. She patted Violette's stomach through the silky skirt. She felt the press of bones, the narrow curve of hip she had slept against for the first ten years of her life. "How could two baby boys fit in there at once?"

Violette laughed. Ingabire inhaled the smells of France from her hair, her clothes. "I've had nearly three years to make myself small again, *ma petite*."

"Violette!" Devota called. She held Gasore like an offering. Joseph, her husband, offered his hand. "Mama and Papa have rented a taxi. They're waiting outside."

Violette took Gasore from Devota's arms. She held him to her face and kissed him. "Such a handsome little man. He'll be a famous *Intore* dancer." She touched his feet—one and then the other. "I can feel it."

Ingabire took Violette's hand as they walked to the taxi. "Violette, I wanted so badly to see you, but you should never have come. You can't believe how dangerous the situation has become. I feel like we are all waiting to be killed. Thank God you didn't bring the children, even though it breaks my heart not to meet them. We just keep praying for things to improve."

"*Ma soeur*, how could I not come? I've dreamed so long of seeing you dance again." Violette bent down and opened her bag. Sun flashed on the gold hoops dangling from her ears. "Look," she said and pulled out a leather book with a frame of gold leaf. "Your clippings from Europe. All your performances are here."

Ingabire was performing her dances in Kigali a week before her twenty-first birthday. Her family took up nearly a floor of the Mille Collines Hotel. Violette had paid for it all.

They sat by the pool in the fickle April sunshine. It was the day before Easter. The rainy season started and stopped this year, as undecided as the mood of the country.

"Hey, *mzungu*! Fancy White Girl, be careful! You'll get sunburned!" called Ingabire. She wiggled her toes.

She shared a lounge chair with her mother beneath a bright umbrella and sipped orange Fanta through a straw. Her father paced in his emerald-green swim trunks. His feet whispered worry and fear into the breeze. She breathed it deep into her lungs and turned it into dance.

"Papa," called Devota. "Come swim." Pink clouds of skirt swirled around her. Gasore floated on the raft of her hands, kicking his feet. Joseph ducked under, came up with water-filled cheeks by his son's head. Gasore squealed as the stream hit his mouth.

"Papa," said Ingabire. "Do you remember when you taught us to swim?"

Her father laughed. He sat by the edge of the pool and swirled his legs in the water. I have this gift from him, she thought. We can never be still. The heartbeat of this country will never let us rest.

"You were so difficult," he said. "Even then you thought you could float by dancing."

Her mother took a sip of Fanta, set the bottle on the ground. Orange-stained orbs spilled across the concrete. "But Etienne, of course she could. Didn't I predict it at her birth?"

Ingabire was thinking about Violette as she adorned herself with feathers and bells under the backstage lamps. She remembered Violette's firm hands pushing her, trembling and terrified, onto European stages. It is because of her courage that I am here, she thought. It was because she had the courage to fly away that I had the courage to follow.

She heard the waves of voices push forward and recede. She heard the beating drums and the women singing. Ingabire stepped, feet first, through the curtains and into the one thousand dances of her country.

A sound like a hammer woke Ingabire. Milky light streamed through the window. The sound grew louder, became a fist against a door. Devota stood beside the bed, pulling a shawl across her shoulders. "Mama, what is it?" she called.

"Wake up! Get dressed quickly! President Habyarimana's plane was shot down. He's been killed."

Devota opened the door. Ingabire saw her father slumped with his head on the table. She heard a mixture of static and shouts from the radio and recognized the voice of RTLM.

"Why are you listening to that hateful garbage?"

"It's started," her mother said. "Soldiers and *Interahamwe* are rounding up Tutsi and killing them. They've set up roadblocks all over the country and ordered everyone to stay inside. RTLM is reading lists of people marked for death."

Ingabire sat at the table and listened.

"The job is not yet finished—*Muhutu*, go out and do your work. Cut the brush. Search the drains and ditches. The grave is only half full. Who will help us fill it?"

"*Mana mfashe*," Ingabire said.

Her father looked at her. "How can God help us when we can't help ourselves?" he asked.

Devota lifted Gasore from his cradle and sat on the bed. "Joseph is coming from Kigali today." She began to cry.

Ingabire held her. "We'll be safe in Butare," she said. "They can't let it happen here. Our *préfet* is Tutsi—he'll protect us. If Joseph can get here he'll be safe."

—⧖— —⧖— —⧖—

Ingabire stood beneath the jacaranda. Purple blossoms covered the earth. Mist caught in the branches of acacia, dripped from bowed banana leaves. She heard a distant rumble. Thunder or mortar fire: she couldn't tell. Above the mountains clouds boiled.

Beyond the boundaries of Butare prefecture, the news was bad. Houses burned, mobs of *Interahamwe* patrolled the streets. Neighbors killed neighbors with machetes and spears. Bodies lay in piles on the roads, filled trenches, rivers and lakes.

A procession of refugees streamed toward the churches. For now, Butare remained an island of safety in a sea of death. Somewhere between Kigali and here, Devota's husband hid among the living or walked among the *abazimu*. Somewhere over the continent of Africa a plane that could have flown Violette to her husband and children saw the plumes of smoke and circled back to France. Ingabire gathered a handful of blossoms and held them to her face. She inhaled intoxicating sweetness before she let them fall and turned toward the house.

For the first time in two weeks, the radio was silent. Mama and Papa stood by the table facing each other like two dancers paused in a dance. A faint breath of perfume rose from Violette's chair.

"What's happened?"

"Papa's name," Devota said. "We heard it just now on the radio, on the list. The préfet of Butare's been murdered, and the *Interahamwe* are urging all Hutu to join them. No Tutsi left alive, they said. They've started searching house to house."

The pulse of her country bounded in Ingabire's feet. Flee, her blood whispered. Grab them all in your arms and fly away.

"We should go to the church," Devota said. She held Gasore and rocked.

Her father laughed. "How easy. Get us all in one place and pour the gasoline. No search, no struggle, just light the match. We could even light the match ourselves. "

"Papa's right," Ingabire said. "We should go to Gisenyi through the forest. Auntie can hide us; they won't bother the Hutu."

The family sat at the table with their identity cards. Ingabire, Devota, and Papa erased the lines through Hutu and crossed out Tutsi instead. "A joke," they said and laughed. "What else can we do?" The furious daylight fled.

"Someone must be left," they said. "Someone to tell the truth. We promise each other. If one dies, the other must live. If one falls, the other must run."

A lantern flung shadows against the wall. An untouched bowl of rice with peppery sauce and bits of grilled meat steamed in the center of the table. Plates formed a semicircle around the bowl. Ingabire thought of a planet with an entourage of moons, floating in the darkness. "In the morning we'll go," they promised. In the morning we'll fly to the moon, she thought.

Ingabire must have gone to sleep because the sound of shattering glass pierced a silence in her head that was like death. The walls shuddered. The floors shook. There were so many screams she couldn't make out one from another. Mama, Papa, the house itself. The air was thick with kerosene fumes and the stale reek of *urwagwa*.

She heard wood on flesh. She heard cracking bone. She heard the sighs of her parents' *abazimu*, torn from their bodies. Violette ran to open the bedroom door, screaming. Ingabire grabbed her and pulled her back. Devota was at the window already with Gasore wrapped against her. She pushed it open and jumped. Ingabire put her hands on Violette's shoulders and led her to the window.

"We promised," she said. "There is nothing we can do for them now. We must jump," she said, and they jumped.

The night air was cool. Torches blazed like stars. Plumes of smoke and flames rose from burning houses.

"We must stay together," Ingabire whispered as they crawled through the vegetable garden and hid in the tall flower beds.

When the killers had gone, they climbed the steep hillside towards the shadows of banana groves. Loose rocks tumbled and clattered. Ingabire slipped on a sharp stone. It tore through her toe.

—₩— —₩— —₩—

"I have to find some antibiotics," the doctor says. He has placed Ingabire's foot in a bucket of hot soapy water. Red lines crawl from foot to calf. Rag and water turn red. She sits up, leaning on trembling arms, to watch him work. Her teeth chatter.

"They said they were bringing more doctors, more supplies today." He sighs, and it is almost a giggle. "They said that yesterday and the day before and the day before."

The doctor squeezes her wound, and white pearls float to the surface. Ingabire smells dead fish, a mixture of blood and foul earth. She remembers the hot breath of the soldier, the stink of banana beer. The doctor scrubs once more and dries her foot. He applies cream, wraps it in a bandage. Ingabire sees that the bandage is made from a doctor's white coat.

"I was born in Goma," the doctor says. "When I was a child, we had so little to eat. We used to look across the border to Gisenyi and think, How lucky they are!" He sighs his sigh that is part giggle. "To us Rwanda and heaven were the same."

It is too much, this weight of me, she thinks. She lets herself sink once more. Down through the bones down through the mud down through the fish with their electric mouths. Orchids sprout from her flesh. The doctor's face floats on the lake's surface. Ingabire sees he is waiting to drift in her terrible words. The bubbles of her story rise from her mouth.

—₩— —₩— —₩—

"When we got to Nyungwe Forest we thought we would be safe—Devota, Violette, myself. We thought the soldiers would never come. Still we crawled like worms through the underbrush. Hunger fed on our bones. We could not drink from the streams because of the bodies. They looked like strange water plants with billowing shirts and *pagnes.* I remembered when we were children we came here. We ate our lunch by the water. The streams swirling over rocks made a sound like a baby's breath. Mama taught us to weave baskets from grass, and papa taught us about trees.

"I don't know how many days we had been walking when the soldiers rose up from the earth. My head was filled with a poisonous fog. Hutu or Tutsi, I thought when they asked us. What am I? What are you? What is anyone in this accursed country? I stepped in front of my sisters with their thin beautiful faces and showed them my Hutu nose.

"If one falls, the other must run. But even if the soldier had not held a gun to my head, even if no one had seized my wrist and bent back my fingers until pain cut my heart from my body, even if I had not been the first to be pushed to the ground and entered again and again like a dog, I could not have run and left my sisters behind. Their blood was my blood. Their breath was my breath.

"The soldiers held Violette and Devota and made them watch. I closed my eyes and begged Imana for death. Then the shot came and I thanked him and I fell into a sweetness of shadows.

"My sisters were cold on top of me when I awoke, their arms and legs entwined like the roots of a fallen tree. Their blood, my blood mixed on my face my arms my legs. The tides of us ran together. I had to swim to the surface.

"I must be alive, I thought. I was shot and bleeding. The *tic-tic* of the hammer pulling back over and over was the only heartbeat left in my head. I saw Gasore sleeping in his blood-red cloth with his head folded in against itself. I promised, I said. And I rose from the dead and I walked. I came to bear witness, I said, when I saw the blue tents rising like waves from a river of mud and blood."

THE DANCE OF AMAHORO, PEACE

Ingabire is dancing in a field of maize. The stalks wave and bend in the wind and wind fills her body until she is as light as a dried maize stalk bending and swaying in the breeze. The sun, afloat in a sea of clouds, spills streams of light onto the earth.

Ingabire sees her mother picking ripened ears from the tall stalks. A basket on her head overflows with maize. Ingabire plants her feet and springs into the air. She flies above maize, hills, trees. She sees her father, a black spot in the distance, but getting larger as he descends the hill. Violette and Devota walk behind him. And there is Gasore! How big he has grown! He runs in and out of the bushes with his dirty feet. His clothes are ballooning clouds of bright colored cloth.

From out of the ground a cloud of yellow butterflies rises. Ingabire feels the wind from their wings. There are more and more until the air is so thick with butterflies she is carried along in the river of their flight. They fan out until they cover all the hills. A thousand butterflies, dancing the one thousandth dance of Rwanda.

DIRECTIONS

Someday, when you least expect it, the afternoon will find you sitting on the bottom step by the back door, lost. There's no use looking for a topographic map, a road map, a neat line drawn that says, Here: you need to get from here to there. You will be talking to your father on the phone like an idiot, watching fingers of eucalyptus wave in the breeze as if you are the same person who sat here yesterday. This morning. Ten minutes ago. The instant before the phone rang. The same person who kissed a mother goodbye on Tuesday and put her on a plane. Today is Friday, and there is a telephone receiver in your hand, and the lace of your left running shoe has come undone.

But really, it is not unexpected. With every good-bye to every visit home you said to yourself, Chart a course, make a plan. The last time you walked down the airport concourse, leaving your waving parents behind, you did begin to draw a map. This is what it would feel like, you dared to think, to say goodbye. For one brave instant you imagined them disappeared. It terrified you. It caused tiny poking needles of guilt as you gazed out the airplane window watching a continent spread between you and your mother's love. She's grown pale. Her fingers tremble, and she often has to stop for breath. So you said, leave it, and turned back to your book.

Announce to the world it was not supposed to happen today. On your fingers, tick off the reasons why: (1) You have been meaning to call since Wednesday. (2) The last time she called, you couldn't keep a tone of annoyance and impatience from your voice. (3) You have dinner to cook, a husband and a dog to feed. (4) Damn it, you just can't let her go.

It's impossible to sit still and listen to your father's disconnected voice, so tie your shoe and resume your march-in-circles. Hold the phone against your ear with your shoulder and count the laps. Soon enough it will add up to ten kilometers of pacing, which is good, because this is the distance of the evening workout you had planned but no longer will get to run.

The words your father says will feel like shards of glass. They will bounce against your skull, tumble down and stick in your heart.

Angiogram
Infarction
Full Cardiac Arrest
CCU
What?
Coronary Care Unit
Oh. See—see you

Call your husband as soon as you hang up. Then call your dog and howl into the thick fur of her neck. Wipe your nose with the back of your hand and call your best friend. Although you keep trying to form the words your father pronounced, you won't be able to fit your lips around the sharp edges. In the Yellow Pages is a list of airlines to call to find the fastest plane. But the person you really need to call is your mother.

Mama, you want to tell her, I am lost at sea.

An earthenware crock sits on the kitchen counter next to a measuring cup filled with brown rice. The multicolored fruits of your garden overflow from a bowl. Sunlight strikes the ruddy skin of a tomato. A glass half-filled with water spills its orb of green-tinted light. Spilled grains of rice form an *I Ching* pattern on the blue tile. What fortune do they portend? Is it *Hêng, the heart and the constant moon*? The image will be stored in your heart under L, The Last Still Life of My Familiar World.

On the flight to Las Vegas, where you change planes on this only available convoluted route from Here to There, squeeze in between the two giggling chorus-line dancers. Don't bother to say excuse me—they are too busy with the day's events to hear. Their hair sparkles with fool's gold, and a weight of emerald dust half-closes their eyelids. They speak across the shadow of your seat, making sleep impossible. Go ahead and ask them, if you dare. What is it that makes you happy? What is it that moves you to dance? And, Excuse me, but have you seen the instructions anywhere for sitting in a hospital to help a mother die?

The runway rises from the blackness, the pinpoint lights of the city like stars in the wrong place. The airplane jolts back to earth. Wait until you are the last one. Take three calming breaths. Walk down the long tube that connects plane and airport and wonder, When I see him, am I supposed to wave? Your father is waiting at the passenger gate, and his skin is the same gray color as the carpet, and your hand signals a feeble hello before falling back against your thigh. Your numb, swollen feet press against the tongues of your hiking boots. They feel like they don't belong to you. In fact your entire body, you think, no longer belongs to you. The sloping carpet becomes a moonscape of felt. As soon as you are close enough, stumble into his arms. Don't even wonder—you won't be able to cry.

The "No Visitors" sign blinks like a rubicund eye as you pass into the forbidden territory of CCU. Nurses swoosh through the hallways in their cheerful scrubs. A nurse sits between each pair of rooms watching screens with squiggly shapes and taking notes. Your mother has a nurse all to herself, and you know that's bad news. Go ahead. Cross the threshold into her room and force air into your lungs. It will be the first breath you've taken since the double doors of the hospital parted to admit you. No matter how many episodes of *ER* you've watched, the shock will be new and fresh. This channel can't be changed. The volume's stuck on high.

A forest of tubes enters and exits her body. They carry murky liquids of intimate colors. Resist the urge to throw a towel over them, because alarms will sound, and they will kick you out for causing trouble. Surrounding the bed, a collection of machines produces a cacophony of notes. They wheeze and whine with a life of their own. Don't be afraid. Let your fingertips find their way through neoprene branches to touch her forehead. Talk to her. "Mom, I'm here." You'll feel like a fool, but these are the only shreds of language that remain. A shadow of movement crosses her face. Where inside this foreign form is she hiding?

Here is the vision that floats up from the waters of memory: following a pair of blue and yellow fins in front of your face mask as they undulate through tendrils of sea grass. Jewels of breath rising like moons. Your mother's hair spreading out in ripples red as ink. As blood. The refracted blaze of sunlight catching coral and fish on fire. It was your fifteenth birthday, and she took you to the Virgin Islands where she taught you to dive. The ocean was a gift your mother gave you again and again since you were old enough to splash. Is it like that for her now? Is she underwater? Can she pretend that this is nothing more than a dive? Attached to a mouthpiece, a regulator, a tank of air? Her swollen body floats beneath the white sheet, and you are both cast adrift. All you can think to do is cover her feet because they are blue and feel like ice. In the watery neon light, her face is the color of bone dust.

Above the bed, the waves of her heartbeat ride across a screen. They seem askew. Ask your father, because he's a doctor and he will know. It's not your imagination, he whispers into your ear. Their shape is all wrong. Your mother has a machine to breathe and one to move the muscles of her heart. Buy chewing gum and candy. Smack and chew and pop to keep the noise of her mechanical metabolism at bay. Hunker down. Tuck your feet underneath you in that uncomfortable chair. You are here for the duration because you know it is only your breath, in and out, that breathes life into her.

Forget about sleeping. Fold the thin pillow in half. Turn the flimsy blanket into a cocoon. Turn the reek of chemical cleanliness that coats nose, bronchial passages, and lungs into the scent of pine. Envision this: a hike in the forest and her braided hair wound around her head instead of a hat and shared sandwiches, the sin of Snickers. Transform the screech of metallic heart and lungs into the rhythmic sound of windshield wipers. There is a child in the backseat of her parents' car, and she is safe and warm. Rivulets of rain careen across the windshield. A father's steady hands on the wheel and his fedora perched on his head, tilted at a slightly daring angle. A mother's hair rain-glimmered beneath the flowers of her silk scarf.

There won't be a television in CCU. Amuse yourself through the insomniac passage of time by painting your own shows across the jagged wings of heartbeat on the only screen you see. A Comedy Hour. A Love Story. An Action Thriller. A Miracle on Main Street where a Mother Rises from the Almost-Dead. Don't close your eyes, because the moon is dangerous. Its lambent light slithers across the floor, slinks into corners where escaped dust motes gather, creeps across the bed rails, greedy to steal a mother's last labored breath.

In the morning, when sunlight stabs at your eyelids, you will discover that you have slept after all. A flash of panic brings you bolt upright before the blip of electrodes tells you nothing's changed. Rub life into your face. Stumble out into the hallway chanting, Coffee coffee coffee. At the end of a maze of corridors, your father is already sipping a

cup in the waiting room for CCU. The room is tucked into
an out-of-sight corner and has the feeling of a drifting ship
for the emotionally quarantined. The passengers whisper
among themselves, press their lips into a smile when you
say hello, then look quickly away. Stifle the urge to climb
on a chair and shout, Let's show a little support for each
other here! We're all in the same boat! The coffee looks
like it's been stewing for hours, but it's free. Pour a cup.
Kiss your father's stubbled cheek. Take a scalded and bitter
sip and start making lists.

Talk to doctor
Go for run
Find important papers
Bring more music for CD player
Bring Mom's cashmere socks

The lists will get shorter daily until only one item remains:
Keep Head Above Water

Grip the doctor's hand firmly when he comes in to talk
to you. Smile when he tells you she can survive, and when
he pats your hand and counsels you to hope. He confesses
that she reminds him of his own mother, gone last year,
and inexplicably you will want to laugh. Don't.

Make up lies. Tell him your mother fought the Nazis
and the Arabs. Tell the truth. She fought her way into medical school and a professorship in pediatrics. Tell him there
is a big difference between survival and life. Survival is not
something she would choose. Resist the urge to tell him
you have spent your life fighting the fierceness of her love.
He won't care.

Gulp the last of your coffee. Chew the grounds that remain in your mouth for the last little jolt of caffeine. Your
father wants to talk to the doctor alone, so run back to your
mother's room, asking directions when you end up on the
wrong end of a hallway in Neonatal ICU.

You've been away too long; it's shift change on CCU.
The night nurse leaves and the morning nurse enters. Their

scrubs rustle like dead leaves blowing across bare ground. The morning nurse has a cup of coffee from Starbucks, a place you and your mother have been boycotting for years. Plug in the CD player you asked your father to bring and play *Eine kleine Nachtmusik*, your mother's favorite piece. Fold her hand inside your own and bring it to your lips. The faint squeeze against your palm is real, although it seems no more than a flutter of butterfly wings. The morning nurse says your mother must rest. She says that noise and touch are stressful. She sips her coffee, leaving a bright red slash across the lip of the cup. Ask her if she would feel relaxed in a dark and soundless cave. Ask her what leads her to believe that Mozart makes one anxious. The conspiratorial press of your mother's fingers will make you giggle, but control the sudden urge to laugh until tears run down your face.

Two nights in the uncomfortable chair are enough. On the third night, go home with your father. Sit in the kitchen with him until two in the morning, drinking tea and telling remember-when stories. When neither of you can stand it anymore, ask if he wants to help clean your mother's office. It's not really order you're looking for; it's the secret hope that you can reconstruct her from the detritus of her interrupted daily life, like a golem out of clay. The things you find will surprise you. Take two pictures from the crumbling shoebox filled with photos. The first is labeled Zürich, kindergarten, 1921. In this photo your mother has round pouting lips and bituminous eyes set in a face that is half heart shape, half moon. She smiles in the second photo, which is labeled Prague, 1939. Her hair forms a halo of braids, and she is stepping forward with her right foot. She wears a woolen scarf about her neck, a man's leather jacket, and loose-fitting pants.

Don't call attention to the ancient packet of letters. Tuck them inside your sweatshirt. They are postmarked Prague, 1938. Pieces of envelope peel away like flecks of skin. Later, spreading the letters out on your childhood bed, you will find a pressed rose and a picture of a dark-haired man standing next to a motorcycle. The leather jacket he is wearing is familiar. A vaguely remembered conversation about a boy who died in a concentration camp will float back. Dismiss it—it's probably a lie.

In the morning, hide the letters in the dresser drawer beneath the scraps of your own discarded childhood. Pack running clothes and running shoes and the two pictures of your mother. There is something else—something you are forgetting—but you left the list you made on the seat of the uncomfortable chair.

When you enter your mother's room, prop the photos on the table beside the bed. Resist the urge to announce to the nurse, Look here. This is my mother. This is who she is. Let her adjust her healing intravenous potions in peace. After skimming the morning paper and telling your mother the important bad news of the world, excuse yourself. Convince yourself—a run would do you a world of good. Just one half-hour.

Step through the hospital doors. Let the cold air sting your face. Breathe in sharp hungry gulps of morning; inhale rocks, flower plantings, grass, trees. Don't be shocked when you realize that the pulse of life has not skipped one beat since you set sail. Sink into the rhythmic footfalls. One foot in front of the other. Follow a path that leads through a neat garden lined with evergreens and oaks.

The last time your mother came to visit, you took her to the butterfly exhibit at the Wild Animal Park. Her feet were swollen from the flight, and you fussed and pleaded until she consented to a wheelchair. All around, mothers pushed babies in bright strollers. You struggled with her bulk up the steep ramp, remembering when she was thin and strong and you couldn't keep up with her on the steepest trails. A bitter taste tugged at your tongue.

Passing through the double doors of the exhibit, a cloud of butterflies suddenly surrounded her. They alighted on her blue dress, the floral scarf that covered her shoulders, the crown of her still-red hair. The closed fist of your heart opened, warmed by the wind of their wings. You bent to touch her cheek with your eyelid. A butterfly kiss.

As you wheeled your mother through the thickness of butterflies, she spoke of her brother who had died before she was born, taking with him her own mother's heart. Trumpet vines, honeysuckle, and jasmine flung fragrance into the air. The sun splashed leaf shadows across the concrete walk.

"When I was a child," she said, "I used to watch my mother sit by the window for hours, her eyes focused on something I couldn't see. I knew she was waiting for her son. I would tug and tug at her sleeve, but she never felt the pull. I was just a shadow she looked through while searching for her shoes, cleaning dust off a shelf.

"That's when I decided to become an explorer. I knew if I found my brother and brought him home, she would love me. I came to believe that he was on another planet, alive and well. I imagined myself shooting through space and calling his name. I imagined hearing him answer, holding him, flesh and blood, in my arms."

"And did you ever find him?" A rebellious swirl of hair had freed itself from her braid, and you swept it back behind her ear.

She laughed. "Of course. All this time, he'd been on the moon."

The path you are running on winds away from the trees into a clearing of grass, and when you enter this clearing you will suddenly be face to face with the setting moon as it slides down tilting mountain ridges. Stop and catch your breath. Feel your full heart flutter. The cold beauty of the full moon's surface will be sharp enough to slice your lungs. And there, emerging from the shadow of a crater, will be the image of your mother as she looked in her childhood photograph. She will be wearing explorer boots crowned with tufts of lamb's wool, a leather aviator cap, and a flowing woolen scarf. By her side is a boy, red hair floating in the freedom of weightless space. They are leaping across the shores of lunar seas with long, confident strides. Your mother is leading her brother home.

Years later, sleepless and wandering through your own silent house, you will stop to watch the full moon from a window. You will press your head against the cool glass and let your breath condense like fog rising from the ocean. The panorama of lunar seas and craters will be vaguely unsettling until a particular memory surfaces: a pair of cashmere socks. You meant to bring them to cover your mother's icy feet, but you forgot.

A Matched Pair

The left sock of Sophie's favorite pair of socks is missing. She discovers this while folding laundry in a swath of sunlight and mesquite-branch shadow that drifts across the bed. It seems breathtakingly important. More important than the perfect creases in her dress pants, more important than the impending emergence of kittens from her waddling cat, more important even than her missing husband.

Kurt's clean laundry lies in a heap on the floor by his dresser. Sophie speaks to herself as she crawls on her knees, tossing his socks, boxers, and shirts into the air.

"I know I washed both socks. I remember distinctly. I turned them inside out, like every other pair of my socks and *his*, goddamn it." She seizes the neck of a shirt and squeezes. "Every one. And I put them both in the dryer." A pair of boxers sails through the open bathroom door. "Old men wear boxers: *old men*," she shouts.

The sock that Sophie seeks is neither extraordinary nor expensive. It is a cycling sock, dark blue with an orange smiling sun that shows off the shape of her ankle. And a hole that lets her big toe peek through. Flames surround the circle of the sun's face. She has, in fact, two similar pairs. She guesses she could substitute a sock from another pair with no one being the wiser, but there is a subtle difference in the artwork of the sun. On her favorite socks, the eyes are brighter, rounder. They have a look of pleased surprise, as if the sun has just been given an unexpected gift by her lover. And the mouth blooms in a sexy 'o'. She rocks on her heels, lets the last of Kurt's clothing fall from her hands and makes a sound that is half sob, half chortle. She collapses backwards, her butt hitting the Saltillo tile with a thump.

"You have nothing to do with the person I married," he had said. He sighted down the gun barrel of his finger. "And I don't like you anymore." He had been drinking, of course, but he spoke the truth.

That was just after two. She knows this because she checked the clock with every hiss that announced the opening of a beer. He was on his fourth. She was ironing her second pair of pants. As she sits with her skin against the cool tile she cannot remember how this particular argument started. Like all the others, she guesses. Some small and stupid itch. She tries to remember when she put away her backpack and it became essential to iron and crease her pants.

Sophie sees two paws protruding like slippers from under the bed, the pink dog nose resting on them.

"Watson," she sighs. She crawls under the bed and sinks against the warm body. His chest rises and falls with the tides of his dream. When Kurt brought him home he rested in her arms: substitute child, the booby prize, runner's legs dangling, bloodhound ears draped over her fingers. Now they lie end to end in the tea-pale light that settles like dust around the safe harbor of the bed.

"Look at that face," she had said. "He looks like Winston Churchill. I'm going to call him Winston."

Kurt snorted. "Winston? You can't call a hound dog Winston. His name is Scout."

She didn't know these things. She had not grown up flinging buckshot into the wild sea of Ohio hills. She had not grown up eating squirrel, unanchored between a thickness of trees and the whorl of scorched stars, saving the eyes for last, fighting over them with six brothers and sisters because of the slippery squish between your teeth. Or so he said.

"Every dog in every book and every movie is called Scout. How about Sherlock?"

Kurt squinted and rubbed his chin. The sun flung flecks of gold at his beard. The nameless dog licked her fingers with his hot tongue. "Watson," he said. "I'll give you Watson."

"Watson." Sophie rolled the name over her tongue. Watson's ears stiffened, slinking up the ladder of her fingers. "We'll take it."

"No trace of my sock," she says. "No trace of rain, no bloody trace of sock." She strokes his ear and he presses his face against her hand.

Sophie has come to believe that the missing Arizona monsoon and the drought of her marriage spring from the same evil seed. Fix one and the other will surely follow. She doesn't know which to work on first. Doesn't know if she should learn a rain dance or steal a lock of hair, stick pins in a doll.

"Hey! Where's Zungu? Where's your cat?" Sophie lifts Watson's ear and speaks into the conch shell of his auditory canal.

Watson found the cat last spring, sniffed out the trembling mud-caked thing wedged between trash can and wall. The kitten cleaned up to a shining white, paws a dusting of gray. From Sophie the kitten got an African name to commemorate her time in Kenya with the Peace Corps, and from Kurt Zungu received a measure of grace, an allowance of love from a man who had always hated cats. But it was Watson who was transformed by kitten into mother and friend, Watson who provided the warm curve of body where she nestled to sleep.

Sophie wiggles out from her safe place. "Tell you what: you find Zungu, I'll find my sock."

She walks to the laundry room, lifts the top of the washer and sticks her head inside the tub. No ball of sock stuck to the barrel. She checks the dryer. No sock disguised by tuft of lint. No sock in the forgotten dust between dryer or washer and wall.

A buzz of fear tickles the back of Sophie's neck, leaves a patina on her tongue. She wonders what unlucky hole in the universe this failure of hers has opened up. For the first time she allows herself to see Kurt's Jaguar belly up, a stranded desert tortoise by the slinking side of road, wheels turning like useless flippers, a rusty stain spreading in the sunburned dirt. *I don't like you anymore.* Sophie wonders if the curse of a mother's disapproval is enough to condemn a love to death.

———

When Sophie first mentioned Kurt to her parents, she stood in their kitchen. A skinny smile of moon swung in the window-framed sky, and the fluorescent glow of the kitchen lights illuminated the azaleas that grew alongside the house, sprayed the pink blooms with silver. Lilacs drooped over the walkway like grapes, perfume spilling into the evening. The night sky of Boston winked in the distance.

"Mama, I have a friend I want you to meet." Sophie held her breath between the drying of plates. In her belly she felt the heartbeat of new life, the sleepy division of cells. She pressed too hard with her towel.

"What's his name?" The predictable response: code for, *Is he Jewish?*

"His name is Kurt," she said, flinging the words at the floor.

Her mother's hands froze in the soapy water.

"Kurt?" She slammed the name back.

"Mama, he's not *German* German. He comes from Ohio."

"And his parents?" She was fishing. Baiting her questions with the hook of the war.

"Ohio. His great-great-great grandparents sailed to fucking Ohio on the fucking Mayflower."

"Sophie, you don't need to swear." Her father's contribution between puffs on his pipe.

The hands rose from the water. Sophie handed her mother the towel. Bubbles of soap shimmered on the floor.

"A German is a German. Just like they said about us. A Jew is a Jew is a Jew."

"For Crissakes, Mama. The war ended forty years ago. Can't you just give it up?"

But how could she? The war would never be farther than the numbers tattooed into the landscape of her mother's arm.

—ᴠᴠ— —ᴠᴠ— —ᴠᴠ—

Sophie walks to the kitchen placing her feet squarely in the center of each tile. *Step on a crack and break your husband's back.* She looks at the clock. Kurt has been gone nearly four hours. She opens the back door and steps across the gravel in her bare feet. The blast of August heat takes her breath. Like I'm treading water, she thinks, arms pinwheeled out for balance.

Kurt's tomatoes, beans, and squash spread tendrils beneath the green shade cloth. A few tomatoes, nearly ripe, float among the pungent leaves. Sophie can't get a weed to grow in this sorry soil.

Running shorts snap smartly on the line, and a few thickheaded clouds are building over the Catalina Mountains. Mesquite branches shiver. "Will it rain?," they whisper. The cruelty of hope. There is no sound of Jaguar ridden hard and coming home wet.

Dinner did not go well. Kurt, nervous, drank too much wine and asked for cream in his coffee. Sophie gasped: how could she have forgotten to warn him?

"We don't mix meat and milk," her mother said, her straight back as unmovable as Mt. Kenya.

"When I grew up," Kurt responded with his wine-loosened tongue, "we were too poor for that kind of luxury. We ate anything slow or stupid enough to be caught."

After he left, Sophie plowed ahead through the clatter of dishes and the flush of her mother's cheek that filled the kitchen like an aura.

"Mom, I'm going to marry him."

The clatter stopped. Her mother wiped her hands on her skirt, tucked a loose strand of hair into her bun. "So. That's how you honor the memories of the dead?"

Strands of Beethoven floated in from the living room. Sophie heard the scrape of a match, imagined the glow of her father's pipe.

"Mom," she began. She had to stop for breath. Had to put her hands in the pockets of her sweater to calm the urge to slap her mother hard across the face. "Whether I marry him or not, no one is going to rise from the ashes of Auschwitz."

"Sophie, you do what you want. You always have. Just don't hold your breath waiting for my blessing." Her mother turned away, scrubbed hard at a dirty plate.

"Mom, I'm pregnant. And I'm going to keep the baby."

The plate sank back into soapy seas. Her mother crossed the room, fished through a drawer and pulled out a pair of scissors. With fingers shaking she cut then tore the neck of her blouse.

Sophie understood what this gesture meant. With the tearing of her clothes, her mother had declared herself in mourning. She might just as well have reached inside Sophie's chest, torn a hole in her heart.

At the kitchen door her father emitted a cry like an antelope calf brought down by a leopard. "Eva, please. Don't be crazy. Think what you're doing to your daughter."

"My daughter wouldn't do this to me. My daughter wouldn't marry a German. I'm going to say *Kaddish*."

Sophie watched her mother walk up the stairs. She supported herself on the banister and incanted the first words of the prayer for the dead. Sophie thought she looked like the oldest woman alive.

—∿— —∿— —∿—

In the kitchen Sophie sprinkles cat food in Zungu's dish and calls her. Kurt's absence answers. She imagines him with the top down, wild-haired and three sheets to the wind, kitten-filled cat rolling across the seat, a clenched fist raised against the wounds of the world. A sunshine sock flaps like a flag from his antenna.

Sophie hears the click of Watson's nails on the floor. He nudges her, bloodhound nose inhaling fish-and-liver bits, bloodhound tail an antenna in the air. She tosses a nugget into the yawn of mouth. He crunches and burps.

Perhaps she could fix some dinner. She hasn't eaten all day. But Kurt took over the cooking years ago; she barely remembers how to fix an omelet. What would he think to come home and find a steaming three-course meal awaiting him? What would she think choking down un-tasted bites, watching the empty chair, the cooling artwork arranged on his plate?

Sophie paces. She peers out the window at Blackett's Ridge. Shadows slide down the green-fuzzed rock. Gathering clouds lift in anvil-topped plumes above the peaks. Yes: it just might rain. The raging light from the western sky glints off her mother's menorah, the copper *Pesach* plate that hangs on the wall.

She thinks of someone to call, to say hello. But what would she say? My sock is missing, and—oh yes, my husband. And to whom could she say this? She had sailed away from the shores of friendship since Kurt's drinking worsened and she ran out of answers to, Any babies on the way? She prefers the comforts of books and Beethoven, the pleasure of long runs with her dog.

Perhaps she could watch TV. She hates TV, flees from it as Kurt stares, feet up, drinking his beer, but the thought of a soothing voice to fill the corners of the room seems suddenly right. She turns it on, flicks through the channels. Fuzz fills the screen. There was something Kurt said about having to use the remote. The blinking eyes of buttons glare. Which ones to push? She tries a few, tosses the thing on the floor, slams the on/off switch with her palm. A Ph.D. in hydrology and she can't force the television to speak.

—w— —w— —w—

"Mama, I did it. I'm a doctor now—a water doctor."

She held the phone like Elijah's cup, wine-filled. Will the prophet come tonight? Will he accept our offering? Kurt danced by the window, twirling her mortarboard on a finger, gulping champagne from her *zeyde's* fancy crystal. Prisms of light slithered across the floor, splashed across the wall. Her father stood beside her trying to pull a mother's love through miles of wires and poles. Sophie listened in the silence for a breath, a hint of a smile, a falling tear.

"That's wonderful, Sophie." A pause. "I'm very proud of you, really. Congratulations." A pause. "Goodbye." A click.

Sophie imagined a trench in a field, a stubble of grass over hard ground. She and her mother, no more than rags of flesh flapping from bones, were shoveling. Electrified barbed wire sizzled at their backs. A gray snowfall mixed with the slurry of human ash blurred the lines between earth and fire-reddened sky. The greasy scent of the ovens' work lay across their skin.

"Near the end there were so many bodies we had to throw them into trenches. The crematoria couldn't keep up," her mother once said. "Then the men poured gasoline over them and burned them."

Into the trench went mortarboard and gown. In went thesis, papers with her name in well-known journals, stacks of A's, nights of no sleep. In went the hope that if she crawled through enough of her own fire, her mother would forgive her.

"She loves me. She almost said it. Really." She replaced the dead receiver and collapsed inside the safety of her father's arms.

—w— —w— —w—

Sophie wonders when Kurt slipped inside and severed the arteries of her independence. It's mutual, she supposes. He needs her to transfer dirty clothes from floor to laundry bin, find missing items, make doctor's appointments, pay bills. Their roots grow together in a tangled mess, seeking water in this arid soil of life.

—w— —w— —w—

The first Sophie saw of Kurt was his shadow. "Excuse me," the shadow said, "do you speak English?"

Sophie squatted in the way she had learned from the Kenyans, planting the last eucalyptus seedlings in the raised bed. The children with their bright, flapping rags, their broad, flat feet, watched from the field. A few boys played soccer with a ball made of tightly wound plastic shopping bags. She wiped her hands on her pants and looked to find the source of the voice. He stood behind her wearing a Boston Red Sox cap, camera vest pockets bulging, a camera with a long lens around his neck.

"Yes," she said. She stood. "I'm from Boston. Are you?"

He laughed. His hair and eyes were the same metallic shade: an alloy of copper and gold. The bones of his face made sharp angles, his beard framing the square jut of jaw. His body carved a space in the mountain air. She sensed a faint wild smell: half animal, half savanna grass in the rain.

"No, I just have undying respect for their losing ways," he said. "I'm looking for the Presbyterian Guest House. Do you know where it is?"

She did. It was next to the Peace Corps compound where she lived. Each morning she awoke to the hopeful songs of the church.

"Take back what you said and I'll tell you."

The children ran behind as Sophie and Kurt walked. "*Mzungu! Mzungu,*" they called.

"What are they saying? Zungu?"

"*Mu-zungu,*" she said, separating the syllables. "They're calling you a white person."

"So what are you? I'm sorry I haven't asked your name."

Sophie pulled her sweater around her. Soon the sun would begin its high-speed plunge behind the Aberdare Mountains and into the Rift Valley. The skies blazed a coppery red.

"I've been working in this dirt so long they think I'm black. I'm Sophie. And you?"

Kurt stuck out his hand. "Kurt."

Sophie took the hand. Oh God, she thought.

He was a photographer. Until last month he photographed wildlife for local outdoor magazines. Then he got a call from a friend who worked for *National Geographic.* A project shooting the elephants and big cats of the Kenyan mountains. He threw everything he owned into a knapsack, loaded his camera gear and stepped with his size-twelve hiking boots into the business-class section of a British Airways plane.

Kurt told her this over a dinner of grilled meat, *suku-ma wiki* and crispy fried potatoes. Tusker beer bottles accumulated on the table, beads of sweat forming puddles on the plastic cloth. They broke chapatis in half and fed each other bites. Painted on the wall beside their table, a man dangled from a branch above a river where a crocodile spread its jaws. A python, coiled along the branch behind him, raised its head. A yawning leopard crouched at the base of the tree. He looked like he could crouch and wait all day.

"What's this about?" Kurt touched the space between the man's foot and the crocodile's gaping mouth.

"*Shari ya Mungu*. God's law, or God's will. To me, this mural is about how Kenyans see life. We're perpetually on the verge of disaster. It's all up to God to get us through. Or not."

It would be two years before Kurt told her of his father watching as he chose the willow switch from the tree and scraped off the leaves and branches. His father forced him to leave the nubs because of the painful welts they left, the better to cure his son's stubbornness. His father's foot tapped out a rhythm on the empty stool waiting by the base of the tree. Then pants dropped to the ankles, body bent over splintered wood, Kurt counted blows while his brothers, sisters, and mother watched from the window.

After dinner, in the small bed at the Presbyterian Guest House, Sophie told him of her degree in forestry, her work with the Peace Corps, her desire to remain in Africa forever. She did not tell him she was AWOL from a war that ended years before her birth. Did not tell him about her mother and her mother's sister, hidden children, swallowing words and breath in an attic for months whose names became a blur of lost time. They almost made it—*almost*—but the soldiers came shouting *Wo sind die Juden*, splintered the secret wall, ripped apart the entwined limbs of sisters. Shot one, pulled the other out by her hair.

As Sophie spoke, Kurt slid his hand over the smooth plain of her belly, gathered the small hill of breast into his palm. Her hair, released from the practical braids, spiraled like curls of peeled bark across her shoulders and down her back. When Kurt's tongue found the bridge of bone at the crest of her thighs, her words turned into a whispered "aah." He entered in soft circles despite the angularity of limbs; his a densely bound frame, hers light and airy as an ibis springing into flight. They slid against each other until morning. The film of sweat and beer caused a slight sucking sound, like a kiss, when they separated.

On the night before Kurt left, his wild Sugarcreek, Ohio, seed went swirling up her own dark creek and nestled against an erudite egg from Boston, Massachusetts.

Six weeks later, after the fifth day of fertilizing fields with upchucked breakfast, Sophie sent a letter, quit the Peace Corps and booked a ticket home. When she came to visit Kurt in Tucson she walked through the back door into blazing light. She stood under the mesquite, reached up into the silver-dusted canopy. She rolled the feathery leaves between her fingers. A thorn left a dot of blood on her skin.

"I could live here," she said, thinking of the wind-flattened acacia with their thorn teeth that rise from the Rift Valley, the lower slopes of Mt. Kenya.

—ₘₙ— —ₘₙ— —ₘₙ—

Sophie is staring at the silent television when she notices. Watson's crate is reflected in the glass, and the top is bare. There is no knapsack with its one frayed strap, its ragged *National Geographic* patch. There is no camera with telescoping lens. How could this happen? Does this man she is married to take up so little space in her world that she doesn't see him lift his camera like a baby, place it inside his bag? Doesn't notice the knapsack draped over a shoulder as he walks out of her afternoon, her day, perhaps her life? She walks into the garage. Tent and sleeping bag are gone.

The sun is giving up. It bleeds color onto clouds and mountains. The fierce teeth of the Tucson Mountains glow with volcanic light. A coyote in the front yard slips through the shadows of paloverde, the waxy leaves of creosote bush. Watson presses his nose to the window and growls. A family of Gambel's quail, persistent, pecks at seeds. The black topknot of the male bounces like a candy dangled from a stick: always just out of reach. In the cloud-dark sky beyond the southern window, heat lightning flashes. No thunder follows.

"Come on, Watson. Let's eat."

Sophie spoons meatloaf into Watson's bowl, pours a bowl of cereal for herself. She flips through CDs, alphabetic by composer, chooses Beethoven's *Emperor Concerto*, cranks the volume. Piano notes rise defiantly, joined by a cascade of strings. They rage against silence, injustice, betrayal. Sophie sits on the couch, facing the TV, and watches a darker image of herself push spoonfuls of food into a mouth and chew.

On the coffee table are two magazines with Kurt's latest photos. Sophie places one bare foot on each. She puts her bowl of cereal, unfinished, on the floor. Watson's dessert. Or Zungu's, if she ever comes home.

Sophie knows it is wrong to let Zungu roam, knows it was incorrect to let her conceive, bring furry fruit into this overpopulated world. But she couldn't bring herself to confine the wild white spirit. She remembers looking through Kurt's telephoto lens at the eyes of leopards glinting yellow in Kenyan moonlight. She remembers their sharp cries tearing through night's silence, the unleashed power of their springing legs, while she held her breath, afraid to let one single ripple of her own existence swirl into the star-crazed darkness.

The sky is deep purple, a shade away from black. Sophie refuses to look at the clock as she turns on lights. She calls Watson, lets him lap milk and cereal, wipes Saltillo tile with the palm of her hand.

"Let's go for a walk." Watson's ears perk up, the antenna of tail wags. "Just let me get the laundry."

Sophie gathers running shorts, pantyhose and underwear from the line. The full moon has cleared the peaks; it must be nearly nine o'clock. A few stars blink defiantly against the numinous glow. She walks down the hall past the closed door of the spare bedroom. The space where a crib would have gone has been taken over by a festively colored futon couch.

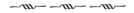

It seemed a simple thing, really. A missed step, a toe stubbed on a rock, a fall with scraped skin and torn running shorts. Three days later she lay in a hospital bed, blood running down her legs, tears streaking her face. "No connection," the doctor said and patted her arm. "These things just happen." But Sophie knew better. The curse of torn cloth, the punishment for her selfish behavior. God's will in its cruel glory.

The second and third miscarriages happened quickly: pregnant and gone. There were carefully plotted graphs of basal body temperature, tests and treatments, surgeries that left her doubled over with cramps for days. The fourth baby dug in its toes, held firm to her rebellious womb. She heard the heartbeat, watched the tiny limbs move on the screen as she lay on the examining table holding her breath. She dared to think about a name. Then the high fever came, her own blood turned toxic, and the unnamed baby let go its grip with a sigh.

Sophie wept in Kurt's arms without tears. "I can't handle the uncertainty of God anymore," she managed, thinking not only of four lost babies, but also of her mother searching for a trace of lost parents and brother for forty years. Thinking of her mother as a fifteen-year-old girl for whom God became an extra sip of watery soup, a stolen crust of bread, a Polish woman who tattooed her arm gently, with small neat numbers, instead of a brutal and painful scrawl.

Sometimes, Sophie thinks as the pile of neatly folded clothes grows, the Arizona heat sucks her life out through her gasping pores. When she beats her fists against Kurt's chest it is not anger but desiccation she feels. Sometimes she screams as if they are strangers in a car wreck and he has slammed into her from behind. "You have nothing to do with the person I married," he said as he left, and she believes he might be right.

"Let's get out of here," she calls. "Let's go find Zungu. Watson, get your leash." She hears the jangle. Watson is at the bedroom door with his leash in his mouth. His tail makes a sound like African drums against the doorframe. "I should have married you. At least you are easy to please," Sophie says as she puts on her shoes.

In the moonlight the desert landscape shines like shells. Zungu likes to hide among the spindly branches of creosote and desert broom. Sophie mistakes every fat, white rock for her pregnant cat.

An occasional arc of lightning synapses between clouds. Each time Sophie counts to thirty, hoping for a crash or bang or just a shudder. Lesser nighthawks trill, swooping at unseen prey with their white-banded wings spread wide. A car comes around the corner too fast. Sophie holds her breath, imagining relief. But the shape of the headlights is wrong, and they are too high off the ground. The car turns in the wrong direction.

Watson is four, maybe five steps in front. His huge head nods with his steps; he holds his enormous ears out as if there were guy wire strung between them.

There is no time to react. No time even to think stick or crack in the road or snake before the rattler raises tail and head and lunges. Watson leaps and yips. Sophie screams and yanks his leash. She wants to run. She wants to bargain back thirty seconds of her life. She wants the headlights to have been right so she could have turned around and followed Kurt's windblown hair as the topless Jaguar leapt toward the driveway.

"Watson, come," she whispers, heart thundering, as she reels in his leash, takes a few shaky backward steps. She sees the bright rattles of the snake disappear into the desert broom. He's not limping, she thinks, daring to hope. She grasps each paw and presses. Not tender. She presses her head into his flank. His breathing is quick but deep. She cups his face in her hands, and he licks her. His tongue is warm and wet; she sees no foam or drool.

"Easy, baby. Let's go home."

—ᴡ— —ᴡ— —ᴡ—

Sophie was listening to *The Magic Flute* when the phone rang. She kept turning the music up, Kurt kept turning it down. It was between her first and second miscarriages, before the house filled up with ghosts.

"That opera makes my developer curdle," Kurt called through the door. Sophie remembers that her mouth was open to laugh, but she had not yet turned it into sound when she picked up the receiver.

"Sophie," her father said. Sophie turned down the music. It was the only word she needed, to know what he would say. Kurt drove her to the airport in the dying December light. She watched the cheerful lights of Tucson twinkle, fade and disappear into a vast and sorrowful darkness from the window of the plane. She felt the uncomfortable pressure of guilt in her chest because she couldn't cry.

Sophie's mother was lost in the tangle of neoprene tubing. She looked like a curled, dried leaf beneath the sheet, and her exposed feet, swollen and blue, reminded Sophie of grotesque balloons. Machines breathed and beat and beeped, turning the hospital room into a factory of noise. Sophie saw the dark liquid that flowed into the catheter tube. She looked around for a towel to cover it up.

"Mama," she said, and folded her mother's fingers into her own.

"They've given her medicine to paralyze her," her father whispered. "Takes the strain off her heart."

But Sophie felt the feather squeeze of fingers against her palm, saw the slightest wisp of smile cross the taut skin. It was enough to reach across four years of silence, to wipe them away with a flicked wrist.

"I know, Mama. I love you, too. Really, there's nothing to forgive. For either of us." She bent across bedrail and tubing and kissed her mother's forehead. It was the color and texture, she imagined, of incinerated bone.

—ᴡ— —ᴡ— —ᴡ—

Sophie leads Watson to the lamp and makes him lie down. She spreads his paws to inspect the pads. He howls and mouths her hand, but she sees no blood, no swelling, no puncture. "You're just cantankerous, I think," she says. She presses his gums with a finger, watches the pink flush return. She goes to the phone to call her friend who is a vet but hesitates. It's been five or six months since they've talked, and she doesn't want to seem crass. She dials the emergency clinic whose number she keeps on the fridge.

"Since there's no evidence of bite, I'd just keep him quiet and watch him," they tell her. "Bring him in right away if anything's suspicious."

"Watson, you're going to be okay. They promised," she says as she hangs up the phone. She sees the red eye of the message light blink. She pushes the *play* button.

"Hey, babe." A pause. She hears traffic and a jingly noise. A cash register perhaps. "Just want you to know I'm okay. I need a little time, that's all." Another pause. Is he crying? "Don't worry." A click.

She seizes the machine in both hands, thinks of flinging it across the room. Instead she wipes the dusty place beneath with the palm of her hand and replaces it unharmed.

"He loves me, Watson. He almost said so. Really."

Sophie coaxes Watson into his bed, but he won't stay. She walks out into the backyard and he follows. A ghost of moon illuminates the clouds that now lie across the sky like a blanket. The wind has picked up, but the effect is merely to move hot air from one place to another. Sophie takes off her shirt and bra, drops them in the gravel.

"It's so fucking hot," she says. "Why can't it just rain?" She takes a few steps, removes shoes, shorts and panties. She raises her arms to the hidden moon and for the first time in years regrets the sensible ear-length bob. She longs for the feel of hair shaken free across shoulders and back. She traverses the yard naked, like a pilgrim offering herself to an angry god. Watson sniffs at a rock. "Please let him be okay," she asks. Wondering if she prays for husband or dog.

Sharp edges of gravel press into her feet. She presses back until pain makes her stop. She lifts her foot and is pleased to find a slight trickle of blood.

Sophie checks Watson every hour until 2 A.M., when she falls asleep on the couch. She dreams she is with Kurt in a tall glass building, on an upper floor. There is some kind of storm outside: a tornado, she thinks, because a furious chaos of black cloud bangs against the transparent side of the building. They are in bed, and she believes that if she can keep him hidden beneath the blanket that covers them, they will be safe. But Kurt keeps popping up. He keeps throwing off the blanket and trying to run. She is terrified that because of this failure the cloud will crash through the window and rip them apart, turning their glass house into a swirl of shards and debris. She wants to cry out, but something rough and wet presses against her face, suffocating sound. She opens her eyes to a still-dark room and feels Watson's panting breath, his scraping tongue.

"You okay?" She turns on the light and checks paws, mouth gums once more. It's four thirty. She goes to the bedroom and checks, but she knows she would have awoken if Kurt came home. She hasn't slept well in years. Watson is nearly tripping on her heels.

"You need to go out?" But it's to the garage door, not the back door, that he goes to whine. Sophie hesitates with her hand on the knob. She is afraid of a purring Jaguar, a body slumped over a steering wheel. Watson scratches at the door. She hears no engine, smells no exhaust.

"Okay," she says. "All right." She opens the door and turns on the light. Watson barges in.

From behind the freezer Sophie hears a purring sound, a soft chorus of mews. She follows Watson and discovers a half-destroyed box between freezer and wall. She counts five pink kitten shapes beneath the purring cat. Zungu's paws expand and contract with her breath. Watson sticks his nose inside and Zungu swats lazily.

"Well, at least someone around here's fertile," Sophie says, shocked at the truth that has come out of her mouth.

She emits a little squeal. There in the collection of rags and papers that Zungu has gathered for her nest is the missing sunshine sock. The face is crumpled, and the expression seems tired, as if it had found the ordeal of giving birth exhausting. But Sophie still sees the triumphant smile across the sun's cheeks, as if the surprise of living is enough—just enough—to keep the sun going.

How to Write a Train Story

Such luck! A snippet of space large enough to sit in. He sees it when the motion of the train opens a passage through the tangle of bodies and squeezes through like Moses, parting the Red Sea. It is filthy with the same black dust that blankets his skin, settles on the inside of his nose, closes like fingers around his throat and lungs. But a treasure trove all the same.

He settles himself in the corner. He sits on the sharpened sticks of his bones. The jostling of the train travels through these bones and into his spine and up to the top of his skull. His jaws knock against each other; the sound of his teeth rattles in his ears.

From his little corner all he can see is shoes. Shoes and pants and legs. The women wear dresses or skirts, and he can see that some of them once were elegant. Faded flowers cling to bruised, scabbed flesh.

Has he eaten? Perhaps. Was it today? Yesterday? Who knows. How long has he been on this train? An hour. A week. A year. There were a few crumbs of bread that he rescued from beneath the heel of someone's boot. And a morsel of a sausage that a man at the station pressed into his hand.

He is still saving a piece of chocolate wrapped in a tissue. It rests in the inside pocket of his jacket next to his heart. This chocolate is the last touch of his mother.

"Take this," she said. She kissed him, folded the miracle into his palm. The smell of chocolate exploded through the tissue. How long had it been since he last smelled it? Years. Endless time. What did he think of? He thought of his lost house. Of candles in a menorah and singing and arms embracing him in a warm room. The taste of roasted chicken. Pain beat against his chest like the wings of a wounded bird. Pain and a hunger as deep as the earth.

His mother took his hands and held them to her cheek. He felt a pulse of heat, a dampness, but there were no tears. For months they had been too thirsty for tears. How did she find the chocolate? With her love. How did she pay for it? It crushes his heart to think.

The gates that held them inside the fetid courtyard in a fetid corner of the ghetto burst open. The earth roared and rumbled with the noise of trucks. The trucks stopped in the middle of the crowd and soldiers leapt from the beds, guns drawn. He thought of a swarm of grasshoppers fanning out.

The soldiers herded the people into lines of five. They stood in a mist of rain, his jacket sagging against his skin. His mother squeezed his hand until he was afraid his bones would be ground into dust.

"Stay with me. Stay with me," she shouted into the storm of noise.

A man in a blue uniform with black boots and golden hair that tumbled from beneath his cap walked down the lines. Fate trembled like a noose at the end of his finger. He paused and pointed, pointed and paused.

"To the center! To the center!"

Those who were selected were pulled into the center of the courtyard. Many fell in the mud. Many did not get up. The finger stopped in front of his nose.

"To the center!" The words floated up as if from a cave. He heard his mother scream.

I sit with my father at my kitchen table drinking tea. Between us, the tape recorder wheezes and whirs. It is August, but a cold rain streaks the windowpane. A thin mist condenses on the glass like baby's breath. The pine floors send a chill through my stocking feet.

Two delicate fingers drum against the floral porcelain of his cup. The veins in his hands stand out beneath the translucent pearl of his skin, and I can follow the beat of his heart in the soft arterial bulge at his throat. A slow steady pulse of life. The seconds tick away on the grandfather clock that belonged to my mother's father. They feel irretrievable and cruel.

I want this story to be beautiful and sad. I want to write that my grandmother was wearing a feathered boa and a glamorous hat that brushed one eye and the corner of her cheek with shadows. I want to write that she watched her son board the truck and called out to him in defiance, "Pincus, never forget to thank God every day that you are a Jew!"

"And then they shot her," my father says.

"They shot her?"

My father is eighty-four. I am forty-two. I have spent my life tiptoeing around these truths. I never had the heart to pull them like scabs from the wounds of his soul.

His mouth opens. He takes in a sharp breath, sips his sweetened tea.

"Yes," he says. "The officer in blue pulled out a revolver. He put the gun to her head and pulled the trigger." He makes the motion with his hand. "Just like that."

"Why? Because she screamed?"

"Because she could not bring herself to let go of my hand."

At the station the soldiers push the people into cattle cars: men first, women next, children last. Bodies shove against him until he has no air to breathe. A stranger presses a scrap of sausage into his hand.

The image of his mother floats in and out of focus. Her hand was outstretched toward him and her feet and legs held the graceful arch of a diver about to plunge into a glistening lake. In the mud beneath her face a red flower bloomed.

There is no room for children in the car. Soldiers grab them by the legs and toss them on top of the waving sea of bodies. Two soldiers seize his ankles and heave. He is flying through space, sailing dizzily through the air that swirls around the black mouth of the train. It is his one moment of boundless freedom. He clutches his jacket tightly around him to keep his chocolate safe. Later, on the rotting plank of a bunk in Auschwitz, he will recall the feeling of flying. He will taste it on his tongue, breathe it into his lungs, sustain himself for one more hour, one more day. Just this? Just this. The smallest drop of water in a sea of thirst. How could it possibly be enough? It had to be.

There is one small window in this train car. It has bars and barbed wire to keep Jews in and curious Polish gazes out. People take turns drinking in the world, gasping a breath of air. If a mother or a father or a kind stranger has the strength, they will lift up a child for a look. If he stands on the tips of his toes, he can see trees, clouds, the tops of farmhouses and factories. Silver fingers of birch branches beckoning. But now that he has found this corner to sit in, he will not give it up. He touches the chocolate with the tip of his finger, watches the shifting of legs and feet. He shifts his weight to ease the stabbing pain.

Did he have any sense of where he was going? How could he? There was neither sun nor moon to anchor him. The train crawled through a black hole of space. Was he cold? Did snow, silent and cruel, fall onto the trees and the roof of the train? Did it muffle the people's cries? Snow? A joke! It was September. Yom Kippur. He suffocated in a blanket of heat.

Why did he have his jacket? It was all he had left of his life. Why didn't he take it off? The chocolate! The chocolate and the yellow star sewn into the cloth above his heart. Without this star he will be shot.

At the stations people beg for water. Sometimes a drink is handed up through a space in the wire. Years later he will learn that the penalty for giving water to the Jews was death.

In the beginning, water is passed around. A sip each. Only a sip. Later, as thirst rips the flesh from the insides of their throats, some snatch and claw at the bottles and cups. Between the legs bodies fall. Eyes open, seeing nothing. He thinks of the lake in winter where he used to skate, the terrible blue depth of ice.

At first *Kaddish* is said. The prayer for the dead. He closes his eyes and lets the words fill him. He sees his mother with her face in the mud.

Yisgadal v'yiskadash sh'mey rabo b'almo khirusey di v'ra. Let the glory of God be extolled, let his name be hallowed, in the world whose creation he willed.

As more bodies take up space on the floor and people must sit on them, too weak to stand, there is only silence to mark the passing of a life. *V'imru omeyn.* Let us say: amen.

As the pile of days grows, he begins to fear that he, too, will slump, forgotten, disappearing into the belly of the train. Just when he begins to pray for this, his head fills with the screech of metal: the howl of a monster with his mouth around the train. The car lurches, then there is the sudden cessation of motion. Outside, he hears shouts and the unmistakable sound of boots on concrete. Inside, as the train comes to a final halt, people stumble and crash against each other. The doors fly open.

"Ausladen! Raus! Los, Juden!" Unload! Out! Get going, Jews!

Men in strange striped pajamas pull them from the cars. They kick them and beat them with clubs. He is puzzled; these men wear yellow stars on their sleeves. He hears the words *effektenkammer, sonderkommando,* but does not yet know what they mean.

He tries to stand, stumbles, falls on his face and hits his chin against the floor. He reaches inside his coat, tears the chocolate from his pocket. Chocolate and tissue have melted together. It sticks to his palm. He shoves it into his mouth: chocolate, tissue, sweat, filth, fear. He chews without tasting and swallows.

My father has finished his tea. He sits at the table with his hands resting on his knees. I want to take his hands in mine and bring them to my face and kiss them. These hands that all the years I have known him have brought forth new life into this world. Coaxed the shining and trembling bodies from between the outspread thighs of women. I cannot move from my chair; the weight of his words paralyzes me. I reach over and turn the tape recorder off, and the shining wheel of my father's words slows to a stop. My father looks up, gives a little laugh.

"It's extraordinary," he says. "What I remember most about that day is the pile of shoes."

"Shoes?"

"Yes. I was standing on the platform. They lined us up in rows of five. Dr. Mengele walked down the lines, pointing left or right. Of course it didn't mean anything to me at the time. Nothing did. I didn't realize that those sent to the left were going to their deaths in the gas chamber. He directed me to the right, and as I followed the others toward the row of buildings, I saw these piles of things: suitcases, clothing, shoes." He clacks his teeth together. "And dentures. Can you believe it? A pile of people's false teeth!"

I suddenly remember the terror, bursting unannounced into the bathroom as a child, to find my father's teeth fizzing in a glass, his cheeks sunken in on themselves. He shakes his head. "But it was the shoes that got to me."

I rise from my chair and kneel by his feet. At this moment I realize that it was on this train that my father became irretrievably lost to life. How can I rewrite that? What can I do? Turn my father into a Christian? Kill Hitler with my words?

No. I must write that on this train my father first came to believe that God himself was spurious. I must write that from this day forward my father came to believe that "chosen" had more to do with the finger of a German doctor pointing right instead of left than with the irrevocable holiness of a people. That because of this train, thirty-five years of cradling life in his hands were not enough to balance three years of death.

I want to plant a garden of his words. I want his truth to bring forth trees, terrible and tall. But what can I do with these strange seeds of empty shoes?

Take Six

Daddy, I have had to kill you.
You died before I had the time—
  —Sylvia Plath

Daddy, you bastard. I've returned home triumphant to make a movie of your life and—just like always— you've skipped town. I wanted to tell you I've been catching the world with my cameras, and people are finally beginning to notice. I wanted to tell you I had a film in a little festival in Idaho, and it was well received. Well-known producers were asking my name.

When I asked if I could film you, you said, *sure*; when I asked if you'd actually be home when I arrived, you said, *of course*. So here I am with my girlfriend, my camera, my DAT recorder, and sacks full of Super 8 film, but you don't seem to live here anymore. We've been here since yester- day, drinking your Scotch, eating a few stale crusts of bread, but no Daddy anywhere in sight. To pass the time, I filmed the birds through the screen of the open window and sun- light waving through the curtains. Since when have you gone for lace?

There are dirty dishes in the sink, and there's mail on the table, some opened, some not. I filmed an envelope, empty, torn open, skittering across the floor in the breeze. I checked out the return address; it's from your current Bitch, the latest one you swear is forever this time. It's the woman you mentioned in the letter you sent last month.

Crumbs from your last breakfast decorate the tabletop and speckle your place mat like tiny ants. A single plate basks in the sun. A knife, shiny with hardened jam, a napkin with the shape of your lips painted in coffee. It appears you ate alone.

When another car goes by the driveway but doesn't pull in, Corina puts her arm around me and hooks a finger under my chin. I collapse against her, and she supports my weight with hers. We rock, bone to bone, like two shipwrecks colliding in the shallows.

–Poor Pearl, she says. But it's not pity I want.

Corina's hair is blacker than squid's ink this week, and it shimmies down her shoulders, plays with spaghetti straps and a thin line of cleavage. I grab a mouthful and suck it in. Her shampoo leaves the taste of lilacs on my tongue.

Where were you going in such a hurry? Were you running away from me again? There were some questions I wanted to ask, a few answers I needed, to plug up the holes in this heart of mine. Holes that still let love out the back door as soon as it comes in the front. You sent me a key in the mail. You said this time we could get to know each other again. Did you decide at the last minute to jump in your car, put the top down and leave rubber by the mailbox?   I can picture you taking the mountain curves like they belong to some woman you want to fuck. Daddy, you could have waited this one time, you bastard.

TAKE ONE

–Are we rolling?
–Yes, ma'am.
–We're here at Daddy's house. Daddy had the nerve to

set out for parts unknown the day we arrived—or there-about—so we're making this movie with the main character *in spiritus*. (I stare hard at the camera, as if searching.) Hello, Daddy, can you hear me? (I pause and listen.)

–Check it out, Corina; you hear that?

–Yeah, man. Your daddy definitely hears us. He's rattling the window frames. (She points the mic at the window.) He is saying he wants to party.

Corina hands me the camera, fishes a joint from her bag, and lights up while I film. She tokes, puts her lips to mine and gives me the gift of the first hit. A raw heat spreads through my lungs and into my gut.

–To your daddy, she says.

–May you suffer the eternal boredom of heaven, I say. (Corina pantomimes a toast.) I hand over the camera after a full shot of her cleavage.

Corina pans across the kitchen. There are four plates, three glasses, one mug in the sink. All the glasses still smell of Scotch. The bottom of the mug looks like the Mississippi Delta. I tilt it toward the camera and make a show of holding my nose. Corina zooms in for a close-up. Daddy always did like his coffee and his women strong.

When I was a kid, he'd lift me high into the air. –Who's my girl? he'd ask.

Then slowly, he would lower me until we were face to face, and we we'd wrinkle our noses at each other and rub them together. A bunny kiss, he called it. The scents of coffee, cigarettes, and aftershave set my skin buzzing. Love made my head whirl until I thought I would faint.

When I told Corina about my dad, I said she'd fall for him. I told her he could make the curly hair on a dyke go straight. She just shook her own straight hair—newly red—and kissed me hard on the mouth.

–No way, she said. My heart is occupied.

I take the camera and pan quickly, out of focus, across tomato-sauce-stained plates. Blood spattered across white skin: that's the effect I'm looking for here.

–I guess we're doing a mystery instead of a history, I say.

Corina replies, –Let's hope it has a happy ending, and a little shiver races up my spine.

There is a vase of flowers on a table next to the telephone. The vase is dry except for a growth of green scum that rings the bottom and sends exploratory tendrils snaking up the sides of the glass. The flowers have been dead for days. I point to the red blinking eye that counts out four messages on the answering machine. I max the volume and push play. I've heard them all before, but I make a show of surprise. Corina's filming away, focused on the Deserted Daughter's face.

–Hi, Joshua. Nancy. I'm here at Dolce Vita. I thought it was tonight we were supposed to meet. Seven o'clock, right? Call me on my cell. I'm going to order a drink and wait.

–Hello, Josh. It's Anne. Just wondering if you'd heard from Pearl. I think she said she'd be there today or tomorrow. When I talked to her Monday she was in Idaho. Please have her call me when she gets in, would you?

–Joshua, it's nine fifteen. I've had a lovely dinner. The waiter even gave me a complimentary carafe of Chianti. I'm going home now. I'm turning off my cell and unplugging my phone. I won't be bothering you again.

–Hi, Dad. It's me. We're in Oakland with Corina's folks. We'll be there by noon, early afternoon at the latest. Keep those choppers shined; we're coming in with cameras rolling. I love you. Bye.

Next to the phone is a shopping list. It's his writing for sure, choppy and thick, like he's impatient with the written word. Like the mundane act of putting pen instead of paintbrush to paper is not worthy of his precious time.

beer
butter
whole grain bread
tomatoes
salad shit
bananas
soymilk
Cherry Garcia frozen yogurt

Daddy, you remembered what I wrote you about the soymilk. And you remembered my favorite flavor. But you forgot the list. Forgot to be here. I can't help it; I bless your pen strokes with the holy water of my tears.

–Turn that fucking thing off, I say, covering the lens with my hand. I'll call my mother when I stop this sniveling. We're having a great time, I'll say. Daddy's just gone to the store.

—ᴡ— —ᴡ— —ᴡ—

Corina and I are on the rug in front of the picture window in the living room. A slurry of rain and blowing leaves slams into the pane and runs down the glass. It's 6 A.M., and we are naked and shivering and hunting for any scrap of dawn to set a spark in this sorry excuse for a sunrise. The distant mountains drown in a soup of clouds. There are too many trees here. They howl and bend and shake and don't let me sleep.

–There's a little wood left. Let me light a fire, I say.

–Mmm, she says and licks my face and breasts. The stud in her tongue tickles, and my nipples are wide awake. She twirls one between two fingers, and I wrap my legs around her like a locked chain. If I could crawl inside her I would do it. Curl up like an unborn baby against the shelf of her pelvis and never come out.

Last night, we started filming upstairs. Even if he isn't here to help us, I'm making this movie to rediscover my father, and maybe in the process discover what he means to me. It's been nine years since I've seen him, and our circumstances of parting were not the best. Our first communication since that episode was the letter I sent last month.

I was looking for his presence, but everywhere I turned the camera, I found his absence. I stirred it up in the hallways—unswept cigarette ashes, a forgotten raffle ticket, a dropped penny—and it hit me in the face when I opened his closet door. Here and there an empty hanger swayed, waiting for him to come back, to open the door, sigh, and hang up a dark-blue blazer. I remembered when my grandfather died, it was his unoccupied clothes that really got to me.

–At least Daddy's not dead, just missing in *in*action, I told Corina, and then that little shudder danced up my backbone again. I handed her the camera and headed back downstairs. –Honestly, I shouted, –he does this all the time. I started shaking and couldn't stop.

That's when she grabbed me and warmed me with the heat of her hands and one thing led to another including a bottle of father's finest Cabernet around 3 A.M. But now we need to get busy; we have a project to complete. A project of a professional nature.

We pull on our clothes. We both wear black jeans, black tanks, thick silver-studded belts. Our navels wink at the world. Corina is wearing motorcycle boots. I am wearing sandals, and my toes are cold. I found two bottles of nail polish in the downstairs bathroom: one gold, one blue. My toenails are a field of flowers and stars. Blue and gold bees buzz on my feet. Corina points the lens at me, and I roll up my jeans to expose a wreath of flowers tattooed on my ankle. The design came from one of my dad's paintings. The wreath was on a table covered with a silk cloth: still life with a bowl of fruit, a plate of cheese and bread, a bottle of wine spilling blood-colored light.

TAKE TWO

–I am remembering a painting you made, Dad. The one with the wreath of flowers. See?

(I balance on one leg, showing off my ankle artwork.) Corina licks her lips and trails the fingers of her free hand across her breast before zooming in.

–That was just before you left us the first time. In the painting, the morning scene is calm, motionless. I guess you thought you could whisk the tablecloth away with your magician's hands and leave the objects undisturbed. Well, we all went flying: bowl smashed, fruit splitting, wine splattered across the walls and floor. Your sleight of hand always seems to come up short, but you never stick around to hear the catcalls.

I signal *cut* and bound up the stairs two at a time. The staircase spirals in a series of dizzying steps that appear suspended in space. How the hell did you manage when you were drunk? I feel some empathy for you now, your Cabernet sloshing away in my otherwise empty stomach. We reach the last stair. Corina motions to me like she's seasick, about to hurl all over the varnished wooden planks. I laugh so hard I have to hold my legs together and squeeze.

–Stop here, I say, in front of a lopsided painting.

Thick blotches of red, orange, and purple erupt like exploded stars. A furious green streak slashes a landscape of spills and swirls in two. Teeth of nails and broken glass glint from the mouth of a screaming man.

Corina puts her hand to her chest and pretends to wheeze. Like we have ascended to impossible heights and there is no air. I gesture toward the picture with my open palm and assume my serious face.

–I haven't seen this painting before, but I remember the period. You thought you were Jackson Pollock then, although the influence of Munch here is a bit too blatant for my tastes. You were six years old when Pollock died, but you swore to me his spirit had jumped inside you. Rattled the bony bars of your cage and kept you up all night. You had just come back from Honduras and were eternally in love with your third wife, a painter herself. Mom and I were living in LA then. We had an apartment with cockroaches and four rooms. I used to stick my finger down my throat to make myself throw up because I didn't think I deserved to eat.

Corina doesn't like the painting, and she is making ugly faces behind the camera.

–C'mon, quit, I say. She is not taking this seriously. I don't like the painting either, but my reasons are different. A child's red footprints traverse the canvas, and they don't belong to me.

TAKE THREE

We're in Daddy's studio now. There are boxes all over the floor. Maybe he was getting ready to move, or maybe he never bothered to unpack from his last change of wives. Three easels hold paintings in various stages of completion. Two are unrecognizable creations that seem unfinished, but the third is a Madonna and child. I stand next to the painting, and Corina pans back and forth between us. We are all holding our breath: me, Corina, Madonna, child.

He hasn't seen me in nine years, but he's stolen my face down to the birthmark that peeks out from the bangs beside my left eye. The Madonna's hair—my hair—falls over one shoulder in a dark chocolate coil. I touch the Madonna's cheek with my finger. The skin shade's right, too: bone, with an opalescent hue. We spend so long on this painting, it's already time to change the film.

The fumes of paints, varnishes, and thinners mix with the leftover fumes of the wine, and I sit down on the floor to catch my breath. I wonder if this painting is a gift for me, and the thought prickles my skin.

Daddy, did you go to the grocery store and just forget to come home? Are you wandering the aisles of a Safeway somewhere, searching your pockets for a forgotten list? Or perhaps you've plunged your car, Jackson Pollock style, into the terrible embrace of a tree.

There are dirty glasses on the worktable. Burn marks in the wood like imprints of fossil snail shells. Brushes stiff with lithified paint. Ashes and butts spill from an ashtray. I rummage through the mess, and sure enough there's a roach, which I slip into my pocket.

A mug rests on the windowsill, half full. An oily film floats on the surface of the coffee while two flies, buzzed on caffeine, swim in circles. I grab the camera from Corina and get a shot. Corina kneels and slits the tape on a box labeled *Pearl* with her fingernail. She tears at the flaps, starts pulling stuff out.

–Pearl, she calls, –get a loada this.

She pulls out sheets of ancient paper, lets them fall to the floor. Flecks of paper, like fragments of bone, drift from her fingers. I remember a cremation I filmed in a village at the base of the Himalayas. Monks in orange robes struck cymbals, sent shock waves through my blood with blasts of their long horns. A light snow fell, flakes coming to rest on my arms, my face, my eyelashes: the ashes of human remains. I set the camera down; I don't like where Corina's exploration is going. She's digging through my past like garden soil instead of treating it like consecrated ground. She holds a piece of paper to the light and squints. She is clicking her stud against the back side of her teeth and it's pissing me off. From the faded splotches that show through the paper I recognize my first painting.

–Fuck you, I say. –That's off limits. I make a grab for it, but Corina's faster. She's panting; brushstrokes of pink spread across her cheeks. She picks up the camera and aims the lens at my face.

–Okay, fuck me then, she says, gyrating hips, flinging spears of light from the studs on her belt. My painting flaps from her fingers. –I thought we were in this together, so stop pushing me out, Pearl. She walks backward with the camera trained on my face and sets the painting down on the table.

I take a deep breath and turn it over. The colors are faded, the paper cracked. I painted it a few months after my dad moved in with some student from his art class, and, weak from guilt or drink or maybe just incurable boredom, he swallowed enough sleeping pills to land him in the hospital.

He's enormous in the picture, and the smile on his face is the same as the smile on the sun that shoots flames above his head. There are pink sheep-backed clouds floating in what was once an intensely blue sky. My own form is tiny, hiding in the lower right corner, scarcely bigger than a bug. "Daddy I love you more than the HOLE world" is scrawled across the bottom in thick gold letters. I didn't know where to send it, but Mom said she'd just mail it to the college where he taught. I always wondered if he got it.

I bend over the box and stick my hand inside. I pull out our past one scrap at a time and read. I guess Corina's filming away.

Report card, first grade: Shows promise but not performing to potential.

Note from my mom: I'm so sorry for what I said. For Pearl's sake please come back. Trust that I love you. Note from Dad to me, never mailed: Dearest Pearl, trust that I love you. Note from my teacher, fifth grade: Remarkably intelligent but prone to outbursts in class. I know what I'm looking for, and I know I'll find it. Papers pile up, and I turn the sound of Corina's breath into tiny wavelets on a childhood beach. I wish she would laugh or shout or just say something. I wish she would grab this damned box and make me stop. Then my hand hits pay dirt. I can tell by the texture: crumpled by all those trips into and out of the trash. Like parasites, words burrow through my fingers in search of the softer organs. After nine years, I can still recite them.

It's called "Poem to my father," and it sounds like a made-in-Taiwan version of Sylvia Plath. I was sixteen, in my own Plath stage, purple-haired, ear-and-belly-button pierced, fucking boys and wondering while I masturbated at night, how it would feel to kiss my best friend's breast.

I wrote the poem after the one time he truly set out to die. I imagined him at his kitchen table, John Coltrane wailing away on the turntable, cigarette smoldering in the ashtray, swallowing handfuls of Oxycodone, chasers of Scotch, until they both were gone. I described a single lock of hair falling over a half-closed eye and wondered, if when his girlfriend found him, he had turned a shade of blue only a painter could appreciate.

My mom and I jumped on a plane as soon as we heard, using money we couldn't hope to have. For six days, I watched him fight for life, like it or not, forced by machines to breathe and move blood through his body. When he opened his eyes for the first time, he twisted a hook into the freshly reopened wounds of my heart.

I sent the poem to the rehab center where they took him. In the last verse I gave him my blessing to leap from a cliff and fly. Then I kicked him off the ledge with the heel of my poet's boot. At first, the thought of him reading it gave me pleasure, but even anger sacredly held eventually dies. Some nights, I still wake in a sweat, the dream always the same: Daddy swan-diving, poem fluttering beside him, the last stanza shredding the space of my sleep.

Suddenly Corina's hand is on my shoulder.

–What's wrong?

Gently she tries to pry the page from my fingers. I don't let her. The urge to surrender to her arms fistfights with the need to smack her hard in the face.

–Keep filming, I say.

–I have something to add.

She stands, extends her hand to help me up. I take it and wobble to my feet.

–Shit, she says. –I need to change the film again. She's shaking too, and it takes two tries to get it right.

With all the meanness I can muster, I face the lens, intending to brandish my message for the camera. Instead, I let the poem fall to the floor. To hell with it, I say. To hell with daddies and girlfriends and love.

I have never figured out if I wished for life or death as he lay in his hospital bed. For him or for me. For years, I walked around with the sound of those machines pounding in my head as if my own heart and lungs were made of metal and rubber: contraptions that needed batteries and oil. That was the last time I saw him. I think I decided to write last month because I didn't want the poem to be our final communication. I think I was secretly hoping it wasn't too late to take it back.

TAKE FOUR

Corina and I are making love in Daddy's bed. The sun is out, and moisture rises in waves from the wet ground. We are listening to Dave Brubeck on the expensive sound system. "Blue Rondo A La Turk" is playing. The bass vibrates my skin, and a frenetic exchange between piano and sax threads through me.

All that jazz between us, Daddy, like mother's milk. You, sitting by the window in your studio at dusk, paint brush clamped between your teeth, cigarette smoke a halo, your body leaning and bending to the beat. Coltrane. Monk. Charlie Parker. Me, on the floor with a book, blue light slipping through the cracks until it was too dark to read, the moment so breakable I couldn't bear to breathe.

–You hear that, Pearl? You *hear that?* You used to whisper. Young as I was, I could see those notes reach inside you, wrap themselves around some secret part of you I would never be able to touch.

–Yes, I said. –Yes, I do.

Daddy, that's one gift you can never take back.

Corina takes my face in her hands. – Hey, she says.

–Where'd you go?

Her eyelids gleam with green glitter. She has chosen a color somewhere between grape juice and blood for her lips. She purses them into a berry shape and paints them onto every inch of the canvas of my flesh. – CQ Pearl, she says. –You keep disappearing on me.

I spread my arms and let her land on me like a butterfly. Her hair tickles my skin, and I feel as if I am sucking air into my lungs through a straw. I hook my fingers under the wings of her shoulder blades and hang on for the ride.

The camera's on, but it's running on empty, and I'm not stopping to change the damned film again. Still, I'd like to have a record of our time together—something tangible to put in a box. I hear the hinges on the gate of my heart swing open. Pretty soon there'll be no one left inside.

TAKE FIVE

I'm sitting on the windowsill in my father's studio. We've finished off the roach from his ashtray and the last of our stash. I'm facing the camera, and in my arms are all the roses we could gather from his garden. Who tended your flowers, Daddy? For sure it wasn't you.

The painting of Madonna and child is beside me. It radiates light and color in the afternoon sun like an incandescent body. I believe it's his best work. We've fashioned a coffin out of boxes, their contents strewn over the floor. Corina steps backward and slips on a magazine, falls on her ass. The camera captures the ceiling. The magazine is from 1994, and it features my dad. We keep starting over because we're laughing too hard to film.

–We come to bury Daddy, not to praise him, I say. I make a sad face, but it falls apart in a spurt of giggling. Tears roll down my face until I don't know if they're from silliness or sorrow. Roses tumble.

–Wait, Corina says, –we can't have a funeral without a body.

She pulls a doll from one of the boxes, but it's my favorite doll, Pitiful Pearl, the only gift I ever asked for. It belonged to my mom before it belonged to me. I tear it out of her hands.

–Okay, she says. –I'm sorry.

I get a pillow from Daddy's bed and a sweater and one of his hats. We dress the pillow in the sweater, lay it down in the box-coffin, and crown it with the hat.

–Yes, I say. –I definitely see the resemblance. It's that pale artist's complexion.

Corina zooms in on the body, then zooms in on me. Dave Brubeck plinks away on his piano: "Time Out." Corina is clicking her stud against her teeth, and I want to shake her. I pick up the roses and place them on the daddy-pillow. I'm crying again, but this time there's no doubt about the source. This time I can't make the tears stop.

I turn away and weep to the compassionate Madonna. My own sad eyes stare back.

–How about if we skip the bury part and praise him, I say, but only loud enough for the Madonna to hear.

The telephone is ringing away, but by the time we separate ring from jazz and stumble down the stairs, the machine picks up.

–Pearl, are you there, sweetheart? My mother's voice asks. –Honey, please pick up the phone.

There's a long pause, and Corina is staring at me, hard. –Well? Aren't you going to?

My heart is bursting its little seams, but I shake my head.

–Pearl? It's important, the machine says. –Please.

Corina makes a grab for the receiver, but I catch her hand and squeeze it.

–You better get it, she says. Her eyes don't leave my face.

I say, –Why ruin a good funeral? I take her fingers in my mouth and bite down until she moans. I hear the click at the other end of the line, and I envision the final shot in a movie: a shadowed door shutting in a bare white room.

–You're right, Corina says, hooking a finger under my belt. –The real Daddy's waiting for us upstairs.

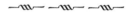

The clock is blinking 3:00 A.M., and I still can't sleep. The full moon bangs on the wall. Corina has kicked the covers down around her waist, and her body is a minefield of shadows and moonlight. I want to bend forward, unleash my braided hair and kiss her open mouth. Instead, I grab her lighter, cover her, and step over the moon's shed skin. I find the hall and creak my way upstairs.

The poem is on the floor where I dropped it. I pick it up and hold it to my face, inhaling the must of stored years. The scent of the forest comes in through the open window, and I kneel on the rickety table. I push my face and upper body out into the night. With one hand I hold the paper, with the other I strike a flame.

Sparks lift and dance like tiny stars finding their way home. With one swift movement I could step through the mouth of my father's house and follow. When I look down at the ground, my head spins with possibility. Would I fly?

The air is so sharp and clear it reminds me of the mountains in Nepal, and I lean further forward, balanced against the windowsill, trying to capture something of my father's life. I hear footfalls on the floor behind me and wonder for an instant if they are real or imagined as the fire singes

my fingertips. Corina screams. I let the flash of burning
cleanse me. Heat slithers up to my wrist before I am pulled
inside and swept to the ground.
  –My God, baby.
  –I thought you were going to jump.
  I welcome the weight of her, holding me to the earth.
Her chin in my cupped palms is like a delicate shell. My
hand begins to throb: a hot, dull pain.
  –I did, I whisper.
  –I flew.

Tomorrow I'll take Corina back to Oakland. I'll gather
up Pitiful Pearl, Dave Brubeck, Madonna and Child, and
toss them in the trunk. I'll take the curves on the road
down the mountain like they belong to a woman I want to
fuck. And there, coming around a corner too fast, barely in
control, will be my father in a red convertible, going the opposite way. The woman named Nancy will be leaned into
his shoulder, a blue silk scarf trailing Isadora Duncan-style
in the wind. They are hopelessly in love. Corina will film
them as they fade into colored dots against a canvas of sky.
I'll wave farewell. I'll hope for the best.

SHEDDING SKIN

Big Red was no longer big, but his hair was still red. Between the feathery tufts that had survived six months of chemotherapy, new bristles sprouted from his itchy scalp. He sat upright in bed, supported by a hill of pillows, and inspected the picture between his fingers. His wife and daughter sat at the foot of his bed. As he tossed the photograph toward his wife, he began to cough.

"No, Kit," he said between fits, "not that one."

Kit picked it up and let it fall into a basket of rejected pictures. Their edges curled like the shells of long-dead insects. She rummaged through the pile at his feet and selected another.

"Here, this is a good one," she said.

Red peered through watering eyes. He leaned forward to take the picture from her. Fingers of pain skittered across his ribs.

"Yes, it is."

The images on the paper floated into focus. He sighed and lay back against the pillows. Bleue, his daughter, wiped his forehead with a cool, damp cloth.

Big Red was dying as graciously as an aging rigger could die. Two years ago, he built laboratories from blocks of concrete and assembled the long mazes of particle accelerators from gleaming secret metals. Two years ago, he moved mountains with his cranes, blocks, and pulleys. Today, it took an immeasurable effort of will to move his body to the couch.

Inside his lungs wild cells grew into jungle vines. Errant tendrils drifted off to sprout in distant soil. They drilled into his bones. They floated past brainstem, twirled through gyrating folds of cerebrum, nestled cruelly in the place that governs speech. Broca's area had become an unpredictable swamp. Sometimes the space between synapses thrummed with electricity; words traveled smoothly down their proper path, and sentences emerged unimpeded. Sometimes synapses fired randomly into the bog, leaving words and thoughts entirely disconnected.

Big Red quit smoking after a mild heart attack. He took up walking, swinging his arms defiantly at 5:00 A.M. past rows of houses filled with sleeping neighbors and barking dogs. He dug out his ancient anatomy texts and memorized the blood flow to the heart. On his morning excursions he visualized the coronary arteries like a pulsing crown encircling his heart. *Left descending, circumflex branch, right coronary artery, marginal branch*, he chanted like a mantra, imagining the arterial walls smooth and shining once again.

He gave up red meat and poured his beer down the drain. But the cancer didn't care. It sailed in his blood, silent and small. It did the backstroke. It bided its time.

"I want to take your picture, Daddy," Bleue said. She fingered his tufts of hair.

Red made primping motions. "Look. Like. Shit." Words meandered from brain to mouth. They plopped like stones onto his tongue.

Bleue sat on the edge of the bed, her camera resting on her lap. She wiped the wet place at the corner of his mouth with her hand and slid her palm across the stained cotton blanket. Kit snorted.

"Remember." Speeding thoughts became a pileup of speech. "Don't remember. Now. See here. Strong." Red offered the photograph that Kit had chosen to his daughter.

In the picture, they are standing beside Red's truck. Red and Kit face the camera, smiling. His arm snakes around her waist. She leans her head on his shoulder. Even in her red flats, she is nearly as tall as he. A cigarette dangles from his lips, and a shock of red hair covers one eye.

Bleue stands on tiptoes and points to the freshly painted door of the truck. Curls of peach-gold catch the sun. It is her fourth birthday. RED WHITE AND BLEUE RIGGING, the sign proclaims. Bleue's legs are long and thin as stilts. Her dress is ablaze with red tulips, yellow daffodils.

"God, Daddy, you were one handsome dude."

"Horse," said Red, then shook his head. No, horse was not what he meant.

Kit laughed. "Looks like Brando, don't he? " She sat beside him, squeezed his shoulder, pecked his cheek.

Red smelled smoke on her breath. He heard disobedient cells chattering in her chest. Although speech failed him, his mutating brain envisioned with startling clarity the hidden spaces beyond what others saw. His crazed cells built bridges into shimmering new dimensions.

"Horse sense," he said.

Bleue rose. She removed the lens cap from the camera, crouched, focused and began to shoot. Her fingers fluttered like butterfly wings.

"You gonna sell me to your fancy magazines, Bleue? "

"I'm a wildlife photographer, Dad. You make a shitty bird."

"He's a lion," said Kit and frizzed his hair.

Red growled. He showed fangs and claws. He flexed his muscles and stuck out his tongue. Red as tough guy. Red as clown. A flash of light, glinting from glossy paper.

Nothing more nothing less. Courageous Red. Almost dead Red.

"Daddy, what is it?" Bleue touched his cheek. Red realized he was crying.

"Shit," he said as unstoppable tears came. He turned his face away, but there was no place to hide. As well as at bones, brain, lungs, the cancer nibbled at his dignity daily.

Kit stood and reached for the pile of photographs. "It's time you got some rest."

"No," said Red too loudly, grabbing at the pictures.

Kit raised her arms. "Sorry, big boy." She kissed his forehead, smoothed his hair. He pinched her as she turned to leave.

Pain thumped at Red's chest. Fists of pressure squeezed his eyes, and teeth tore into his hip, his right leg. "Bleue, is it time?"

She looked at her watch. "No. It's only been an hour."

"Please, Bleue." He pointed at the vials on the dresser, the neat row of syringes. Red measured out his remaining life in doses of morphine.

"I shouldn't," she said, but she walked to the dresser and tore the wrapper from a syringe. She upended the vial of morphine, drew out a dose, tapped out air. Leaning over him she pointed to his leg. "I can't resist you, you know," she said. Bangles flashed on her wrist. They sparked a fire in Red's brain.

He clutched her arm and drew her closer. He whispered in her ear.

"She smokes. Right here on my bed. Sits down next to me and lights up."

"Daddy, don't be ridiculous. That's your guilty conscience sending you dreams."

Red sighed. Who was to say these days when someone sat on his bed, if they were made of flesh or fog? "Well, she hates me."

"She adores you. She's mad at you for dying."

Red released her arm and laughed. "No. Mad not dead yet." He pulled the covers from his leg, raised it in the air and examined it. Skin flapping on sticks. He used to have limbs like redwood trunks.

Faint bruises brushed the white thighs. Bleue found a spot, pinched, injected. "You should have been a doctor," he said.

"Please, let's not start that."

Beneath the spot a poppy bloomed. Red sank into his pillows. The pulsing heart of warmth spread slowly through his body. His eyes began to close. He willed them open and pointed at the photographs. "Another one," he said.

Bleue took a handful from the middle of the pile. She shuffled them and held them facedown in a fan. Her red curls waved in the breeze. "Pick." He touched each one, then picked.

In this picture, Red and Kit stand before their small house. Red stands behind, his chin resting on her shoulder, his thick arms supporting her. Bleue is a tiny blanketed bundle pressed to Kit's heart. Kit is pale, and there are dark shadows beneath her eyes. She looks as if she could collapse into herself and sink onto the stone steps. It is only the miraculous bundle with its crinkled pink flower of a face and curled petal fingers that breathes life into her and gives her strength. The bundle that took eleven years and four miscarriages to make.

Kit wanted to name her Margaret. Too common, said Red, who had his eye on a fancy truck and a small rigging business of his own. Her name is Bleue, he said, seeing the letters in fancy scroll on the door of the truck. Kit shook her head and laughed. She rolled her eyes. Too vain, she complained. Red knew it, but the name stuck, the truck was purchased and his rigging business roared down the road to wild success.

"God, Bleue, you were perfect." Red stroked the outline of the blanket in the picture. He paused, touched the image of Kit's face, her dark, tumultuous hair. His eyelids closed, opened, closed again. Morphine vapors drifted across the room. His hand dropped. He weighed anchor and floated on a calm sea. His pain became the faint slap of waves against his bed. The photograph fell from his fingers and bobbed, a waterborne leaf on the swells. Red struggled to remember who had taken the picture but could not. He struggled to burn the images of his wife and daughter into his brain, but there was no place permanent enough to store them. He clutched at consciousness and beckoned. "One more."

Bleue turned the photos face up. He saw summer vacations, rigging jobs, fishing trips. He shook his head. Bleue cocked her head, regarded the photos and wrinkled her nose. The intertwined gold hoops in her ears shivered. "You're right. Boring." She dropped the rejected pictures into the basket, shuffled, chose another stack. She dealt them face down.

"One for me, one for you. One for me, one for you." The past piled up between them. "Okay, you first," she said.

"No, you."

He watched her delicate fluttering fingers. Between them, an imaginary shutter closed, freezing time. She turned over a picture of soldiers in a war.

Red heard her whispered fear. She reached for the picture. "Sorry. I'll choose again."

"No," he said. He covered her hand with his. "I want you to listen. To know." He heard planes rumble, guns tear through earth, chopper blades slice falling snow. "How-how-house. Fish." He sighed, shook his head. He reached into the ravine that split mind from mouth. He scratched clawed and dug for words. "Heart. Break. Heart Break Ridge. Yes." He pointed to the men, one by one. "Dead. Dead. Survived, Purple Heart." There was one soldier left. Red's finger hesitated, trembling. A thin pencil of light pierced the insignia pinned to the soldier's lapel. Dead or alive?

"Daddy, that's you!" Bleue treaded water with her words. "In all these years you've never shown me a picture of you in uniform. No wonder Mom fell for you."

Tracers split the photograph's waxen sky. "Dead or alive?"

At first she did not seem to understand. Then tears came, and she squeezed his paw of a hand.

"Alive, damn it," she whispered.

"Scared shitless," said Red. Then and now.

In the photograph, four soldiers stand on a steep slope. Above them, a barren ridge rises, rocks jutting up like teeth. Even in April, a crusty snow covers the ground. The camera has captured the breath that curls like smoke from noses and mouths. The air is so cold it pulls tears from their eyes and turns their souls to ice. Behind them, the convoluted peaks of dead mountains reach toward North Korea.

Red left behind two years of college, two younger brothers, and a mother with indigestion, arthritis and failing vision to enlist. He planned to go to medical school. He planned to cure the world because he grew up too late to cure his father. He was tired of working night jobs and studying until his head, too heavy with words, formulas, and lack of sleep, would hit the desk with a thump. Fatherless since fifteen, fighting with his fists since the age of eight, he was ready to go to war. Win a few battles, come home, let the GI Bill pick up the tab for school.

Red was a crack shot. Before dying a slow nightmare of a death, his father had taken him to the woods and taught him to hunt. Red's father said he killed a British soldier in Black Rock, County Louth. Dropped him like a stone and watched him die.

Shivering with cold, his fingers red and numb as they curled around the rifle's trigger, Red had watched his father sip from flasks and breathed in his stories with the winter air. He imagined his father, pale as snow, crawling belly to the ground in the silent Irish hills, his earth-black hair falling over his eyes, watching, sighting, squeezing the trigger. The uniformed soldier, no older than his child-father looking up, momentarily startled, then crumpling, falling suddenly down. Stone. Cold. Dead.

What he did not yet have the power to imagine was the sickness in his father's liver. He could not see the tissues swelling and dying, hear them sinking into an alcoholic sea. He could not feel the weight of his father drowning in his own poisonous soup.

In Korea, Red trained as a medic. He joined the Wolf-hound Regiment of the 25th Infantry Division. It seemed like destiny, the son of an Irish rebel fighting with the Irish dogs.

They marched north into the mountains until they saw the flare of Chinese rifles firing across the razor-sharp ridges. Mortar rounds exploded in bright flashes. Careless feet stepped on mines.

They dug through driving snow and hacked at ice to make their trenches. They blew on frostbitten hands and stomped their boots to bring blood to frozen toes. They listened in the dark for the creak of snow like un-oiled hinges that betrayed the enemy's approach.

Big Red, with his tree-solid body and defiant shocks of red hair, received his nickname. The docs taught him how to shove the insides back in, how to squeeze a tourniquet above shredded stumps of arms and legs to stop the blood that felt like a heart leaking out in violent liquid beats. Red learned to divide the wounded into those who might live and those who would die, to silence a doomed soldier's screams with morphine.

The hill in the photograph changes hands almost daily. Fighting has been fierce for months, and the ghosts on both sides are running out of room to roam. On the morning the picture was taken, Red doesn't know that this hill has the nickname Heart Break Ridge. On the morning the picture was taken, there were orders to seize the high ground.

Red is standing with his buddies as the sky turns the color of milky tea. Gray flecks of snow drift down. They stick to eyelashes, lips, and hair. He has asked another soldier to take the picture. He doesn't remember if that soldier lived or died.

The silence of night is not yet broken. Cold surrounds them like a windowpane. It kisses their cheeks and cuts their lungs. Red feels he could shatter the brittle air with his fists. He imagines the bright timbre of breaking glass.

By evening, there is only Red to pose for a picture. One man has no jaw and the ragged hole at the base of his skull has the shape of a rose. One has a hole in his heart. Small, neat, polite. The third lived, and Red stuffed a fist of gauze into his shoulder that gaped like an angry mouth. There is also a Chinese or North Korean soldier on the far side of the hill. He has holes in his chest and holes in his throat and a cave where his nose used to be, because the finger on Red's trigger squeezed and squeezed and squeezed. He is the first man Red killed. He will not be the last. Stone. Cold. Dead.

Red lifted the photograph like a sacrament. He placed it in Bleue's palms. "I thought war would be easy. A snap."

Bleue tipped the photograph toward the light. The finish was cracked like old varnish around the edges. The faces of the men looked scarred. Red felt the weight of them as one by one they walked into the room and sat on his bed. The last to sit was the North Korean with a hole for a nose. Red could tell now that's what he was; his skin was dark and his eyes formed hollows in his broad face.

"What were their names?" asked Bleue.

Red pointed at the ghosts. "Pinky. The best." He hooked two fingers together. "Brothers." He remembered how the blood made the rocks slippery as he crawled toward him, knowing there was no reason to keep going, but not understanding he could stop. He remembered the sharp pain in his hand, lifting it to see a fragment of jaw stabbing his palm.

"This is Sam. Went down like that. Boom." Red snapped his fingers. "And Ian, who got the medal and went home. Was it Oregon? Lawyer now." Red saw the jagged wound through Ian's shirt. He wondered if he could have done a better job if his own heartbeat hadn't hammered in his fingertips.

The North Korean turned to face him. He smiled at Red and pressed his palms together in greeting. Red sucked in his breath and began to cough. "Sorry. Don't. Don't. Know name. Sorry."

"You okay? Want some water?" Bleue bent over him with a glass in her hand. He shook his head and the men vanished. "You having visitors again, Daddy?"

Red shifted his weight. The fist in his lungs relaxed. "I killed him because I had to. He had a goddamn bead on us."

Bleue took the picture from the blanket where she had dropped it. Her brow folded into mountain ridges. "Killed who? What are you talking about?"

Retreat. Full retreat, whispered Red's heart. "Nobody. Nothing," whispered Red.

The picture trembled in Bleue's hand. "Is that why you changed your mind about being a doctor? The war? It's what I've always guessed, but you would never talk."

Red closed his ears against his traitor heart. He reached for his daughter's hope. "No more blood. I couldn't stand the sight or smell of blood. Or goddamned stinking death." He stroked the back of her hand with a finger. "Bleue, I was too dead tired to think anymore." He grabbed a handful of photographs, flipping them over one by one. He chose and smiled. "And then there was her." He let the photograph fall between them.

Kit stands in front of a brightly painted house at the bottom of a hill. Flowers spill from pots beside the doorway. They are in Sicily visiting her grandparents. A stone path behind them rises toward the heavily clouded sky. She wears a red sweater and a blue skirt that hugs her hips and legs. One foot is forward and her hips are cocked. Her mouth makes a shape like a new bloom on a rose.

Red remembers the flower-sweet smell of her lipstick that was a little too close to the shade of blood. He remembers her hair so thick he could bury his face in it and feel like he was lost in deep woods. He knows that it was she who plucked him from a sea of numbness and brought blood back to his dying heart. He knows that she reached inside the Korean ice of his soul with her Mediterranean fingers and burned him with life.

"But I know you regretted it. Not being a doctor, I mean," Bleue said. She smiled. "Why else would you shove it down my throat all those years? If you could have bound, gagged, and dragged me into med school, you would have. Harvard, preferably."

Red shook his head too hard. "No, never regret."

His father's ghost appeared at the window, with his wild hair and bilious eyes. He ripped tubes from his arms, his abdomen, his chest. His skin had the color and texture of a saturated sponge. Red remembered being afraid to touch him because the pressure of fingers left deep craters in his father's flesh. He feared the dark poisonous liquids that filled the tubes would begin to seep from every pore.

"Get me outta here now," his father screamed. "They're tryn' ta kill me."

Outside, tree limbs bowed with the weight of sunshine. The too-long grass dipped and swayed in the breeze.

"You lying bastard. You left Ireland when you were ten," Red said. His father shook his fists. He beat them against air. "British soldier my ass," Red shouted.

"Who is it? Who are you talking to?" Bleue gripped his hands.

Retreat. Full retreat. Red let his head sway. "You never killed anyone but yourself," he said.

"Dad, why don't you try and rest. I'm going to do the same."

Bleue raised his hands to her lips and kissed them, first one then the other. She left behind a wet film of salt. He let her gather the pictures.

"I'll save these for your scrapbook," she said, holding up those he had chosen. She moved to close the curtain.

"No, Bleue." Red raised his hand. "Can. Can need. Shit. Sunshine. Leave it."

A few clouds puffed and swirled in the unreachable sky. Light spilled over the wisps of hair that framed Bleue's face, tumbled in speckled patterns across her shoulder. "I'll take you for a stroll when you wake up," she said.

"Fucking wheelchair," said Red.

"Fucking wheelchair," said Bleue and sighed.

The cane had been dignified. Kit bought him a varnished maple one with an ornate handle. He twirled it and did Fred Astaire impersonations.

The walker was a punch below the belt. Score one for the cancer. Bleue brought out her nail polish and painted flowers, wild animals and fancy trucks on the legs. She painted an American flag and "Red White and Bleue Rigging" on the attached tray.

Big Red fought it from the first day to the last. He kicked it with his good leg. He knocked it over with a tray full of breakfast. Still the cancer was not satisfied. It munched and gnawed until Red's bones turned to doily lace. The cane and the walker went to the closet. The wheelchair came in a truck.

"Bleue," he whispered. His hand searched her out. She took it. He remembered a young child encircling a wounded bird in her cupped palms, tears streaming down her cheeks. He felt sorrow beating like a heart inside her. He felt her trembling love. But there was something else. He closed his eyes. Yes; an unmistakable tiny second pulse. In the dark space behind his eyes the image formed. The folded, floating curl of body with its fisted hands and tiny toes. He squeezed her fingers. "Pregnant," he said and smiled. Her hand flew away leaving his to flop onto the blanket.

The bed creaked as Bleue sat. Heat spread between them like a tide. Red listened to her breathing. The fist of the baby inside her opened like a flower.

"What did you say?"

"I said it right," said Red and smiled again.

"How the hell did you guess?"

"Loud love. Too loud love," he got out before the dark waters enveloped him. Red sailed away on a sea of sleep.

Beneath Red's pillows is the picture of a woman. In earliest morning, after Bleue has given him his shot and gone back to bed, he takes his journal from the bedside table and begins to write. He keeps the picture tucked between the pages. Sometimes, when the edges of her face become blurred, he takes it out and summons her to sit with him. If he places her image beneath his head, her quiet breathing helps him rest.

In this picture she is standing at the top of a sand dune on Cape Cod. Her short hair is blown into wild, frizzy tufts, and the bright green scarf that she has knotted at her throat trails behind her in the wind. Red took the picture with a wide-angle lens from the bottom of the dunes.

Elisabeth is a pediatrician. She was the wife of an orthopedic surgeon until her husband drank a quart of Glenlevit and drove his Jaguar into the Charles River shortly after 2:00 A.M. on an unusually warm December night. She is the only woman beside Kit and Bleue that has ever mattered to Red. She is the only one that made Kit threaten to leave. Red had to beg on bended knees. He had to sob and swear to her *never again, I promise never again.* Red has kept his promise and buried Elisabeth's laugh deep inside his heart. But try as he might, he cannot silence the pulse of her that beats in his blood.

Red met Elisabeth when she was a graduate student at MIT, the year before she decided to go to medical school. He was installing a weather station on the top of the Earth Science building. She was intrigued by the system of blocks and pulleys, she said, and demanded that Red explain them. Red felt a subterranean heat from her fingers when she tapped his shoulder. Electromagnetic fields arced between them when she laughed and trapped his stare with her bright green-yellow eyes.

Bleue knows the journal is hers after his death. She has promised not to tell Kit. When she finds the photograph, she will read the message on the back: *Please inform Elisabeth of my passing. (617) 432-7459.* Perhaps she will call.

Red awoke with a two-fisted hunger banging down his door. The curtains quivered in the afternoon breeze, and

an apricot-tinged light spread across the walls. Big Red took
a big breath of his last summer.

"Bleue, I want a banana," he called. "Please."

The door opened. "You want a banana?"

Red growled. "That's what I said."

"Just checking if that's what you meant."

Red threw a pillow. Sharp teeth clamped into his ribs.
They sucked his air.

"Roger, Daddy. One banana. Over and out."

Bleue closed the door. She came back with slices of
banana, peaches, strawberries on a plate. She must have
been sleeping; he saw tiny creases from her pillow pressed
into her cheek. Sometimes she still seemed no more than
a child herself.

"Thank you," he said, taking the plate. He held a slice
of banana between two fingers and took a bite. "Bananas
in summer. Ever notice?" He chewed. "You can watch
them ripen. One minute green, the next, boom! Brown
spotted mush."

Bleue nodded, watching him eat. He reached forward
and patted her stomach. "Kit. Bee. Beautiful. Pregnant."
He swallowed, clearing the pathways. "Marry?"

Bleue threw back her head. Beads of laughter tinkled.
She dug her toes into the hardwood floor and rocked. "No
way. One man to take care of is enough." She touched her
stomach. "Well, two, I think."

"A boy?" Red ate a strawberry, a juicy piece of peach.

"Bet?" She held out her hand for Red to shake. "A saw-
buck: ten bucks."

In five, six months dead or alive? "Bet," he said and
shook.

Red took another slice of banana. As he put it to his
mouth, the right side of his face began to twitch. The banana dropped onto his chest. "Ka-Ka-Kit," he called. His
tongue felt thick, stuffed with cotton. He sucked breath
through a cold fog. His right hand reached out. Someone
was with him. Who was it? Someone grabbed his hand. It
jerked free. His arm tried to pull away from his body, his
right leg followed.

"Ka-Ka-Ka." Was he shot? Had he stepped on a mine? His body twisted and bounced. Hot stars of pain exploded in his core. Yes, a mine. Medic, he meant. "Mmm-mm-mma," he yelled. He dug his fingernails into dirty ice. He clutched at the hand that grabbed his, but the blizzards of Korea buried him.

When Red opened his eyes, there were rails around his bed, tubes in his arms, wires pasted to his chest, his fingers. Machines made urgent beeping noises. Words drifted down on him like snow.

Daddy Red Hear Me Squeeze Finger.

He tried to move, but pain seized him, made him moan. A hand touched his chest. He felt warmth and worry through the fingertips. He breathed in love.

"Easy, big boy," a voice said. He smiled.

Three faces orbited around him like blurred planets. "Red, do you know where you are?"

He squinted. The faces came into focus and attached themselves to bodies. Kit was there, and Bleue. The one who had asked the question had a white coat and mountainous pale flesh. Red set an anchor and dug deep.

"Fat," said Red. It was what he meant, but not what he meant to say.

"Yes, thank you," the woman said and smiled. "Do you know who I am?"

The anchor pulled taut. Red felt solid earth beneath his keel. "Doctor Arbuckle. Hospital. Oink. Oinkology." He remembered this was his joke. He couldn't think why it was funny.

"Very good. How are you feeling?"

Red looked to Kit. "What I in for?" His words floated, then sank.

She touched his forehead with a cool hand. "Bad behavior," she said. Bleue giggled into her fist.

He tried to sit up, but the pain in his hip nailed him to the bed. "Farfel," his mouth said. "Aaah." Bleue arched over the bedrail and kissed him.

"Red," Dr. Arbuckle said, "you've had a nasty seizure. And possibly fractured your pelvis. Bleue called me; I came right down."

Bleue cleared her throat. "What does this mean in terms of the cancer?"

Dr. Arbuckle adjusted the drip on Red's IV. "Let's wait and see. We'll get the X-ray, a CT scan of the brain. The seizure doesn't necessarily mean the cancer is growing again."

"Are there options? We'll try anything. Experimental chemo, clinical trials."

Bleue tugging at hope like a rigging line. Cinching him to life with her love. The thoughts formed images rather than words.

"Honey, let's save that for later. Your father needs to rest," said Kit.

"Rest," repeated Red. He felt immeasurably tired. Fatigue covered him like stones. He fought. He reached his hands upward into life. Kit took one, Bleue the other. Grounded. Electric current sparked through him, shattering rock. He broke the surface and began to float. Life. Goes. On.

Big Red let his eyelids droop. He saw grass through a window, diamond-sparkled and new. He saw the Japanese maple in his front yard bursting with bloom. Encircling the trunk, sugary pink tulips yawned.

Red, Kit, Bleue and a young boy sat on the bed, turning the pages of a scrapbook. Forsythia-yellow curls made defiant fists across the boy's forehead and stuck out from behind his ears. Red sat between them, taking up no more space than the morning breeze.

The boy pointed at pictures and giggled. Red as rigger, Red as soldier, solid tree-trunk Red as two-fisted fighter, devouring life. Bleue and Kit told stories, their voices honey-smooth. Red smoothed the boy's hair with fingers of air.

Red squeezed the hands that held his. His eyes opened. *Forgiveness,* he thought. He cradled the image like a newborn in his arms.

"Wait," said Bleue. She searched her bag, found her travel camera. "News flash. Big Red pulls through again." She clicked and caught him with his upturned face.

Laughter bounced against the walls of his chest. Bubbles of laughter floated from his mouth.

"Sha-sha-sha," he said.

"Daddy, what is it? What's the matter?"

"Shedding skin," said Red. He began to shake his head no, then stopped. Yes, that *is* what he meant. That *is exactly* what he meant.

LUNCH

So I'm sitting in the park eating a sandwich—roast beef, rare like I like it—and the sky so sharp and cold-glass blue I could lick my finger, run it along the rim: *vaarrring, vaarrring,* a champagne glass of sky and this dressing I got (mayonnaise/ ketchup/ relish) is running down my fingers making a beeline for my elbow and my hand-knit sweater (my sister brought me that sweater from Ireland—right off the sheep) and this guy sits down at the next table (god I wish that baby over there on the grass would shut up she's got her mouth full of grass and dirt and snot and the mother so busy talking to that guy maybe the father who knows these days—that mother don't give a shit about her poor baby so hungry it's eating grass) BUT THIS GUY at the next table he's nearly naked no shirt just a pair of—I swear—PAJAMA BOTTOMS and his hair a Rasta rug (bet if you took your fingers, poked and picked through that mess you'd find living growing weeds maybe a few lettuce or tomato plants) he's got these DOLLS a Batman a Spiderman a bloated puffed out babydoll bald as a bat and naked and (of course) a Barbie; he pulls out I'm not kid-

ding a tea set and proceeds to set up a tea party JESUS now
that kid is crawling right over to the path that goes around
the park and those two runners with their matching shorts
not watching where they're going (my sister's a runner does
that Boston marathon); that kid's gonna end up under their
expensive running shoes while her mother lights up a cigarette, could care less about that baby she brought into the
world and THIS GUY having tea with his dolls is not the
tea-and-doll kind of guy more the kind you go up to and
say: *have a bite of my roast beef sandwich* and he would slip
over your body with those glassed-over green-as-moss eyes
and *sswwwaaaam* suddenly a knife wags out from under
your ribs and your breath sighing outta that smile in your
skin but no—he's having tea with his dolls which is more
than I can say for that bitch of a mother smoking away and
playing with the hair of that goddamn man (I bet he's not
the father I bet she has no clue who the father is) that baby
still screaming and it's getting into my brain a bit but she
can't unfasten her lips from misterwonderful's neck don't
she care that not ten feet away from her bouncinbabygirl
there's a nearly naked man with trees growing outta his
hair just waiting for that baby to crawl over so he can stick
a knife in her heart (I was born early so early they thought I
would die Peanuts they called me, skin swirled like the skin
of a nut; my mother used to tell me that story when I cried
and she couldn't shut me up) damn that sandwich was
good I could eat another; wish I had a Coke, maybe some
chips with vinegar and salt—wow: there go those runners
again; bet my sister could kick their color-coordinated asses: say—is it raining no that's the sprinkler and the grass
so green I could scoop it up, put it on a picture postcard
like the one me and my sister sent my mother when she
took me to the Grand Canyon, well misterwonderful there
is DEFINITELY not that baby's father, that baby is brown;
she has a hand on the bench where pajama-man is having
his tea party; the sprinkler is spurting on my sneakers and
that baby's little pink suit with the snowboarding dogs is
full of mud and snot and now it's getting soaked but she

has pulled herself up and smiles at pajamabottoms who is just waiting for her to get closer so he can reach down her throat and tear her heart out he is bending down and the baby for the first time is not crying she is laughing and he takes one of those little teacups for his trashbin family and holds the damn thing with his pinky finger sticking up like EmilyFuckinPost and smiles: *spot-o'-tea* says he, just like on those shows my sister watches (I got no TV where I live it's a halfway house but halfway to what no one says) and that baby squeals, pushes up-down-up-down on her fat legs, her hand on that pychokiller's knee; finally mommy remembers she has a baby; she and misterperfect (his pants are all crooked I know what's inside them pants) run over—she is yelling "GET YOUR FUCKIN HANDS OFF MY BABY" and the psychokiller's looking like this lady's gonna torture him with her lit cigarette; her boyfriend grabs that baby who starts screaming and it's getting into my brain real bad now and the psychokiller has his hands up like this guy is a cop gonna hit him with a nightstick and FUCKIN PERVERT the mother screams those runners run by like we are in some alternate universe not even visible no the Rasta rug shakes *no don't hurt my dolls* and the boyfriend pushing on his chest, squeezing that baby so hard I'm afraid she's gonna pop— all this noise tying my stomach into a twist that psycho guy rocking back and forth the mother screaming in his face her boyfriend's the one squeezing the stuffing outta that poor baby had no choice about getting born into this shitty world; I close my eyes, lick my finger, run it around and around the rim of the sky *vrrrrraang, vrrrrraang* filling the park vibrating trees benches business executives eating lunch *vrrrrraang* ringing the edge of the sky it vibrates our bones till they burst: all our bones and the benches and the sandwiches and the salt and vinegar chips flying up into the air coming down in a pile of shards (my sister took me to the Grand Canyon Museum; we saw the pot shards— all that's left of those poor Indians—I remember that word SHARD it stuck in the part of my brain that keeps things).

Hunger—Like an Onion

Owl

I f there is one thing I learned early in life, it's this: you need to snatch what's yours and then keep on snatching. Otherwise, you are going to starve. Whether it's food or cars or love, it is not going to drop into your lap of its own accord. Owl, goddammit, my mother used to say, you are going to get yourself in trouble with your hot little hands, but I never believed it until now.

I mean—who the hell names their kid Owl? Only my mother, may she rot in peace. I was born under a full moon, and when she went into labor, she said there was a great big owl *who-who-ing* on the highest branch of a winter-bare tree. She thought it was portentous. She was sure I was going to die, so when I came out whole and perfect and screaming, she named me Owl just to laugh in the face of it.

I know better than to trust one word from my mother's mouth—she saw a lot a shit that was or wasn't there. But I'll tell you what, when it came to aiming something at her mouth or up her nose, her vision was twenty-twenty.

I must confess I have been ground up slow by that mill and spit out the butt-end. But no more. My change goes in my pocket not up my nose. I got an old Econoline van that belongs to my girlfriend and a job delivering her flowers to the rich folks in their fancy houses where the forest meets the clouds. I have carved out my space in this town, and I intend to keep it. In the mornings I load my flowers in the back, kiss Celeste goodbye, stick my coffee on the hump between the seats and throw that baby into gear. There's always a slight grind, like the moan of a woman who protests when you both know that sooner or later she's going to sink into your arms the way she sinks into the cushions of her couch.

By the time I light up the first joint, the perfume of my cargo has wrapped itself around me, rubbed my skin tingly and teased my senses into full alert. Sometimes I change my mind and put the joint down next to my coffee just to keep from ruining the moment. I let the breath of the flowers lick my neck and play with the pocket of my T-shirt. Then I put on the jazz station, and those little electric fingers of sax or horn travel up my spine one vertebra at a time. With the bass cranked up, every exhale of the snare drums hums in the space between my tongue and teeth. I conjure up a vision of Celeste sitting by her dressing table to light a candle, bare knees crossed, taking off her earrings and then her silver and turquoise bracelets one by one.

I used to drive like a maniac, not happy 'til the scream of the engine shook my body. And let me put it this way: those cars were rarely started with a key. Now I look around. I sip my sweet black coffee slow. I watch the mountains arch up out of the morning fog, keep my place in traffic, and let the town of Santa Fe disappear in the rearview mirror on its own unhurried time.

There's a point on the road where I switch gears both in my van and in my brain. It's not marked by a stoplight or a particular bump that I feel under my boots, but I know it as clearly as if it were marked by a bright red X. The suits have all gotten on the freeway to Albuquerque or parked in front of their historic-front adobe offices surrounding the town square. Their wives have valet parked their Jags by the Ten Thousand Waves Spa.

That leaves me and the Sangre de Cristo Mountains and the junipers and pines. I open the window, take a breath of air sharper than a surgeon's scalpel, downshift into second gear, and let the radio rip. I give my baby the green light to climb. When I've finished in the neighborhoods by the National Cemetery and turned off into the developments by Wilderness Gates, where you could fit the trailer park I grew up in on one person's property, I slip my van into third and point her bumper at the clouds.

By then the sun has come up, and the sky is so blue it looks like a piece of colored paper pasted to the backside of the peaks. The road turns into a landscape of curves, and a bit of that old craziness comes back, that feeling like death is nothing more than some woman I'm cheating on. I swallow those curves as if heaven was waiting around the bend. And like I said, I never gave a thought to heaven trying to cheat me right back.

JUDITH

Sometimes in Santa Fe you feel and smell the rain long before it gets there. Especially where we live, nestled like trolls in the toes of the mountains. Here the gray clouds sink down over the peaks until they wrap around you, a blanket that brings ice instead of warmth to your skin. The tips of ponderosa pines moan and sway, and the brittle fingers of chamisa chatter in the breeze. The scent of piñon prickles my nostrils and settles in my lungs. I start to feel frosted, like the inside of my mom's martini glass. I start to feel as if the slightest touch of a twig could cause my bones to shatter into splinters. But maybe that's because it's been two days since I've eaten a meal, and I don't know when I'll get to eat my next one.

Today we got out of school early, so I decided to go for a long run. We're not supposed to run over six miles during the week, since it's track season, but I love this overcast, almost-rain weather. I can run out my back door and be on miles of dirt trails in five minutes. Let's see. Write paper for American history or run eight miles in the mountains with my feet flying over rocks, my legs pumping and my brain buzzing on electrified mountain air. Plus I get the challenge of trying to beat the rain.

American history is boring. I wish I had been a teenager in the sixties when kids my age were going to jail and getting beaten for upholding their beliefs. Instead I am growing up with a president whose great claim to fame is co-starring with a chimp named Bonzo in a B movie. I am still trying to figure out how a guy like Ronald Reagan gets elected by a landslide.

These days, the important things have moved across the pond. Northern Ireland is a volcano about to blow. Bobby Sands is forty-eight days into his hunger strike. I am two days into mine. I picture my stomach as the size of a dried-up leaf. I have to cheat because I need fuel to run the way I do. I'm trying to get a scholarship to the University of Oregon, alma mater of Steve Prefontaine, the greatest runner who ever lived. I need a top finish in the state to do that.

I wrote Bobby Sands a letter. I told him how much I admire him, and how connected I feel to his struggle. My dad was born in Belfast, and I want to study art. Lately all my paintings have to do with The Troubles. I told Bobby I was fasting in solidarity with the IRA prisoners. I didn't tell him I eat the raisins from my raisin bread toast.

My mother would have me committed if she knew what I was doing. The way she looks at me, I think she'd like to have me committed no matter what I do. That is when she remembers to look up at all and notice I'm here. Who am I to be interfering with my mom's work?

I know Bobby won't get my letter. They don't give political prisoners any mail. They didn't even give them proper food when they were still eating, and the guards beat them whenever they let them out of their cells. But I know if he did get my letter, he would be proud.

I'm amazed at how good I feel. I was weightless climbing the grade, like Peter Pan in little green twinkle shoes, every step taking me higher off the ground. And coming down was like skiing. I imagined the swoosh-swoosh of skis in a fifty-mile-an-hour slalom, windblown rooster tails of snow hitting my arms. I was so far into my winter wonderland that when I saw that nasty van parked in front of my house, I jumped, and cold shivers shot up my spine. The rear windows were blacked out, but the steady thump of bass on the radio was loud enough to vibrate my feet through the soles of my running shoes. My arms and legs broke out in goose bumps, and my breath froze somewhere in my chest.

OWL

Today I had a special assignment. The usual deliveries in town for get-well wishes and upscale weddings, then a straight shot out to Wilderness Gates. This was the weekly delivery to Dr. Hochberg, but I was told to put that high-dollar armload-full of flowers personally in the doctor's arms. There had been some problems with previous flower theft— or so the doctor said. Celeste straightened the collar of my blue-jean jacket, dusted off my shoulders, and gave me a long, hard kiss. Her mouth was coffee-warm, caffeine-jazzed enough to give me a little buzz for the morning.

I arrived early, and a cold wind was blowing down out of the mountains. The clouds had started to bunch over the peaks, threatening rain. When Dr. Hochberg didn't answer the door, I decided to smoke my doobie, full blast the heat, kick back and take out my James Joyce.

I love to read. I've been devouring books since I first got my hands on the alphabet. To fully appreciate the experience, I built myself a little tent out of sheets and cardboard boxes in my corner of the trailer. I checked out my limit of books every week from the library. While my mother was busy doing what she did best with whatever bottom fish was her catch of the day, I would hunker down in that tent

and read. Rock and read, read and rock. Hum to myself to
keep the noise away.

For my birthday, Celeste gave me a copy of *Ulysses*. I am
her pet project, and she is bound and determined to make
a poet out of me. Cut up my rough-hewn parts and rear-
range them, the way she arranges the exotic flowers from
her greenhouse.

I read *Portrait of the Artist As a Young Man* and *Dublin-
ers*—no problem. But I have started and stopped this damn
book so many times every page is dog-eared, and I still can't
get past the part where all those crazy, little chapters start.

Well, after a few hits on my joint, the literary universe
began to shift. Those unpronounceable words lined up
front and center and started making sense. You sneaky
Irish bastard, says I, now I know what you were doing when
you wrote this scrambled-egg shit. I held my joint in the
air and offered ol' James a toast. I toked until my lungs
burned and my heart kicked into overdrive. Maybe it's
true, I thought—maybe I *am* a poet.

My fingers trembled as they turned the chewed-up pages. I was so in tune with Mr. Joyce I have no idea how long
the fist had been pounding at the window when I looked
up to see a girl peering in. If I'd known what I was in for, I
would have thrown those goddam flowers in her face and
hightailed it down the mountain. Instead, that girl is taking up all my dreaming space, slithering around my good
conscience like a snake in the Garden of Eden with her
skinny, goose-bumped legs and her evil, yellow eyes.

JUDITH

I snuck up so he couldn't see me in his rearview mirror.
I don't know what I thought I would do when I got there.
*Extra: Ninety-pound teen fends off crazed murderer with running
shoe.* But he was listening to jazz, not some awful punk. I
mean, do murderers listen to Miles Davis? When I got close
enough to read "Celestial Flowers" on the side of the van I
remembered. Mom had an emergency appointment with

some kid who was about to dive off the deep end, and she had asked me to sign for her flowers. Oops.

I had to yell at the guy for five minutes before he looked up from his book. When acknowledgement of my presence finally made it through the smoke, his head almost hit the roof. You would have thought *I* was the psycho murderer. He rolled down the window, and a fog bank hit me in the face. I don't do drugs, but I didn't crawl out from under a rock either. I know marijuana when I smell it.

"Can I help you?" I asked.

His book flew from his hand. He opened the van door and it floated out, borne on the cloud. I almost laughed. Strange taste for a flower deliveryman. I picked it up and handed it back. I felt a feather touch of his finger as he took it, the kind where you think, Was that on purpose or not? He had shoulder-length hair, shiny and black, and he tucked it behind his ear. His skin was the color of New Mexico red clay.

"I have a delivery. You live here?"

Wow. Profound. "Yup," I said.

He hopped down, prancing from one foot to the other, and I could have sketched every inch of his quadriceps through the skin-tight jeans. He looked like his energy was too big for his body, like some god or spirit had tamped and pressed until they got it all in. I kept trying to look away, but my eyes disobeyed.

"Sign," he said. He thrust a clipboard at me and grinned. I signed.

"Judith Doyle. Hey, I thought you said you lived here. This delivery's for Dr. Hochberg."

"I do live here. Doyle was my dad's name."

His head jerked up. "Was?"

This flower deliveryman was starting to scare me. Things I didn't mean to say popped out of my mouth. I studied the double knots on my running shoes. "Yup. Was."

He opened the back of the van, threw around some boxes and found ours.

"What's with the weekly flowers?" he asked.

"My mom's a shrink. She thinks flowers cheer people up. In the summer we grow our own."

"Hey, you know the names of all of these?" He put the box on the ground and opened it. He dropped into a cross-legged sit in one swift motion, then patted a patch of rock next to him.

"Nope," I said, although I did. I sat next to him, the cold stone coaxing goose bumps from my legs.

One by one he named them, recited the warm tropical countries of their origins. One by one he laid them in the place between my shivering knees.

OWL

Jesus. Celeste is about to split me in two and string up my halves from her fence posts. And it serves me right. For some reason, every time I do get something in my life worth having, a part of me tries to turn it into just another piece of crap.

Celeste is nearly old enough to be my mother, or one of those sisters who goes away to college the day after you're born. But she is one fine piece of feminine humanity. When I see her walking down the trail, her long, cornflower-blue skirt all ripples and waves and her silver concho belt throwing off spears of sunlight, it makes my heart and other parts of my anatomy swell with pride.

Her mother's a botanist, and her father wears expensive suits and works in a glass-walled building in Albuquerque. Needless to say, they are not too fond of their daughter's taste in male companionship. Every day I have to wonder what she sees in me, and every day I want to fall to my knees and thank someone that she sees it. So I should give myself a prize for saying what I said.

We were in her handcrafted, lodge-pole bed. I was making her sing my praises and shaking and trembling and about to cross over with her to that land of heavenly glory. I dove my face into her hair, found the sweet pearl of earlobe with my teeth and nibbled. Then I whispered, "Judith." Holy fuck.

I'm not even balling the chick. I hadn't kissed her before last Thursday, and she started that. Celeste may think I am ready to jump on anything that moves, but I'm no cradle-robbing pervert. I grew up around too much of that shit; there's nobody knows the half of it.

She sat up like I had poked her with a cattle prod. Her eyes lit up, and she pushed me off with her thick-muscled arms that toss around hundred-pound bales of hay to pass the time before breakfast. Silver bracelets flashed and clashed.

"What did you say, *Owl*?" She said my name like it was a foreign substance on her tongue, sticky and foul tasting.

My brain was spinning and digging, searching for a way to lie myself out of this mess, but all I accomplished was to sink my wheels in my own mire. The only idea that came to me was to tell the truth, and as little of that as possible.

I told her I didn't know where the hell that came from. I said the only Judith I knew was the shrink's kid up in Wilderness Gates I had delivered flowers to. I had been preoccupied about that, I said, because I didn't know if she remembered to give them to her mom, or maybe ate them instead in some drug-induced state. You know kids these days. Hah-hah.

Celeste looked at me like I was unworthy to be dropped out of the butt end of her horse. She pushed again.

"How did you know she was a psychiatrist, *Owl*? I never told you that."

I shrugged. Nailed to the cross, I was.

"Get the fuck out," she said.

My jeans were hanging off a flagpole, but I got them zipped without losing any skin. I looked at her long and hard and hungry 'til I thought I would cry.

"I love you, Celeste. I swear to God I do," I said and got the fuck out.

How the hell was I supposed to make it up to her? How do you say you're sorry to the woman who owns the flower shop?

What I didn't tell Celeste is that I have seen Judith almost every day since we met. I'm not entirely to blame for this mess. She has this way of blinking her eyes and sticking her nose in the air before she speaks that makes you think what she has to say is life-or-death important. She read *Ulysses* cover to cover not once but twice. And *she* asked *me* did I want to have a Coke, not the other way around.

I met Judith on a Thursday. Friday we spent an hour talking at Le Buzz café. I've never seen someone put down so many Diet Cokes. Must've been at least four or five. I asked her did she have a Diet Coke abuse problem. I meant it as a joke, but she got real quiet and looked down at her shoes.

"Makes me feel like I've eaten," I thought she said, but I couldn't be sure.

By Tuesday I was resting my fingers in the hollows between her knuckles. Her bones stuck up like little bird wings. I watched the blood move through her pearl-colored veins.

She wears a necklace with a Jewish star and a cross. The heat of her neck seared my skin as I touched it.

"What's this mean?"

"I'm a half-breed," she said, then clapped her hand to her mouth.

"Hey, that's okay. Me, too." I had to pinch myself to make sure I said that—I'd never used those words to anyone before. Beneath the chain I felt the tiny pulse of her artery keeping time to some internal jazz. I closed my eyes, and I didn't know where her pulse ended and mine began.

"I feel like I'm hugging your heart," I said.

"You are, Owl," she said.

It was flower-delivery day for Dr. Hochberg when Celeste kicked me out, and I told Celeste I'd work until she found someone else. What could she do but accept? By the time I drove into Wilderness Gates, the engine was smoking, and the clutch was throwing sparks. Dr. Hochberg answered the door. I had to fight the urge to throw the flowers and shove her down, but hell—it wasn't her fault. Lately feelings come from nowhere, boiling up 'til they burst out of my chest. I have this hunger that sits like a fist inside me. I could eat all day and never fill it up.

I jumped in my van and drove. I drove like a crazy man, up streets, down streets, craning my neck out the window and praying to see those skinny legs come bouncing out from behind some house or around some corner. I was on my way to Le Buzz when I saw her duck through the fence at the high school.

"Get in," I said, my voice louder and shakier than I intended.

She was wearing a long, green skirt cinched with a belt that must have been on the twentieth hole. Her face looked even paler than usual, and she wobbled like her legs were thinking about non-support.

"Owl, I have to be at track practice in an hour."

"Then give me half of that. Get in." I reached across the seat and jerked her arm.

"Okay. Take me home." She got in and touched my cheek. Her fingers felt clammy and hot. Looking out the window she said, "You don't have to hurt me."

When I saw her room, I knew for certain she was nuts, but by then it was way too late to quit. She had painted the walls black, with sparkles that globbed and ran like drops of silver blood. I wanted to jump out of my skin. Weird creations of streets on fire and bleeding-Christ-looking men stared out from easels. Above her bed was a gold cross on top of an iridescent-purple Jewish star, and on the points of the star were three of the craziest-looking dudes I have ever seen. Some runner and a psycho in a blanket. The guy with the big nose, thick mustache and frizzy hair I recognized.

"Oh, Albert Einstein," I said and puffed out my chest. "I read a couple books about him."

"I painted him because he understands that physics— that the order of the universe even—is art."

What could I say to that? I pinned her against the wall and kissed her.

By the time I finished delivering flowers it was nearly dusk, and a light rain streaked the windshield. The Rolling Stones came on the radio, one of Celeste's favorite songs. I cranked the volume and pressed down on the accelerator, turning rage into raw speed.

You fill my cup, babe, that's for sure
I must come back for a little more

I took a corner too fast and braked too hard. My back end lost traction, and I started to spin out, sliding toward the drop off. "Whoa, baby," I said, teasing the gas and steering into the skid. My whole body tingled with adrenaline, and I felt that really alive feeling I used to have when I was stealing cars, like I had reached in and grabbed something back that life had tried to take away.

JUDITH

This is the sixteenth day of my hunger strike, and my mother still hasn't noticed. What a joke. Dr. World Famous Psychiatrist, and she doesn't realize her only child is starving. But I have my system down; it's not entirely her fault.

In the morning I make a PB and J sandwich and pour a glass of skim milk. I drink the milk, eat about half the sandwich, look at my watch and jump up.

"Oh! Gotta run, Mom," I say. I wrap the sandwich in my napkin, grab my knapsack, and give her a quick kiss. If she looks up, which is fifty-fifty, she'll frown and stare at the napkin. "I'll eat it on the way, I promise," I say, and I'm out the door. The PB and J feeds the birds in some neighbor's yard.

At night I practice the art of Illusion Eating. When I serve myself, I push everything into big, tall mounds so it looks like I have a lot of food. Then I scrape it around —take a bite here, a bite there, until I have distributed the mess into discrete granules over the entire surface of the plate. It's geometry, really. All the white space makes it look like I've licked the plate clean.

The problem is this other hunger I hadn't planned on. This flower-deliveryman hunger that has invaded parts of my body I don't ever mention. I don't know why I like him. I don't have time for boys. Maybe it's because my mind doesn't have enough fuel to work. I've started having dizzy spells, and when I run hard, my heart skips and bangs against my ribs.

Owl didn't even know who Bobby Sands or Steve Prefontaine were. Pre I can understand, even though he ran in the Olympics and held every American record on the track between 2,000 and 10,000 meters. But Bobby Sands? He makes the newspaper once a week. Yesterday he was elected to serve as MP in the government of Northern Ireland, even though he's been a prisoner in Long Kesh since 1977.

"Who's the weirdo in the blanket?" Owl asked. Dumb.

I told him about the hunger strike—Bobby's, not mine. I said the IRA prisoners were striking for recognition of their status as political prisoners. They refuse to wear prison clothes, so they wrap themselves in their blankets. I showed him Bobby's poems printed in the *Phobhacht/Republican News*, which is an underground newspaper my aunt in Belfast sends me. My father came from a long line of rebels. I explained how Bobby smuggles the poems out on toilet paper, and they are printed under his sister's name.

Owl read the poems over and over. He put his arms around me and said he had never met anyone who cared about things as much as I did. He said having a cause made me shine inside and out. I didn't tell him it was just the light shining through my disappearing body.

My mouth keeps trying to tell him my secret. Something about Owl makes me want to tell him everything I've ever felt. Last week I started to say it, so instead I took his face in my hands and kissed him. I felt a rush of hunger, warm and cold, his and mine that filled my head until I felt like fainting. Today when he kissed me, I wished he would swallow me whole.

OWL

She finally asked the question I know she's been itching to ask since she met me. We were lying in the grass in back of her house with our tongues trying to braid themselves together. I felt the little BBs of her nipples pressing into my chest, and I had to be careful not to hold her too close so she wouldn't feel certain parts pressing into her. She unsucked her lips from mine and planted kisses over every inch of my face. Then she started in on my hair. She took a strand and wound it around her finger.

"Owl, are you Native American?"

"Yes. I was born in Arizona, U-S-A."

She frowned her cutest high-school frown, but I was starting to feel that familiar pressure in my chest.

"That's not funny. You should be proud of your heritage."

Before I knew what I was doing, I jammed her down hard. All the old anger came pouring out. "Shit, Judith, shut up. I'm sick to death of hearing that crap. My heritage my ass." My hands grabbed her shoulders and squeezed. "My heritage was ten minutes in the back of a broke-down pickup truck at some powwow. Fifteen if the dude was good and my mother didn't pass out before he got his rocks off. Oh, she went on and on about love-this-love-that when she was floating in her whiskey bath, but I know better. She wouldn't recognize the guy with clothes on and a full-blown, Native-American-heritage hangover."

Judith started to cry. Here I go again, I thought, fucking up every good thing that comes down the pike. I pulled her close. I kissed her head. She sobbed until her whole body shook. I rocked her and held her and pretty soon we shook together and before I knew it we were shaking and starving for each other and crawling back into the woods. By that point all the exit signs were turned off, the doors bolted shut.

"What about your mom?"

She closed her teeth around my neck and nibbled. "Seeing patients 'til six," she said.

I put my hand up her skirt, worked a finger inside. Her bones felt sharp enough and near enough to cut me. She sat up and pulled my hand away.

"Owl, I'm a virgin."

"So am I," I said like the jerk that I am.

But she was, and I know I hurt her, and now I carry some crazy responsibility for her soul like a cross on my back. Especially after what she whispered in my ear.

JUDITH

When I was five, I painted my first picture: my father with a hand nearly as big as the rest of his body. In the palm of his hand a tiny stick figure of a daughter reached upward toward his unattainable heart.

When I was six, my father killed himself. I was the one who found him. He was in his car in the garage with the engine running, an empty pill bottle on the seat beside him. He wasn't quite dead. I thought he was playing a game, so I sat on his lap. The blue of his body and the odd shape his lips made when he tried to speak scared me.

Dizzy with fumes, I ran to get my mother. I had to pound on her office door; the rule was I couldn't interrupt her when she saw patients. She left me rocking and crying by the banister. My old basset hound Buster nuzzled my foot as if he knew what was wrong.

I closed my hands around the dusty scrollwork and traced the pattern over and over. The knobs on the ends felt like onions. I dug my fingers into the wood and tried to peel the layers. To this day, I can feel splinters under my nails.

I am twenty days into my hunger strike, or is it nineteen or twenty-one? I am too sick to get out of bed, have been since yesterday. My body is peeling off in layers. Above me, Albert Einstein, Steve Prefontaine, and Bobby Sands, the gods of my life, float in black space.

I haven't seen Owl since we had sex. After, I made myself throw up. I retched and retched, but all that came up was a little blood. Then I passed out at practice, and Coach sent me home. The pains in my chest are getting worse.

My mom brought me a letter from my aunt with the latest copy of the *Republican News*. "Bobby Sands Near Death," the headline said. She brought up a tray with some soup and crackers. She felt my forehead.

"How are you feeling?" she asked.

My heart wanted to tell, but my lips stayed shut.

"Please try and eat." She put down the tray and left.

When I started fasting, I didn't really think about what I was doing. Now it's too late. I want to quit, but I can't make myself—I just can't. I wish my mom would sit down and hold my hand and make me eat. How blind can she be?

I wish I could be strong like Bobby or Pre. My mom took me to a track meet when I was eight to watch Pre run. We were in the front row, and I could see his face so clearly, completely twisted by sweat and pain. He knew what price he had to pay to be the best, and he was willing to pay it. And the final reward for all his work was an early death. Which, if I don't stop soon, is all that's facing me.

Owl, how did this happen? Let me fly away tucked in your wings. Bird of Death, Bird of Life: which are you?

OWL

Celeste took me back. I brought her a necklace and a box of books, ones I know she's been wanting to read. I got down on my knees, I did, begged her forgiveness. She forgave me. Hell, no one who didn't crawl out of some gutter would deliver flowers for the sorry excuse of a wage she pays me.

I was feeling my oats. It was a magnificent day, and I could still smell Celeste's sweet perfume on me. I had fooled myself into believing I had put Judith out of my mind. What choice did I have? That relationship had nowhere to go but down, and I had my own rosy future to think about. Didn't I?

I decided to drive to the newsstand to get a paper. Where that decision came from I'll never know. Before I met Judith I hadn't thought about current events since I flunked the subject in sixth grade. But there I was with a steaming cup of coffee and the sun beating down on my jeans and *The New Mexican* turned to page three. The headline caught me like a sucker punch to the stomach.

"More than 70,000 people attend funeral of Bobby Sands. Violence erupts across Northern Ireland in protest."

Suddenly I remembered what Judith said to make me sneak out of her life. We were lying under the trees, shivering from sex and love and late afternoon. She put her lips to my ear.

"Tell me a secret, Owl," she said, "and I'll tell you one."

I told her some stupid shit. The girl was making my mind all crazy, and my feet were getting ready to run.

Her breath was sending waves of heat through my brain. "I'm on a hunger strike, too," she whispered. "I can feel death in my heart."

That's when I got scared. I guess that's when I realized maybe I had this little girl's life cradled in my arms and I had got into this mess with not one measly thought of how to get out the other end or even considering that there would be an end to get out of.

"Don't make up shit like that, Judith," I said.

"Sorry. You're right." She reached for her clothes. She looked like I had punched her in the teeth.

Maybe it was my "Native American Heritage" finally kicking in. Maybe it was just a pair of skinny legs and a milk-pale face with spooky, yellow eyes that had got hold of my soul and wouldn't let go. But when some universal spirit or Albert Einstein or Bobby Sands calls you on the phone, you have to answer.

I put the paper under my arm. I left my dollar-fifty fancy coffee on the table, got in my girlfriend's van, and stepped on the gas. I yelled for all the world to hear, "Please don't let me be too fuckin' late."

JUDITH

It takes me a minute to realize I'm not dreaming. My mom and Owl, bending over me. My mom is sniffling, Owl is crying silently, like the tears are sharp and hurt his face.

I'm in the hospital now. I have been here a day or maybe two. I'm starting to feel a little better, starting not to be so scared. The doctor said I was lucky my mom called the ambulance when she did. She said my heart couldn't have lasted much longer. She says I'm going to be okay.

"It's over, honey," my mom says. "I'm so sorry. Why didn't you tell me what you were doing?" She says this last thing a million times, like Hail Marys, like this is what she has to do to forgive herself.

"You won, baby," says Owl. His voice comes out Jell-O, all quivering, or maybe now I am just obsessed with food.

"What did I win?" I say. I can't make my mind stay in one place.

Owl tells me about Bobby Sands. He tells me people like me have to stick around so we can change things. He puts a newspaper in my hand and says everything will be all right. I have forgotten how to read, and I don't think anything will be all right. I try to cry, too, but my tears are too weak to make it outside my heart. My heart that still flutters like a bird.

Owl takes me in his arms. I am so light I worry I will float away if he doesn't hold on tight. My mother kisses and squeezes and won't let go.

"Mom," I say. "When I get better I want a dog. A big hound dog with floppy ears. I'm going to call him Bobby or Pre, and he's going to run like the wind."

I can hear him howling now—there must be an ambulance pulling into the hospital. But I can see him, too. He's white with black splotches, like Buster on stilts. He has more energy than fits into his body, as if some god or spirit pressed and tamped just to squeeze it all inside. His legs are prancing.

Hope: Entwined
With a Lock of Hair

This story is dedicated to the people of Denmark, who by their acts of defiance saved more than 7,000 Jews from death in 1943.

I am old. I have seen the grandparents of your grandparents cross through my doors, heads bowed, feet shuffling, breath soft with the miracle of worship. For the countless turning of seasons I have watched over the thatched and tiled roofs of this small town. I have watched my people with their wind-caressed skin scratch gardens from rocky soil, glean nets of herring from the sea, bring babies into the hardness of this life.

My bones are the bones of ships. Borne by waves onto the rocks, they were collected one by one and carried across the dunes. And what of the sailors on the ships from whose timbers I was born? Alas! Their bones caress the rocks. I hear them still, crying to me from the foam-flecked waters of winter storms. Today I rest on a firm foundation of stone, but in the beginning my timbers rose defiantly from bare earth.

"We will build our own church," the fishermen declared. "We will bring our own minister and worship here where we live, cradled in the teeth of an angry sea. We will sing to those we have lost to her depths and pray for those who set out into her fickle arms."

Today my red roof shines. My walls gleam white. This modern face reveals nothing of my secret. But that is why you have come: to hear the whispers of spirits that rattle inside my bones. In my attic you will find a plaque, a testimonial you can read. On Sundays my bell cries my story to the heavens.

Perhaps you have walked across the pier and seen the statue of a man blowing the shofar, a trumpet made from a ram's horn, that looks out from the harbor of Gilleleje toward Sweden. From the highest point of my spire he is merely a spot against the narrow sea that separates Denmark from Sweden. On Rosh Hashanah, the day of the Jewish New Year, the song from his curled trumpet splits the wind that swirls across the water. His song calls out to the ghost flotilla with its huddled and frightened cargo, the flotilla whose memory he honors. Today the bay is filled with bright pleasure boats, but in the days of the flotilla, working boats strained against their anchors, wooden planks creaking in the wind. Some had motors, some sails, many no more than a pair of long oars.

Come closer! Put your ears to the walls. Do you hear it? My story is the pulse of the ocean inside a shell, the breath of a moth's wing against a light. You will not read it on the plaque. It is not in your guidebook. But if you press your fingers against these old bones, you will feel it. It will run through your blood.

Who can say when this story began? The first I saw of it were the ships filled with soldiers on a spring day, but I felt the tremor of their boots for weeks before their coming, felt the fear of my people swirl like fog across the newly green fields.

"The Germans are crawling like rats over our country," they whispered as they passed each other on the streets.

Mist rose from their mouths. "We have surrendered," they cursed, fire burning in their eyes.

For the first few seasons, it was difficult to tell that life had changed. The fishermen spat behind the soldier's backs as they passed, and farmers leaned against their hoes with darkness in their eyes. But when spring had turned three times to winter and back again, when the sun had chased the night into hiding, its cloak of stars following close behind, my people shook off their seasons of slumber. The rocks shifted and trembled, and the surface of the sea began to swirl. Men and women came, heads bowed, to meet inside my halls. They sat at my pews as if in worship, but it was not religion they discussed.

"We must fight," they said. "We must fling the Nazi dogs from our backs." Light from my windows washed their cheeks with reds, greens and blues. "For three years they've stolen our produce, the goods from our factories. Now they want us to turn over the Jews. We've heard about the fate that awaits them."

"We're all Danes," another said. "Even those who have streamed across our borders in fear for their lives. We've welcomed them here. They have worked alongside us, worshipped alongside us, suffered with us. Are we now to abandon them?"

"Worse," said a woman. "We're to lead them into hands bloody with the slaughter of their people."

The men and women left, came back, left again. The seeds of their whisperings grew and bore fruit. As summer turned on its heels, the wind was heavy with whispers of resistance. Tree branches sighed with its story.

"Truckloads of supplies have been stolen and businesses working for the Germans have been set on fire."

"The factory workers are on strike. They are marching through the streets, and people are lined up to cheer for them."

"We have blown up a German train."

"German soldiers have been ambushed."

"The Gestapo has caught a resistance fighter. He is sentenced to death."

The teeth of winter had torn into the sun on the Sunday the letter was read. A salt-kissed wind blew in from the Kattegat, beating against my doors and whistling through my belfry. Rain-filled clouds swooped down from the north and opened their mouths over the harbor. My bones shivered with cold.

Pastor Jensen stood behind the pulpit, brandishing the words of the bishops before the congregation like a holy sword. Although it was winter, his cheeks glowed as if the summer sun had painted them with brushstrokes of dawn.

Two days prior, he read, on Rosh Hashanah, the Nazis had begun their *aktion* against the Danish Jews. Believing they would be home for their holy day, the Germans swept through the neighborhoods searching for *Juden*. But warning had come from a German shipping attaché named Georg Duckwitz, and the terrible news was passed on by Rabbi Marcus Melchior in the synagogue of Copenhagen. Now a network of Danes spread through the countryside to sequester the Jews.

They were hidden in attics, hospitals, and empty rooms. They were transported in taxis, ambulances, carriages, and trains. Since the day of Rosh Hashanah, Pastor Jensen said, they had been arriving in Gilleleje and other fishing villages that looked out across the Sund to the safety of unoccupied Sweden. From these villages they were loaded into the holds of ships and ferried across the straits to freedom.

I had seen our fishing boats coming and going day and night. I had watched the *Maagen*, the *Tyborøn*, the *Haabet*, the *Fri*, and the *Wasa* held fast against the docks as people bundled in heavy clothing boarded the ships until the surface of the waves nearly nearly touched the gunwales. Their whispered pleas and their fears were carried to me by the stormy wind, but the words were chopped and broken; I could not understand.

Pastor Jensen held the letter from the Lutheran bishops high above his head. "Our church has spoken. It is your duty to protest the persecution of Jews. Was not Christ a Jew? Did Christ not say we must love our neighbors as ourselves? Are we not bound by the blood that runs in our veins to stand up for justice and freedom? Even our King, Christian X, has spoken out. He has declared that there is no 'Jewish question' in Denmark."

The air inside my halls trembled. I felt the breath of the people, breathing as one. Husbands, wives reached for each other's hands. Children shifted in their seats. In the harbor I saw the wind turning the tops of waves to lace, felt the straining of ships against their anchors. I shook to my frame, but I held my people tight.

Three times day turned to night. Winter snapped up the few lingering traces of summer into its jaws. A cold wind swept across the grasses, the dunes, the barren fields. It rattled against the thatched roofs. It blew across the *Kattegat* and turned the sea to foam. Waves rose toward the sky, and ships careened down their mountainous slopes. Rain drummed against the windows and turned the streets to streams.

The fleeing Jews filled the town until I was afraid it would burst and spill us all into the sea. Families opened their doors to the unexpected guests. The villagers of Gilleleje turned into magicians. In the mornings the town swarmed with strangers, but by evening, they had disappeared into darkness. I watched the occasional flicker of a candle in an attic or a deserted summer home, saw a momentary wisp of shadow cross a room. The bare branches chattered with the whispers of the hidden, tossed their sighs of hope toward hidden stars.

When morning came again, the rain had turned to soft gray mist. I heard the iron gate creak, felt my door open. Pastor Jensen entered with two men I did not know. They shook the water from their coats and rubbed their hands together.

"The Gestapo has closed the harbor," one of the men said. "No one without a valid fishing card will be allowed to sail."

The other man laughed. The notes of his voice were like a rumbling of stones. "And who will enforce this ban? Our Danish Coast Guard? They've been smuggling arms to us for years."

"Even so, it will slow things down," Pastor Jensen said. "There's no place left to hide anyone. The Gestapo is bound to come soon; we need to act quickly."

There was a knock on my door. Two men entered, their hats pulled low over their faces. I knew the high school teacher, Mogens Schmidt, but not the other. He stood nearly a head taller, and I knew that if he were here in summer I would see the muscles of his arms ripple like the taut anchor lines of a ship. He spread his work-hardened fingers wide and grasped the outstretched hands of the others. His fingers looked like the roots of some enormous tree.

The men shifted their weight as they talked. The tall one spoke with hands and arms sweeping wildly in the dim light. The dawn that seeped through my windows was as pale as milk. Rain streaked the glass.

"Agreed, then," said Mogens Schmidt. "I'll go to the harbor and speak to the ships' captains. We'll collect what payment we can from our guests and move them down to the beach as soon as we can find someone to take them. Let's pray that nightfall will find them on their way to Sweden."

The men shook hands again. I could see in Pastor Jensen's eyes the same light that burned on Sundays, when he spoke the word of God to his people. It flared like the sleepless summer sun, the fire so strong it chases the dark of night away. It glowed in the cheeks of the men. It smoldered in my bones despite the winter gale.

You will read about this day in your books. You will perhaps even meet an old fisherman smoking a pipe or a woman bent over her patch of garden who will tell you, "I remember. I was there on the wharf and saw." If you search, you may even find someone feeding the gulls from a bench along the dunes who will describe holding a frightened child against his body in a wave-tossed dinghy, passing him to the waiting arms of a fisherman on a schooner, where the smell of herring rose in a cloud from the holds.

But listen! Hold fast to the rails and climb the narrow wooden ladder that leads to the dizzying air of my belfry. If it is a sunny day, the bell will glint golden, and the orange-bodied crossbills with their black-and-white-tipped wings will flit from branch to branch in the tall spruce. Now, thrust your face into the wind and look down at the harbor, and I will speak to you of what I saw.

Word of the exodus swirled in the wind. It beat against the houses, seeped in through the cracks, shook awake the frightened Jews who lay huddled in attics, under beds, inside wooden barrels.

"Hurry," the clouds called. "Run to the docks or you will be left behind."

All morning I watched the people tumbling from houses and crawling out from the smallest spaces of buildings. They dragged suitcases and boxes; they pushed babies in carriages filled to overflowing with clothing and books. Children ran down the streets while their parents called to them or grabbed for their hands. Their hair streamed wildly in the wind; drops of rain nested like jewels in the tangled locks.

At the jetty's end, the schooner *Flyvbjerg* strained her bowsprit toward the restless *Øresund*. Her crew stood on deck, reaching for the trunks, suitcases, and children that were handed up. Words and cries rose up from the harbor. They mixed and tumbled in the air and carried across the town in a symphony of sound. My bell strained to call out to them. *"Håbet,"* I sang to them, have hope.

Gulls careened in the waves, their long, curved wings tipping toward the sky. "Hurry," they cawed. "The Gestapo is coming."

Suddenly the crowd began to scream. They swarmed toward the ship. Panic roiled through the press of people. I saw a rising tide of coats, hats, arms, legs, heard a roar like crashing waves. Sailors pulled up the gangplank and ran to cast off lines. The Jews reached toward the rigging. A few were strong enough to hoist themselves on board. The captain waved his arms and called to his crew. The *Flyvbjerg* freed herself from land and headed out to sea.

Those who remained on the jetty reached out toward the safety of the ship. Those on board cried out toward the family who had been left behind.

"We are abandoned," the gulls screeched. "We shall surely die."

"We shall find a way," the waves called back. "We shall hide you in our night until we find a way."

"Bring them here," I shouted into the trees. *Bring them here, bring them here.* My words rolled like pebbles down the cobblestoned streets. They rolled across the dunes and onto the beach. They stopped in the sand by Pastor Jensen's feet.

Have you imagined this? Have you heard their voices in the wind that now touches your reddened cheeks? Have you tasted their salty fear that still swirls in the waters of the harbor? Yes, you have. So. Loosen the collar of your coat, but not too much. Place one foot and then another on the rungs of the ladder and climb down from the belfry back into my loft.

Look around you. Take off your shoe and touch my sturdy bones with your toe. Below you, my nave breathes softly with the breath of God. To your left, your right, the limbs of my timbers support the red roof that reaches toward the heavens.

Put out your hands and turn around. Did your fingers touch the timbers? Can you feel them leaning toward you in the afternoon light that washes over the whispers of ghosts? How many are you? I count fourteen shoes: you are seven.

Imagine now that summer sunlight is replaced by a wintry dusk. Imagine that a shivering darkness swallows the remaining day. In the morning, yes, you may have been seven or eight or ten. But the footsteps have come and come and come. You grew first by fours and fives, then by tens and twenties. You are wrapped in all the clothing that you own, for you were forced to abandon your bags and trunks, forced to leave behind the last anchors to your lives. You are floating in a sea of strangers. They press against you. You huddle against the bodies of strangers for the warmth it provides. Your breath forms ice crystals that you watch in the dying wisps of light.

Have you imagined this? Yes! I feel you tremble inside your comfortable summer coats. I see you reach for the hand of your husband, your wife, caress the smooth skin of your child's face. *You are safe here*, I whisper. It is what I whispered to them.

All that day the people of Gilleleje brought the Jews to my doors. "We must have a password," Pastor Jensen said.

"*Håbet*," the men agreed, *håbet* for hope.

All that day and into the evening someone guarded my doors. All that day and into the evening there were knocks, the password *håbet* whispered to the listening ear, my door groaning softly open. By nightfall, there was no space between the people in the loft. They strained against my timbers. My ceilings sighed with their weight and their sorrows.

"What happened at the docks?" the Jews whispered into the darkness.

"We heard the Nazis were coming."

"Who said this? We never saw them. They never came."

The people shrugged. "We heard it in the wind."

The words I have whispered to you are known to be true. It is also known that the man with the hands like tree roots, whose name was Arne Kleven, stood guard that night. He had returned from his home in Copenhagen with a group of rescued Jews. It is said by the people of Gilleleje that when the night was darkest and the teeth of winter gnawed at feet and hands, there was another knock.

I will tell you this is so. I will tell you that when the knock came, Pastor Jensen stood beside Arne Kleven. "*Håbet*," a voice whispered into the frozen air. Once more my door opened.

"Thank you for coming, Dr. Fremming," Pastor Jensen said.

He cupped his hand around the flame of a small candle and led the doctor to the loft. The two men stepped between the bodies. Despite their care, my beams creaked and moaned.

They reached a corner under the eaves where a woman shivered beneath a pile of coats. A small boy sat beside her. He held her hand as if without his grip she would rise and fly away. He wept silently, his breath rising in sad white curls. Pastor Jensen held the candle by the woman's face while the doctor knelt beside her and felt her forehead.

"Bless you," she said.

"I'll leave you, then," the Pastor whispered. "There are another thirty people at the parish hall, and only Miss Frederiksen to care for them. I'll be back as soon as I can." He handed the doctor the candle.

The doctor introduced himself and peered into the woman's eyes. "You're very warm," he said. He melted drops of wax on the floor and set the candle there. "Is this your grandmother?" he asked the boy. The boy remained silent except for the sharp intake of breath.

"He doesn't speak Danish," the woman said. Her voice was a shadow of sound. "He's German. His parents sailed on the *Flyvbjerg* today. They had gone aboard first and asked a cousin to hand him up when the panic started. The cousin abandoned him and scrambled up a rope onto the ship. He was screaming on the breakwater, watching the ship disappear, when I found him."

The doctor's sleeve rustled as he reached to touch the boy's cheek. "*Freund*," the doctor whispered, friend.

"*Freund*," the boy replied.

"And you? How can I help you? Where is your pain?"

"For an old woman like me there is not much you can do. A drop of belladonna if you have it, for I suffer from spasms. I am afraid if the pain gets worse, I will moan aloud. I couldn't forgive myself if my weakness gave us away."

"Belladonna I have. Your fever worries me, but there is not much I can do here in the darkness. We will get you to a hospital if you feel you are in danger."

"No, I'm not in danger, doctor. I'm strong and stubborn. Just something for the pain."

"If you open your mouth, I will put some drops under your tongue."

This story I will tell you now cannot be found in your books, no matter how hard you search. You can ask every villager in the town of Gilleleje; they will shrug their shoulders. You can scour the countryside for plaques; you will not see them. The story I will tell you is a sacred trust. It was breathed into the terrible darkness of that night. Close your eyes and you will feel it, for it beats in my frame like a blessed heart.

The woman reached up and stopped the doctor's hand. "Wait," she said. She had a story of her own to tell, and no one to tell but the doctor. The little boy held the woman's hand in his. He held her love with his eyes while her whispered words filled my shadows.

"My name is Rachael," the woman said. "I was an opera singer in Cologne. My dearest friend, also an opera singer, was named Sophie Hiller. Her husband, Paul Hiller, was a musician, and the son of a famous composer and pianist. Although they had converted to the Lutheran faith, this mattered little to the Nazis. All that mattered was the centuries of Jewish blood that flowed like a river of curses in all our veins.

"When Paul Hiller died, he bequeathed his memorabilia to the museums and libraries of Cologne. But there was one piece of his collection that Sophie could not give up. She kept it hidden, folded in a cloth in her dresser. The thought that this treasure could fall into the hands of the Reich was unbearable to her. She did not even tell her children she had kept it. When she learned that I planned to escape to Denmark, she entrusted me to carry it to safety."

Rachael held the boy's fingers to her lips and kissed them. *"Eins minute,"* she whispered. She took back her hand and struggled to find the inside pocket of her coat. A tiny gasp of pain escaped.

"Take this," she said. She pressed something into the doctor's hand. "I myself had two sons. One night, when I was gone, the Nazis came and took them away to a work camp. It was when I gave up hope of finding them alive that I decided to escape to Denmark. Please accept this as a gift of gratitude. It is all I have to give you, and I believe Sophie would be pleased that you have it. I ask only that you do everything in your power to protect this little boy and see him reunited with his parents." She held her hand against her lips a moment before continuing. "I know only too well the suffering of such separation. If I can save another human being from enduring such pain, that will be my *mitzvah*, my good deed in the eyes of God."

The doctor put the gift in his pocket. I heard the dry rustling of paper. I breathed in the breath of a hundred years. He took the belladonna from his bag.

"Are you ready?"

"Yes, doctor. Thank you."

Soon I heard the soft breath of her sleep. The doctor stroked the boy's hair. The boy touched the doctor's hand with his small fingers. *"Danke, Herr Doktor."* He had a voice like the tiny sparrows that rest beneath my eaves.

Dr. Fremming blew out the candle, closed his bag, and stood. He had taken two steps, perhaps three, toward the ladder when the knocks came.

"Get everyone out! The Germans are coming," a voice said.

"The password; say the password," Arne Kleven replied with his ear pressed to my door. There was only the sound of footsteps running in the darkness.

Fear stirred in the people. It settled in their lungs and rose from their skin. It shook Rachael awake with its icy hands. The boy began to cry. He pressed his tiny body against Rachael as if he could crawl inside her coat. Dr. Fremming held a finger to the boy's lips. "Tell him we will protect him with our lives." Rachael gathered the boy in her arms. Softly she began to sing, the notes of her song burning holes into the chilled darkness.

"We must flee. We must run for our lives," some people cried.

"It's a trick," others said. "The password was never spoken."

Dr. Fremming descended the ladder. I felt the press of his fingers as he felt his way along my walls.

"What shall we do?" he whispered at the door.

"I heard no password," Arne Kleven said.

"Did they speak Danish?"

"Yes, but there are dogs among the Danes as well. The people are safe inside the church. Can I take the chance of sending them out into the sights of German guns?"

"You're right. I'll go back to the loft. I'll tell them to be ready but to stay quiet for now." Again I felt the press of fingers as Dr. Fremming guided himself to the ladder.

The doctor had reached the boy when the second knock came. Had he been beside the door, he would have recognized the voices that whispered, "They've captured the parish hall. Get everyone out quickly." He would have known them as friends.

But Arne Kleven was a stranger, hearing only the voices of strangers. Once more he asked for the password. Once more there was only the sound of footsteps hurrying away in the dark.

Dr. Fremming knelt and put his lips to Rachael's ear. "I know a hiding place for him. There is barely room, but if he tucks his chin to his knees he will fit. Please tell him he must not fear. Please tell him he must be quiet and trust that I will come for him when it is safe."

Rachael held the boy to her. She whispered the words while she stroked his hair. Her sorrow spread to the eaves. The boy cried when the doctor reached for him, but the touch of Rachael's lips against his cheek calmed him. I am the only one who knows that she cried into her coarse woolen sleeve when she was alone.

There is a secret hidden behind my altar. It is a small trapdoor cut into the boards that conceals a space no larger than a bailing bucket. Come down and see it now; you are ready. Walk slowly with your eyes to the floor. With the toe of your shoe feel the tiny hollows pressed by centuries of footsteps into the wood. You could cross this door twenty times and never find it. But inside this space, the scrawled notes and sketched maps of resistance fighters were left to be passed from hand to hand.

The boy shivered and shook in his lonely cranny. He drew his coat tightly around him, but he could not stop the trembling. I tried to warm him with the smallest scrap of sunlight that remained in my bones. I pressed my arms around him. I sang him the hymns of my people. "*Håbet,*" I whispered over and over, you must have hope. I filled his ears with a rushing of air so he would not hear the shouts of the Germans as they surrounded my walls.

"Open the doors!" they shouted. "Come out and live or stay inside and die." My doors shook until I thought they would splinter from the force of fists.

Arne Kleven pressed his body to the door. He became a tree, his legs growing roots to anchor him. "You are safe here," he called to the Jews. "We will protect you with our lives." The key rattled and jangled inside the lock, but my doors held fast.

When the stars began to slide down the back of the sky, the Germans brought torches and gasoline. The flames crackled and hissed like an eerie dawn.

The Jews saw the glow from the flames and called out. "Open the door! Please, let us out!" Pastor Jensen wept. I caressed him with my fingers of wood. "Arne," he said, "we must open the door."

I heard the scrape of a key in the lock. I groaned with a hundred sorrows. The doors flew open, and the Germans rushed in with their guns. In twos and threes the Jews came out, their trembling hands above their heads. They came out until there was nothing but night inside my walls.

The Nazis scraped against my pews. They pulled the

hymnals from the racks and threw them to the floor. They struck at pulpit and altar with rifle butts and poked my rood screen with bayonets. They violated my presbytery with their guns, but they could not hear the sparrow breath of a boy who lay cradled inside my heart.

Håbet. Do not give up your hope. Open your guidebooks and read. Seek out the statue by the waters and listen to the triumphant call of his shofar that sings into the harbor winds. We kept our promise. We never ceased our work until nearly all the Jews in Denmark escaped to safety. Those who were caught that night were never sent to their deaths. Many have returned.

Bend down and touch the secret space beneath you with your fingertips. Listen. There is more. Last year a man came here with his wife and daughter. At his daughter's side a small boy stood with hair the color and texture of flax. The man held the hands of his wife and daughter in his. His fine silver hair shone in the summer light. He bent to the floor until he felt beneath his fingers the secret of his salvation.

"Eva, Rachael, come. Here it is. Franz, come. Give me your fingers, little one. Let's open it."

The four knelt beside my altar as if in worship. The man and his grandson removed the door and peered inside. The boy shrieked with delight.

"Can you believe it? Me tucked like a ball inside this tiny room? I was just about the age you are now."

The tiny miracles of their lives rose like a hymn through the loft. They circled the belfry. They touched the patina of my bell and swirled upward into the clouds.

And what of the gift given to a kind doctor by an old woman? Ah! What can I tell you? I heard the whispers on Sundays. A gift of great value! A treasure beyond words! But the doctor never spoke of it.

You must imagine for yourselves. If you search the archives of Copenhagen's newspaper the *Politiken,* you will find a small article from December 1994 with the title

"Beethoven's Hair." You will notice that the name of the silver haired woman who sold the lock of hair was Michele Fremming, and you will learn that she was the adopted daughter of a local doctor. Then you will remember that it was this doctor who helped a woman and a boy on a cold October night.

Do I believe that a paper-wrapped parcel passed from the hand of a grateful woman to a village doctor contained within it such a gift? I say only this: if you stroll by the dunes in the soft light of a midnight sun in summer, you will see the golden notes rising from the rippled surface of Øresund. And if you listen closely you will hear it. A thousand joyful voices rising in a chorus. "Ode to Joy."

Author's Note

On March 27, 1827, a young Jewish musician named Ferdinand Hiller paid his last respects to the man he had revered above all others: Ludwig van Beethoven. He asked for and received permission to snip a lock of the composer's hair, which he then sealed in a wooden locket. It is documented that the lock of hair was passed to his son, Paul Hiller, in 1883. Paul Hiller married an opera singer named Sophie Lion, and they had two sons. They lived in Cologne, Germany. All trace of the Hiller family vanishes during the late 1930s, when Hitler's reign of terror spread. Their fates were discovered in the late 1990s, following the sale of the hair to a retired American businessman, Ira Brilliant, who was interested in discovering the history of his treasure.

The locket next surfaced in 1943 in the small Danish fishing village of Gilleleje (pronounced Gill-uh-lie-uh). It was in the possession of the village doctor, Dr. Kay Fremming. It is unknown how the locket came into his possession beyond the speculation that it was given to him by a grateful Jew. The lock of hair was sold at auction in 1994 by Dr. Fremming's adopted daughter Michele.

This much is true. The story of the resistance of the Danish people and their heroic rescue of the Jews is also true. The statue of a man blowing a shofar does exist in the town of Gilleleje, as does the commemorative plaque inside the church. The names, and for the most part the deeds, of the people of Gilleleje are historic. What I have filled in with my own pen is the story of how a lock of Beethoven's hair came to rest in a small fishing town of Denmark during a time when history was made.

See also

Beethoven's Hair by Russell Martin, New York: Broadway Books, 2001.

Naomi Benaron's fiction has appeared in *CALYX, Red Rock Review, PRISM International Journal, Green Mountains Review,* and other in-print and on-line journals. She was the winner of the 2005 Lorian Hemingway Short Story Competition. Before pursuing her MFA at Antioch University Los Angeles, she worked for many years as a geophysicist. She has lived in Israel and the West Indies. Currently she lives in Tucson, Arizona, with her husband and two dogs. She teaches writing and geology at Pima Community College and has just completed her first novel. *Love Letters from a Fat Man* is her first book.